THE WITCH'S BLOOD

KATHARINE & ELIZABETH CORR

HarperCollins *Children's Books*

First published in Great Britain by
HarperCollins *Children's Books* in 2018
HarperCollins *Children's Books* is a division of HarperCollins*Publishers* Ltd,
HarperCollins Publishers
1 London Bridge Street
London SE1 9GF

The HarperCollins website address is:
www.harpercollins.co.uk

1

ISBN 978-0-00-826478-9

Katharine and Elizabeth Corr assert the moral right to be
identified as the authors of the work.

Typeset by Palimpsest Book Production Ltd, Falkirk, Stirlingshire
Printed and bound in England by CPI Group (UK) Ltd, Croydon, CR0 4YY

MIX
Paper from
responsible sources

FSC
www.fsc.org
FSC® C007454

This book is produced from independently certified FSC™ paper
to ensure responsible forest management.

For more information visit: www.harpercollins.co.uk/green

THE WITCH'S BLOOD

Katharine and Elizabeth Corr have been writing since they were children. They keep in touch any way they can, discussing their work via phone, text and Skype, and have been known to finish each other's sentences – and not just when they are writing!

www.corrsisters.com

Books by Katharine and Elizabeth Corr

The Witch's Kiss
The Witch's Tears
The Witch's Blood

For Rebecca and Sam, the two brightest stars in
my universe
E.C.

For Neill, Georgina and Victoria, with all my love
K.C.

PROLOGUE

'LEO? LEO, WAKE up.'

A man's voice. Leo could feel the weight of someone's hand on his shoulder. But he stayed where he was, curled into a ball on his side, trying to remember. The pain in his chest was fading, but he was cold. Cold to the bone. And his mind was full of shadows, as if every minute of his life before this present moment had been walled off by a thick screen of smoked glass.

There was the sound of wood against stone, and sunlight hit his face. He blinked, half-opening his eyes.

'Ronan?' Leo reached up to touch his boyfriend's face.

They'd been at Ronan's campsite together, and then they'd walked to the lake, and Ronan had lit a fire, and then…

And then.

Leo gasped and scrambled backwards, away from Ronan, to the edge of the room. 'What did you do to me?' He clawed at the pattern burnt into the skin of his chest, making it bleed.

'Leo, don't—' Ronan took a step nearer.

'No! Stay away!' Leo remembered now. The figure of the King of Hearts, emerging from the water. The unbearable, suffocating pain as it took control of his body. And then his sister –

Merry. He'd tried to warn her. To scream at her to run. But the thing inside him had laughed. And Ronan had laughed. And then his sister and Ronan had started fighting, hurling spells at each other. 'Merry?'

'She's alive. Safe.'

'You tried to kill her.'

'I didn't—' Ronan broke off and dropped into a wooden chair, crossing his legs. 'I just couldn't let her stop me, Leo. I had to get away. Even in our world, I'm not,' his mouth twisted, 'not normal.' He meant the world of witches, and wizards, and half-remembered magic. 'I needed the power that was trapped under the lake.' Ronan looked up again, and Leo could see the hunger blazing in his eyes. 'I still need it. And I needed you to act as,' he waved a hand through the air, 'a vessel, to transport that power. But even if I hadn't, I would never have left you behind. I love you. I thought you loved me.'

'Love?' Leo shivered and took a deep breath, wincing as the skin across his chest stretched. 'How can you even use that word after what you've done?' He glanced around, taking in his surroundings for the first time: a stone room, like the inside of a castle; rushes on the floor; a low bed with furs strewn across it. Nowhere he recognised. Panic twisted his gut. 'Where are we?'

Ronan shrugged slightly. 'Somewhere safe. Another time. Another reality. Somewhere I can properly exist.'

'I don't understand.'

'I couldn't stay in our time, Leo. D'you think I liked stealing from other witches and wizards? Living on the dregs of their power? Knowing that I would always be despised, always hunted?' He laughed; it was a hard, bitter sound. 'I was a parasite! At least, that's how they saw me. The King of Hearts has taken us to a place where I can use its power and the power of the shadow realm. Permanently. No more stealing. But there's no way back, for either of us now.'

Leo swallowed hard. 'The King of Hearts...'

Ronan leant forward, steepling his fingers. 'It's not inside you any more. I promise.'

Was he telling the truth? The King of Hearts was a creature of the shadow realm created by the evil wizard Gwydion – a malevolent, bodiless entity that needed a human host to exist. Leo remembered being sealed inside his own head at the lake, remembered the suffocating presence that had taken his limbs and mouth for its own. He felt as if he was in control of his body again. But was he truly free of the creature?

His abductor was watching him. 'We can be together now, Leo, and no one can—'

'She'll come for me.' Leo hugged his knees to his chest, digging his nails into the flesh of his arms, focusing on the pain to keep from screaming. 'Merry will find me.'

Ronan shook his head.

'No, she won't. They won't let her. The coven, I mean. Besides, she has Finn now.'

Finn, the wizard who'd shown up in Tillingham just after Gran had gone missing? It was true that he and Merry had been spending a lot of time together, but Leo couldn't quite remember whether his sister had actually been dating the guy. Finn had been there too, hadn't he? At the lake, that night. Ronan was still talking.

'Finn will take her back to Ireland and she'll forget all about her big brother. He'll make sure of that.' Ronan stood up, dragged one of the furs off the bed and tossed it to Leo. 'That's what you never understood about witches and wizards. We're selfish. We might try to hide it with oaths about helping plebs and so on, but that's just a veneer. Even for your precious sister. She has her power. And now she's with Finn, she'll have position and wealth as well — everything she could possibly want. To be sure, she'll grieve for you, for a while. But then she'll move on.'

'No. You're lying, you're—' Leo tried to force himself back through the wall as Ronan walked towards him. 'Merry wouldn't leave me here with you. She wouldn't.'

Ronan crouched down in front of him. 'We'll see. But in the meantime, you need to trust me, Leo. You belong to me now, and I'm going to take care of you…'

ONE

JACK.

Nearly five months had passed since they'd last stood face to face. But Merry would have known him anywhere. Sure, his hair was shorter. And his clothes were different. Gone were the princely garments with the rich embroidery and fur trimming. Instead, he was wearing coarse woollen trousers, a cloth shirt and a ragged leather tunic. His forearms were painted with patterns and symbols, dark blue lines swirling and interlocking. The only hint of luxury was a gold belt buckle, which gleamed with hints of red and green, despite the dull grey light. And he looked older. Wearier.

Still, she knew him.

He was the same boy she'd fallen in love with. The same cursed prince who had been put into an enchanted sleep fifteen hundred years ago and had woken in her own time, still possessed by a creature summoned from the shadow realm. Of course, he'd been a corpse the last time she'd seen him. *Actually* seen him, not just dreamt about him. His dead body had been lying on the floor of the wizard Gwydion's chambers, beneath the Black Lake. She'd knelt by him, wept over him, kissed him –

The temptation to run to him now, to throw her arms round his neck, was almost too strong to resist.

But Jack – this Jack – was holding a long, angular knife to Finn's throat. Finn was on his knees in the snow, panting, his face pale and rigid. Jack had hold of Finn's hair, and as Merry stepped forward he yanked the wizard's head further back, making the other boy cry out in pain. The blade was hard against Finn's skin now, and Merry could see a bead of blood welling up against the dark metal.

Jack frowned at her. There was no recognition.

'Who are you? And how do you know my name?'

She tried to read his feelings, to use that ability to pick up emotions that she'd gained a few months ago. But there was nothing. Either the people were different here

– wherever here was – or the passage through the point of intersection had done something to her. She could sense her magic clearly, running like a current beneath her skin. But nothing else.

Finn whimpered as Jack pressed the knife further into his flesh.

'Answer me!'

Jack had forgotten her. Or...

Or maybe, in this place, he and I have never actually met.

'Jack, please—' She stopped short, felt her eyes widen. The unfamiliar syllables of Old English felt strange in her mouth, just as they had done under the lake all those months ago when she'd confronted Gwydion. Her magic must have just taken over, and her brain switched language automatically. She didn't know how it had happened, any more than she knew where she was, or why Finn – a powerful wizard himself – hadn't disarmed Jack with a spell, or why Jack seemed so different from the gentle, sad prince that she remembered. Any more than she knew what to do next.

Merry pressed her hands to her eyes. The frost-laden air hurt her nose and throat. The dense forest that surrounded them breathed out a dark, velvet silence that seemed to suck at her eardrums. Still, with her eyes closed, she could almost imagine she was back home in her room in the middle of the night, Mum asleep at the other end of the corridor and Leo in the room opposite hers, even the cats quietly dreaming on top of the boiler in the kitchen…

'Well?'

Jack's voice jerked her back to the present. She had to get Finn away from him. Not through magic, though: whoever this Jack was, she didn't want to hurt him.

'We're not enemies. We just need your help.' Merry spread her hands wide, palms up. 'Please, let him go.'

Jack didn't release his grip on Finn's hair. But he did shift the knife slightly, loosening the pressure on Finn's neck.

'You have not answered my question. How do you know me? And what manner of creature are you?'

'I'm not a creature. I'm just a girl.'

Jack looked her up and down. 'You are not clad as a girl.'

'Well, I am a girl. You're going to have to take my word for it. I'm not… I'm not from around here. And as to how I know you –' Merry paused, thinking quickly – 'I have a friend who knows you. She's called Meredith.' Meredith, her ancestor, the witch who had placed both

Jack and Gwydion into the enchanted sleep. The witch who had sworn the oath that had got Merry involved with Jack in the first place. Merry peered into Jack's eyes, looking in vain for a reaction. Perhaps in this reality he hadn't met Meredith yet, or perhaps she didn't even exist in this world. Or maybe he *did* know her, but he had a really excellent poker face. 'Finn's my friend too, so if you could just—'

'What are you doing here? Were you following me? Spying on me?'

Merry pinched the bridge of her nose; she was starting to develop a headache.

'No. We're not spies. I'm looking for my brother. He was taken against his will, and I think he might have been brought here. Maybe a few days ago.' She glanced at the brooding forest around them, hoping for some sign that she was right, that Leo had been here too. The daylight was fading quickly, and the darkness of the forest was nearly impenetrable. Merry shivered, wrapping her arms round herself; she had two jumpers and a long-sleeved T-shirt on, but still the chill was worming its way into her bones. 'Please, Jack. I need your help.'

Jack gazed at her for a few seconds. Then he let go of Finn and stepped away. But he kept his knife drawn, his stance suggesting he could spring into action in the space of a breath. Finn sagged forward, clutching at his neck.

Merry edged closer. 'Do you need help?'

Finn pushed himself upright and staggered over to stand next to her. He was trembling. She took his hand, peering up into his face, but he avoided her gaze. 'Finn?'

'Just, um… just give me a minute. I'll be fine.' Sliding down against the trunk of a tree, he dropped his head into his hands.

Merry turned back to Jack. 'Leo, my brother – he's blond, like you, and he's wearing trousers, and has this strange mark on his chest…' She winced, remembering the ugly scrawl that Ronan had burnt into Leo's skin. 'And he was with another guy who has dark, curly hair, and he calls himself Ronan, but—'

'Ronan?' Jack laughed, but there was no humour in it. The sound seemed dead in the cold air. 'I know of Ronan. Everyone does. There's neither a village nor a hamlet in the land that has been left untouched by him and his… creatures. He turns all to darkness and ruin. The kingdom was cursed from the moment he came here.' He thrust the long knife back into the scabbard that hung at his waist. 'I am sorry for you. Truly. But if Ronan has taken your brother…' He shrugged. 'There is nothing you can do.

Apart from pray to whichever gods you serve that your brother is already dead.' He brushed his fingers across marks tattooed on to the insides of his wrists. *Runes of some sort*, Merry thought, though she couldn't see them clearly. 'You should leave whilst you still can. The borders are closing fast as the black holly spreads.' Jack turned and pulled something out of the undergrowth: Finn's bag. 'Here.'

Merry made no move to take the bag. Jack had to be mistaken. He was making it sound like Ronan had been here – wherever here was – for ages. But Ronan and Leo had only left Tillingham and their own world a few days ago...

'You must go.' Jack thrust the bag into her arms. 'The king...' Jack's voice faltered for a moment, 'King Aidan still holds Helmswick. But Helmswick has been under siege from Ronan and his forces these two months past. The citadel cannot hold out much longer.'

Two months?

'But – but what about Edith?' The Helmswick Merry knew of, the place Jack had told her about, had been ruled by a queen: by his mother, Edith, not by his father, Aidan.

There was a pause. Merry heard a shriek in the distance – some sort of animal, or bird. The first living sound she'd heard in this place apart from their own voices.

'The queen is dead: Ronan murdered her. A few weeks before the siege began.'

Merry stood there, struggling to comprehend. Jack's voice was flat, emotionless, almost as if he didn't care. Didn't he know that the queen was his blood mother? Or was he just as heartless as he seemed?

He swung away from her. 'The road to the Kentish border lies there. I suggest you take it.' Jerking his thumb over his shoulder, he began striding in the opposite direction.

'But you're wrong: the Ronan I'm talking about can't possibly be the same person who's attacking your lands,' Merry cried out. 'He isn't that powerful.' She'd fought with Ronan at the lake and had almost destroyed him – until Finn had got in her way. Finn had been trying to save his own brother's life; she knew that now. But still, Ronan had escaped and he'd taken Leo with him. 'And besides, Ronan would only have arrived here a few days ago. Days, not months.'

Jack didn't respond – he just kept walking.

In desperation, Merry hurried after him. 'Wait!' She hooked the necklace out from beneath her T-shirt and opened the locket that was hanging from the chain. 'This is my brother. Are you sure you haven't seen him?'

Jack glanced at the photo in the locket. His eyes narrowed. 'I have seen him. I saw him with Ronan.' He ripped the chain from her neck and hurled it away from him. 'Standing next to Ronan, as a free man.'

Merry raised her hands and started to back away.

'No, it isn't like that: my brother isn't with Ronan through choice. He was kidnapped! Whatever you think you saw, you've got it wrong.'

'You're lying.' Jack drew his knife again.

In the next instant Finn was at her side. He looked ill, and there was a streak of blood on his neck, but he held Leo's sword – the one they'd brought with them – firmly in front of him.

'Merry, I don't understand whatever language he and you are speaking, but this… this isn't the Jack you described to me. He isn't kind, or compassionate. Hit him with a binding charm, quickly!'

Merry still hesitated.

'But we need him to help us –'

'He can't! Or he won't.' Jack was circling them, looking for a way past Finn's blade. 'Hurry up!'

An unearthly wail split the stillness of the forest. Jack swung around, scanning the treetops. Finn grabbed Merry's hand.

'If I didn't know better,' he murmured, 'I'd say that was a banshee.'

'A banshee?' Merry peered into the shadows around the edge of the clearing. 'But they don't exist.'

Another long, drawn-out shriek, nearer this time. Finn shifted so he was back to back with Merry.

'Are you sure about that?'

As he finished speaking, a creature exploded out of a clump of dark fir trees. Merry gasped and flinched, raising her hands in defence even as her brain clamoured in denial. She recognised this creature. She'd seen it in a school library book about ancient Greek myths. Wide, bronze-feathered wings, monstrous sickle-shaped talons, and the head — the head of a woman, with feathers for hair. Its mouth was open, screaming, revealing razor-sharp, needle-like teeth.

Not a banshee. A harpy.

The creature swooped towards Jack. He threw his knife at it, but the blade missed. Screeching with rage the harpy banked and descended again, raking Jack's up-flung arm with its claws, forcing him to his knees.

Finn grabbed Merry by the wrist. 'Let's go.'

'No.' She wrenched her hand free. 'We can't leave Jack. We need his help...'

Finn gritted his teeth, but he raised the sword again. 'Fine. Go on, then. Help him.'

The harpy had started shredding Jack's arms and neck, scattering dark red droplets of blood across the white snow. Merry summoned two balls of witch fire and launched them at the creature. The seething, coruscating violet strands encased the harpy and it screamed again – screamed in pain, this time. As it flapped around, trying to shake the magic from its wings, Finn leapt forward and brought the sword round in a great arc, slicing the creature's head from its neck. Body and head tumbled to the ground.

Jack, still crouched on the snow, dragged his gaze away from the dismembered remains and the pool of blood that was rapidly sinking into the frozen earth, and stared at Merry and Finn.

'You saved me.'

'Yeah.' Merry sighed. 'We saved you.'

All three of them watched the dead harpy for a bit longer. Merry had no idea what to do next.

Finally, Finn bent down to clean the blade of the sword on a bit of moss that was sticking up out of the snow. Jack's knife was lying nearby; Merry picked it up. 'If I give you this back, will you promise not to attack us?'

Jack hesitated for a moment, then nodded. Merry handed him the blade. He pushed himself up off the ground and shoved the knife into its scabbard.

'So,' he looked at her, the hint of a smile on his lips, 'just a girl?'

'I am a girl.' Merry shrugged. 'But I'm also a witch.' She glanced up: two large carrion crows had settled on the branch of a nearby tree, eyeing the bleeding carcass. They were probably just regular birds, but she hadn't forgotten the crow that seemed to be following her and Leo through the woods a few weeks back.

'We're attracting attention.' She nodded towards the harpy. 'Let's get rid of this thing.'

Twenty minutes later, Merry had magically incinerated the remains of the harpy and had healed the injury to Finn's neck. She walked over to Jack, the pot of Gran's healing salve still in her hand. 'Here: this will help.'

Jack peered at the jar. 'What is it?'

'It's an ointment my grandmother made. It will heal the cuts on your arms.'

He drew back. 'How do I know you're not trying to poison me?'

'Poison you?' Merry shook her head, slipping back into

modern English as she exhaled sharply. 'And why would I be trying to poison you?'

Finn was sitting beneath a tree nearby with his arms wrapped round his legs and Leo's sword stuck into the ground next to him. He glanced up. 'If she wanted you dead she'd have let the harpy kill you. Idiot pleb.'

Jack flushed. He couldn't have understood Finn's words – and it was doubtful he had ever heard the word *pleb* used the way wizards used it, as a dismissive term for a non-magical person – but he obviously recognised Finn's tone of voice. Still, he held out his arms and allowed Merry to dab some of the ointment on to the gashes dealt out by the harpy's claws. Almost immediately, Merry could see the wounds begin to heal as his skin puckered and pink scar tissue formed: Gran's potion was working.

Jack winced, flinching from Merry's touch.

'The pain won't last long,' she reassured him.

He nodded and gritted his teeth. 'Tell me: are you and Ronan kin? Is that why you speak the same strange language as him?'

Merry stiffened. 'Can you understand what Finn and I are saying to each other?'

Jack shook his head. 'I merely recognise some of the

words. Ronan's creatures speak the same way, and I have spent time around them.' He shuddered, either with discomfort or remembrance – Merry wasn't sure. 'Too much time.'

'Well, Ronan and I are definitely not kin. But we're both witches.'

'He is a witch? Not a wizard?'

'No. Ronan is a male witch – there's a difference. He inherited his magic from his mother. Male witches are really rare, and they're usually unstable and have some sort of magical… deformity…'

Jack was looking confused.

'But Ronan and Finn and me, we do all come from the same place.'

'But he,' Jack nodded towards Finn, 'is not a witch.'

'No. He's a wizard.' More confusion. 'And no, I don't know why he didn't just put a spell on you.'

Jack gasped as Merry spread the ointment on a particularly deep cut. 'Neither of you dress like any other witch or wizard that I know of.'

'Really?' Merry said, trying to appear thoroughly absorbed in what she was doing. 'How many other witches and wizards do you know?' The line of Jack's jaw tightened, but he didn't reply. 'There. All done.'

Jack closed his eyes and slumped against the tree stump behind him as Merry sat back on her heels. 'Now, you need to tell me a couple of things,' she started. 'When did Ronan arrive here? And when exactly did you see him and my brother together?'

'How long has Ronan been here? I do not know. But I do know that he began his attacks around harvest time, and the year is nearly over. As for your brother, I saw him the day Ronan and his creatures first attacked Helmswick. The day the queen died.'

Merry's stomach lurched. If Jack was right, at least three or four months had passed since her brother had arrived here, possessed by the King of Hearts. She couldn't bear to think about what Leo might have suffered during that time. She'd seen Jack possessed, of course; had seen him slowly consumed by the King of Hearts, but she'd been able to cast the creature out and had broken Gwydion's curse. Still, the King of Hearts had survived. Which meant that Ronan had been able to summon it, and place it inside her own brother.

What if the King of Hearts had already taken Leo over entirely? Perhaps there was nothing left of him. Perhaps he *was* already dead.

'What was Leo doing, the day you saw him?' Merry

asked. 'Did he look ill?' Fear turned her stomach. 'He didn't... He didn't help Ronan murder Edith, did he?'

Jack glanced up at her. 'No. The queen died by Ronan's blade alone. Your brother's hands were not tied, that much I know, but he could have been under a spell...' He shook his head. 'I cannot say for sure.' He sat up straighter, looking about him and frowning. 'The morning is wasting. I must find my horse. She bolted when your friend blundered into the clearing.' Jack got to his feet and wandered off into the forest. Soon he was lost to view, though Merry could still hear him calling out the horse's name.

Finn hadn't moved all this time.

Merry went to sit next to him. 'I'm going to try a spell on you, like I did on Leo once. It was so he could understand what Jack and Gwydion were saying. Hold still.' She pressed one fingertip lightly against his forehead. Finn's eyes widened as Merry used her power to reach into his mind and share her understanding with him. There was probably a more orthodox way of doing such magic, but she hadn't learnt a formal spell for it yet. 'Hopefully that's worked. I suppose we'll find out when Jack comes back.'

'If he comes back,' Finn murmured, running the tip of one finger across the old scar on the inside of his wrist.

'What happened before I arrived? Why didn't you disarm Jack when he attacked you?'

'I tried to, but...' Finn shuddered. 'I couldn't cast properly. None of the spells worked.' He clutched her hand. His skin was clammy, and his chest was rising and falling rapidly, as if he couldn't quite catch his breath. Merry realised that he was scared. Terrified. And that frightened her, because she'd never seen him like this before. Not when they'd first met, and he'd been trapped by a binding charm. Not when they'd found her friend Flo's body in the woods. Not even when – overwhelmed by anger and grief – she'd attacked him at the Black Lake.

'Finn, what is it? What's wrong?'

He gripped her hand even more tightly.

'I think I've lost my power, Merry. I think it's gone.'

TWO

MERRY BRUSHED THE fingers of her free hand across Finn's cheek. 'Perhaps it's just the effect of going through the point of intersection. It will probably come back soon.'

'You think?' She could hear the doubt in his voice. And in truth, she was guessing. She'd only recently learnt about points of intersection: places where normality was stretched thinner, where it was possible to pass from one realm of existence to another, if you had the skill. The Black Lake was just such a place. A gateway. Ronan had been able to exploit this gateway to escape, and she and Finn had followed him.

Finn was tugging on one earlobe, frowning. 'But why hasn't it affected your magic, then?'

'I don't know. Perhaps you were in shock after Jack attacked you?' Somehow, she and Finn had become separated as they passed through the point of intersection, and Merry had woken up on her own in another part of the forest. 'Why don't you try again now?' She stood up and looked around. There was a beech tree close by with shrivelled brown leaves still clinging to its branches. 'Get those dead leaves to fall off the tree.'

Finn sighed, but he pushed himself to his feet and stared at the tree. Stretching out one hand, fingers extended, he muttered a couple of words in Latin. Nothing happened. He held both hands up and said the words again. Still nothing. Pushing up his sleeves he strode towards the tree and began chanting a longer spell:

'*Iubeo folia cadere, evolare, evanescere sicut aer…*'

He repeated the spell over and over, his voice getting louder, until he was shouting at the tree, pressing his hands against its trunk – but the leaves remained stubbornly in place.

'Finn…' Merry put her hand on his arm.

He let go of the tree, dragging the back of one hand shakily across his face. 'It's no good. I just can't… feel it.'

Merry bit her lip. What had happened to him? And was it going to happen to her next? Sighing, she pushed the thought to one side: there was little point worrying about it now. 'I'm sure it's not permanent. And in the meantime, we'll just have to manage the best we can. At least you can handle a sword. The way you decapitated that harpy was pretty impressive.'

'Huh.' Finn didn't sound particularly comforted. 'All the boys in the Kin Houses know how to fight with pleb weapons.'

The Kin Houses: families of wizards where the sons – and *only* the sons – inherited magical ability from their fathers. Kin House wizards were at the top of the social pile: better than other wizards, and infinitely superior to witches. At least in their own eyes. They were also, in Merry's experience, sexist and arrogant: even Finn, although he tried hard to overcome his upbringing. Merry guessed the Kin House girls, non-magical and mainly valued as pawns in dynastic marriages, didn't get to learn how to use a sword. They probably had to stick to needlework. She sighed and laid her head against Finn's shoulder.

'Don't worry. We're going to find Leo, and get back home, and then everything will be normal again. You'll see.'

There was a noise behind them. Jack was standing there, watching them, his horse next to him. The expression on his face was softer; perhaps he pitied them? Tying the horse's reins to a branch he drew nearer. 'It's nearly midday. We should leave this place.'

For a moment, Finn's gloom was replaced by surprise. He could obviously understand what Jack had said. But his expression soured again as he looked up at the other boy. 'Where are you proposing we go?'

Jack controlled his surprise better, but he pointedly addressed his answer to Merry, not Finn. 'There's a cave, less than a day's walk from here. You can rest there while I seek out news of your brother.'

Finn stood up, shaking his head. 'C'mon, Merry. Jack's already told us everything he knows. I can't see the point of wasting a day walking to this cave. We need to start looking for Ronan ourselves. Leo's probably still with him.'

'I would not reject my offer of help if I were you.' Jack's voice sharpened. 'You may be happy to put your companion in danger, or to rely on her protection. But the land is no longer safe for her kind.'

Finn squared up to Jack, reaching for his sword. 'I don't know who you think you are, pleb, but I assure you, I'm perfectly capable of looking after myself and Merry…'

Merry jumped up and put a hand on Finn's arm, gently tugging him backwards. 'Finn, please don't. Jack's right: we need to get our bearings. This place just isn't what I was expecting...' She glanced uneasily at the ashes of the harpy. 'I think we could use a little local help. We could definitely use more information. I mean, shouldn't we work out what we're up against? What Ronan's been doing since he arrived?'

Finn's eyes were stony. But he turned his back on Jack, brushing some dirt off his sleeve. 'Leo wouldn't even be here if I hadn't stopped you killing Ronan while you had the chance. So, it's your call, Merry. Whatever you think best.'

Merry squeezed Finn's hand, then turned to Jack. 'Very well. We'll go with you – hopefully we'll find news of Ronan and Leo. But no funny business.' It didn't come out right in Old English, but Jack seemed to understand what she was saying. He led the horse forward and tied Merry's pack on to its back.

'Sorrel here can carry your bags. We have a long way to go.'

At some point, Merry had lost track of how long they'd been walking. And now it was impossible to tell where they were. The forest seemed to stretch on forever, in all directions: acres and acres of almost identical trees. Sharp-needled yews, so dark a green as to be almost black, or broad-trunked oaks, twisted with age, their leafless fingers stretching out above the narrow path. Snow lay everywhere on the ground, and as the day waned they all stumbled more and more often into deep drifts. Merry had wanted to use magic to clear the path, but Jack wouldn't let her; he didn't want to risk attracting the attention of the creatures, magical or non-magical, that lived in the wood. He even objected to her using witch fire to light their way. Merry, peering into the darkness between the trees, shivered. She couldn't make out anything lurking in the shadows. But still, there was a vigilance to the forest that set her teeth on edge. Something was watching them; something that didn't want them there. So, she hadn't argued with Jack. Instead, they toiled on, hour after hour, even after the daylight was gone.

At least there was a full moon tonight. It had risen high, and was now hanging in the strip of sky directly above them. Merry, trailing behind the other two, stared up at it. She wondered where Leo was, whether he was looking up at the same moon and asking himself why his sister had abandoned him. Tears clouded her vision. She stumbled into yet another deep, snow-concealed rut and plunged forward on to her face.

Finn hurried back and pulled her out of the drift, hauling her upright and brushing the snow off her legs. 'Are you all right?' It was the first time he'd spoken for hours. He waited for her to nod before turning on Jack. 'This is ridiculous. It's almost pitch-black, we're slowly freezing to death, we've been walking for ages, and we're not getting anywhere. Where the hell is this cave you're supposedly guiding us to? If it's not near, we should stop to rest.'

Jack raised his eyebrows. He whispered something to Sorrel and walked over to Finn and Merry. 'Do you not trust me? *Wizard?*' His voice was low, but the sarcasm in it was unmistakable. Finn flushed and half-stepped towards Jack, one hand raised, before abruptly turning away.

Merry glared at Jack; he shrugged slightly. 'Finn's right,' she said, 'we should camp here for the night, if this cave is much further.' Her limbs ached with cold, even though she was now wearing almost every piece of clothing she'd brought with her. 'I'd really rather not lose my fingers and toes to frostbite.'

Jack sighed.

'We are nearly through the forest, though you cannot see the edge of the trees from here. The cave I spoke of is not so very far now, no more than an hour away.' Sorrel snorted and tossed her head and Jack narrowed his eyes, staring into the shadow beneath the surrounding trees. 'And it's our only choice: you cannot sleep in the woods. Not if you wish to be alive when morning comes.'

'I'm pretty sure I can deal with whatever this wood might throw at us.'

Jack bent his head towards hers.

'Perhaps so. But what about your friend? Would you risk him?'

Merry glanced at Finn. He was slouched on a fallen tree trunk a few metres away, staring down at the snow. Jack had a point. Despite his earlier show of bravado, without magic, Finn couldn't defend himself so well, and if he got captured...

She wasn't about to have another person she loved turned into a bargaining chip.

'OK. Let's go.'

Jack nodded, strode over to Sorrel and began pulling the bags off the horse's back.

'You should ride.'

'No. I don't know how, and I don't want to. I can keep walking.'

'You're shorter than the –' Jack paused, cleared his throat

– 'than Finn and me. You're slowing us down.' He tilted his head, watching her. 'I can tie you on, if you wish.'

Merry gritted her teeth.

'No, thanks. I'll manage.'

Luckily, Sorrel was standing quietly. There was a saddle of sorts, but no stirrups: Jack had to hoist her up on to the horse's back. Once there, Merry had to wedge her knees underneath two horn-shaped bits that stuck out from the front of the saddle. She leant over and wound her hands into the horse's mane.

A howl ripped through the stillness of the forest. Sorrel shied and Merry lurched precariously. Jack grabbed the reins and drew his knife, urging Sorrel into a walk. Finn picked up his and Merry's bags and took up position next to her.

'Finn? Are you OK?'

He didn't reply; just dropped his head and jerked his backpack further up on to his shoulders.

'Finn?'

'I'm fine, Merry. C'mon, let's get you out of this cold.'

He didn't sound fine.

Merry tightened her grip on the horse. She really needed this day to be over.

★

Perhaps Jack's estimate of the distance to the cave was accurate, but to Merry it seemed like one very long hour. A couple of times she nearly fell asleep, nodding over Sorrel's neck, catching herself just in time as she began to slip sideways. And once she thought she saw a face peering at them from the trees nearest the path. But by the time she'd blinked and straightened up to get a better look, whatever it was – if it was anything at all, other than her imagination – had gone. Finally, the trees thinned and petered out. Spread below them in the moonlight, which now shone only fitfully between the clouds, was a wide, empty plain.

Not entirely empty: Merry could just make out scattered groups of buildings, or the remains of buildings. But there was no firelight, or torchlight. No signs of life anywhere.

'This way.' Jack turned right, away from the path that meandered down the side of the hill, leading them parallel to the wood in the direction of a rocky outcrop. He was walking faster now, guiding Sorrel past boulders half-submerged in snow, until they came to a clump of Scots pine. Beyond the pines was a sort of… fold in the ground, which deepened into a steeply sloping channel. Finally, after another few minutes of anxious scrambling, they reached the bottom.

'Here.' Jack pulled aside an overhanging curtain of trailing ivy. Behind was a tall cleft in the rock face. 'It widens, inside.'

Finn dumped the bags on the ground by the cave entrance, wincing and rolling his shoulders back. 'We need a fire.'

'I can take care of that.' Merry tried to dismount elegantly. But after sitting for so long, her arms and legs were too cold to obey her; she managed to swing one leg across the saddle before losing her grip and sliding sideways.

'Careful—' Jack began, but Finn was quicker. He grabbed Merry and lowered her gently to the ground. Her knees buckled under her immediately.

'Sorry,' Merry murmured. 'Pins and needles.'

'You're frozen.' Finn picked her up. 'Let's get inside.'

The cave was a lot larger than it looked from the outside, stretching back a long way into the hillside above. As they passed behind the ivy Merry conjured several globes of witch fire, sending most upwards to hover by the roof of the cave and keeping one in between her hands to warm them. The flickering violet light cast strange shadows, but at least it revealed their surroundings: a sandy floor in the front sections of the cave, giving way to moss-covered rocks further back. The twisting shape of the cave – from the middle of it, Merry couldn't see the entrance – gave protection from the wind outside. Someone had dug a pit in the ground that was filled with ash; clearly, they weren't the first people to have sought refuge here. There was even a small spring that bubbled out of a fissure in the wall before seeping away into the earth. Watching the water, Merry realised how hungry and thirsty she was. She glanced round to locate her bag and saw that Finn was sitting with his head in his hands again, tapping his fingers over and over against his skull.

'Finn…'

He looked up at her – there was so much grief and fear in his eyes.

'I can't feel it any more, Merry.' He touched the centre of his chest, and Merry remembered how he'd talked to her in the garden back home about sensing and controlling her power. 'There's just… emptiness.'

Merry slipped an arm round his shoulders. 'Have you tried again to cast a spell?'

Finn shook his head. 'There's no point. I know it won't work.'

Jack came in carrying a few branches and twigs. 'This is all I could find. And it's damp.' He glanced uncertainly at Finn. 'But the spring water is good to drink. It may revive you.' Arranging the wood in a rough heap in the pit, he brought out two stones from a pouch hanging off his belt and struck a spark. But the fire wouldn't take.

'Let me help.' Merry came to crouch next to Jack. The branches were thin and sodden; even to her untrained eye, they didn't look like good bonfire material.

They need to be dryer. And much bigger.

There had been a collection of household spells among the books that Gran had given her. Merry could see it now: a blue cloth cover embossed in black. And inside had been all sorts of charms that Merry hadn't found that interesting. Cleaning spells and darning spells and charms for making your bread mixture rise. There had also been spells for drying clothes and one for getting a tree to produce larger fruit. Some combination of those would surely work here? Merry closed her eyes and tried to remember…

Her power was strong and instant. Before she'd even finished murmuring the makeshift charm, she could feel heat on her face. And light. She opened her eyes again. In place of a few damp bits of wood there was a substantial pile of logs. Flames blazed brightly from the centre of the pile, licking around the edges of the outer logs and making them glow. Merry held her hands up to the fire and sighed as her cold, cramped muscles finally began to relax. She looked at her companions. Finn was staring at the flames, but otherwise he hadn't moved. And Jack… Jack was busy getting food out of his bag, almost like magical fire-starting was something he saw every day. So far, he'd produced a few small yellow-brown apples, a wooden bowl full of nuts mixed with a kind of berry that Merry didn't recognise, and a large, flat disc of bread that he was tearing into three pieces. Little enough, but better than nothing. Merry took a piece of bread and one of the apples, got a cereal bar from her bag – all she'd been able to bring since she hadn't wanted to risk raiding the kitchen before leaving home – and went over to kneel next to Finn.

'Do you want something to eat?'

He shrugged.

'Please, try. It might make you feel better.' She went to get a blanket out of her bag, and fill Finn's water bottle at the spring. When she returned, he was picking at the bread. She shook the blanket out and wrapped it round his shoulders, crouching down in front of him. 'Why don't you come and sit nearer the fire?'

Finn glanced over at Jack, who was eating rapidly and

cutting slices off something – cheese? – with a smaller knife.

'No. I don't feel like chatting. And I'm not really hungry. I, um… I guess I'll try to get some sleep. I'm already useless enough without being exhausted too.'

'Don't say that: you're not useless. I need you. Besides, the magic – it'll come back.'

'Maybe.' He gave her a small smile, took her hand and dropped a kiss into her palm. 'Don't worry about me, Merry. Eventually I'll stop feeling sorry for myself. And I'll probably feel better once I've had some sleep.'

'Well, give me a shout if you need anything.'

'I will.' He wrapped the blanket round himself and lay down, facing the wall of the cave.

Merry went back to the fire, settled herself next to Jack and took a hunk of bread and a handful of nuts.

'Here.' Jack poured something from a leather bottle into a horn cup and passed it to her. She took a sip.

'Mead?' Jack nodded. Merry felt the honeyed liquid warming her as it slipped down her throat. She was tempted to drink more. But the fire was already making her drowsy, and there was still too much she needed to know. 'So. Ronan arrived in the autumn, if not earlier. And ever since then he's been laying waste to the countryside. And he's killed the queen, and is besieging the king, and if he takes the king he'll control the kingdom.' It sounded like a game of chess. 'Do I have it right?'

'Yes.' Jack stuck the small knife into one of the apples, splitting it in half. 'I was only told a few months ago that my parents – the people who brought me up – were not actually my kin. I travelled to Helmswick and met the king and queen, my natural parents. I spent a day with them. One day. And then…' His features twisted with anguish. 'And then I watched my birth mother die.' He hunched over, wrapping his arms round his knees. It was so familiar a gesture. Merry began to reach out her hand towards him. But she stopped, remembering: this Jack didn't know her. Had never kissed her, or held her.

'I'm sorry, Jack.' She hesitated briefly. 'How did Ronan kill the queen?'

'He cut out her heart.'

Merry shivered and took another sip of mead. It sounded as if Ronan was working blood magic, of the darkest kind.

'My father,' Jack continued, 'my blood father, I mean – the queen's death broke him, I think.' He nudged a stray brand back into the fire with his foot.

'Has he given up?'

'No. But his mind... King Aidan was not, from what I've been told, an intolerant man. But now...' He glanced up at her. 'He believes magic was responsible for his wife's death. He blames your kind: witches and wizards. He's outlawed them, ordered them to be hunted down and executed. And Ronan, he has been searching them out too, offering wealth and position in return for their aid, taking by force those who refuse. Some have joined him willingly, eager for gain, although there are many more who have gone into hiding. It is not a good time to have magical power.'

Now, Merry understood Jack's earlier caution. If both Ronan's forces and the king's servants were searching for witches and wizards, then neither she nor Finn were safe. 'What about the harpies? Did Ronan create them, or bring them from somewhere?'

Jack looked confused by her question.

'Harpies? No. They've always been here. They're far more dangerous since Ronan arrived, of course. They thrive in the dark magic he has unleashed across the land, and have grown bolder and more numerous. Do you not have such creatures where you dwell?'

'No. Only in stories.' Merry felt a current of panic snake through her guts. 'What about, um, unicorns?'

'Yes. Not in the forest we journeyed through today, but further south.'

Oh. 'Mermaids?'

Jack nodded, frowning at her, as if the existence of mermaids was so obvious that only an idiot would even ask.

'Dragons?'

'No, no dragons. They were mostly killed by the elves.' Jack's eyes narrowed. 'Where exactly are you from, Merry?'

'I'm from…' Merry hesitated, trying to picture a map of England and remember which counties had been around in Anglo-Saxon times, 'Northumberland.' It came out sounding more like a question, but Jack seemed satisfied: he grunted, though, in a tone that suggested he didn't have a high opinion of people from Northumberland.

Did that mean they were in fact in England, just in a different time? Merry wasn't convinced. Given what Jack had just told her, she wasn't sure this was a real place at all. It sounded more like she and Finn had fallen into a story book…

A huge yawn overtook her, and she wondered what the time was; she didn't have a watch, and her phone was dead. Past midnight, probably. Definitely time to sleep. But she had one further question. 'Have you ever heard of a wizard named Gwydion?'

Jack face darkened. 'I have. He was a monster. But no one has seen him for years.'

'Oh. So, Jack, how old are you?'

'Nearly nineteen, I believe.'

Nineteen? *Her* Jack had been snatched by Gwydion just after his eighteenth birthday. Had Ronan's arrival just messed up the sequence of events, or had Ronan put a permanent stop to Gwydion's plans? Or was Gwydion still alive and plotting?

Jack stood up. 'I must check on Sorrel. Then I'll take the first watch. You should get some sleep.' He hesitated, turning the short knife he'd been using on the food over and over in his fingers. 'Thank you. For saving me from the harpy earlier, instead of leaving me.' He nodded at her. 'I am in your debt.'

'You're welcome. But I would never have left you. I…' Merry paused. Because what could she really say?

I thought I'd lost you…

I used to love you…

At least, I loved someone almost exactly like you…

Jack tilted his head, quizzical.

'What?'

Merry pressed her hands to her cheeks.

'The fire's hot. I should check on Finn. Then I'll sleep.'

'Good.'

Jack grabbed the sword and the belt he'd discarded earlier. Merry waited until he'd left and then tipped the remaining nuts back into a leather pouch and took the empty bowl over to the spring. There was one other thing she had to do before she could rest. Filling the bowl with water she took off her silver bracelet and murmured the incantation.

Show me my brother.

The water went black. And then… And then, she saw Leo. He was alive. Her heart quickened and she squinted at the little picture, taking in every detail. He was alive, and sitting at a table, and he was concentrating – she could tell, because of the way he was biting on the side of his lower lip, the same way he always used to when he was studying. There was something in his hand – a pen? Or maybe a brush? She smiled a little; his hair was much longer now, falling in loose waves on to his shoulders. It suited him. He obviously wasn't tied up. And he looked so much like himself – so different to the way he'd appeared back at the lake, when the King of Hearts had controlled him.

Leo, please be OK…

Leo shivered and straightened up quickly, looking

around as if he had heard her. Merry hurriedly waved her hand, causing the vision to vanish. Surely, he hadn't really sensed her presence? She'd said the charm properly, in full, and Leo was no wizard.

But perhaps, if there was something from the shadow realm still inside him…

Merry poured the water away into the ground. Rest, that was what she needed now. She needed to be at the top of her game, so she could rescue Leo and make Ronan pay. Taking the second blanket from her bag she went to lie next to Finn.

'Finn?'

There was no answer. Hopefully, he was asleep. Merry touched him lightly on the shoulder, by way of goodnight, wrapped the blanket round her body and lay down.

THREE

LEO SHIVERED AND reached for a blanket lying nearby, pulling it tightly round his shoulders. *Someone just walked over my grave.*

That's what Gran would have said.

But there was more to it than that, he was sure. The sensation of his sister being nearby had felt impossibly real: as if she'd physically been there in the room with him. Maybe… maybe it meant something. Maybe Merry had finally found a way to follow him to wherever this place was, and now she was here, planning her attack on Ronan. And because their bond was so strong, he could somehow guess, he could somehow *know*, when she was near…

He shook his head, still slightly disorientated.

Maybe.

At first Leo had dreamt about Merry rescuing him almost every night. She'd show up, sometimes alone, sometimes with Gran, or with Mum and the rest of the coven. There would be a vicious, bloody battle. The details would vary, but every time Merry would destroy Ronan, annihilate him, burn him into the earth until there was nothing left of him but ash, drifting across scorched ground. But over time – as weeks, then months passed – the dreams had become less frequent. Merry had not shown up, and Leo had not been rescued. He swallowed hard, trying to force back the now familiar tide of fear. Although he didn't want to admit it, he was *terrified* at the thought that perhaps Ronan was right: Merry was never going to come for him.

It wouldn't be because she hadn't even tried. Despite Ronan's taunts, Leo was certain that his sister would never willingly give up on him. He knew she would have tried – over and over – to find a way to free him. Hadn't he seen her determination himself, on the day Ronan had kidnapped him? He could remember her fighting Ronan, just before Ronan dragged him back through the gateway, or portal, or whatever it was that had opened in the space by the Black Lake. Merry had been hurling spells at Ronan, and she'd almost defeated him. But then something had gone wrong. Leo blinked, trying to recall what he had seen. But the image was gone. He hadn't been fully in control of either his body or his mind that day. And there had been so much pain…

Still, what did any of it really matter now? He knew that Merry loved him, and she was certainly a powerful witch. But perhaps she wasn't powerful enough. Not this time… That sensation he'd felt earlier? It was most likely nothing more than the by-product of his increasingly fragile state of mind. Despair had driven him to hallucinate, to conjure up the ghostly presence of his sister when he needed her most.

It was late now, and the chill of evening was creeping in through the narrow, round-arched windows of his room. Leo lay on his bed and tried to sleep for a while, but he couldn't stop thinking, couldn't stop unwelcome thoughts intruding. Turning his head, he glanced at the marks he'd been carving into the grey flint wall to keep track of the days. By his reckoning, at least four months had past. Four whole months! Anger swelled in his chest. Four months of living – no, this couldn't be called living – of merely *existing* in this place. Four months of waking every morning to panic, to a suffocating realisation that he was not in his bed at home. That he was not dreaming. That the everyday nightmare was, in fact, reality. Four months of Ronan professing his love for him, offering Leo everything he could possibly want or need; except, of course, his freedom. Four months of, for the main part, having no one else to talk to other than Osric, the servant who had been assigned to him. And Ronan, of course.

No wonder I'm starting to lose it. One way or another, I need to get out of here. I can't wait for Merry any longer.

Looking towards the window and the dark skies outside, he sighed. The day was at an end. He picked up a stone, carefully carved another mark into the wall, then shut his eyes. Eventually, he fell asleep.

Leo gasped and sat bolt upright, his heart hammering on the inside of his chest. Someone was pounding on his door, making it shake in the frame, screaming his name over and over. Just in time, he jumped out of bed. The door flew open and Ronan staggered into the room, clutching a leather bottle. Mead, almost certainly; the scent of honey had filled the air. Every muscle in Leo's body was singing with tension. But at the same time, he tried hard to wipe any emotion from his face, to stay calm. He had learnt some time ago that it was best not to do or say anything to antagonise Ronan when he'd fallen into one of these… moods. Instead he stood by the table, his hands clenching the back of the chair as Ronan approached.

'It's been months, Leo. Months since the King of Hearts brought us here. But still, you refuse to join your life to mine as I've asked. You refuse to swear your allegiance to me. You won't even come to the hall to celebrate my victories. I offer you the chance to rule this land by my side, but you'd rather waste away, locked up in this tower instead.' He rubbed a hand roughly over his face. Had he been crying? 'Why can't you understand how much I love you? Everything I've done, I've done for us. For you. So why do you deny your feelings for me? I know that you love me, Leo. That much you've shown me, in the past.' Ronan reached one hand out to touch Leo's face, grazing his cheek softly.

Once, Leo would have done anything to have Ronan look at him, to touch him in that way. But not any more. He couldn't help it: he flinched.

Anger blazed in Ronan's eyes, and Leo swore silently in his head.

Ronan stared at Leo for one long minute, then shook his head. 'Fine. Have it your own way.'

Ronan turned and clapped his hands together. Moments later, two guards – human ones, at least – dragged someone through the doorway. It was a boy, about the same age as Leo, perhaps a couple of years younger. His face was mottled with bruises, and there were bloody gashes running across his forehead. Ronan gestured towards him. 'I have someone I'd like you to meet. This is Edwin. He and his family were captured this afternoon.'

Ronan began writing in the air with his forefinger. Glowing blue lines appeared, forming shapes: fire runes. Ronan's favourite form of magic since he'd acquired the power from the King of Hearts. The runes floated across the room towards the boy. He shrieked in fear, trying to twist out of the grasp of his guards. But it was no good. The runes settled on him, searing his skin, and the boy began to scream and writhe.

It was unbearable. Leo wanted to hit Ronan, to force him to stop. But he knew that it would just goad Ronan to more violence. There was nothing he could do to help the boy. Not yet. He lowered his gaze to the floor, wishing he could shut out the shrieks, and the stench of burning.

Finally, the screams faded into sobs.

Ronan took hold of Leo's chin and raised his head. 'It didn't have to be this way, Leo. I offered the boy a choice.

Told him he could serve me willingly, or pay the price. Is it my fault if he doesn't know what's for his own good?' He grabbed Leo by the shoulder, shaking him. 'Is it?'

'No, Ronan.'

Ronan took another swig from the bottle. 'You know what's going to happen now, don't you, Leo?'

Leo nodded, his chest tightening painfully. He'd seen it before. Too many times to count.

'Don't be shy, Leo.' He flung an arm out, pointing at the boy. 'Tell Edwin here what will happen to him. What will happen to his family. Because he chose to defy me.'

'But he won't understand what I'm saying. We speak a different language—'

'Oh, but he will understand you.' Ronan went and stood behind the boy and, placing his hands on the boy's head, muttered a spell. 'Now, tell him, Leo.'

Leo gazed steadfastly at Ronan; he couldn't bear to look at the boy. 'He will enslave you, Edwin. He will enslave your mind, and put one of his demon creatures into your body to control it. He will make you another of his servant army.'

The boy let out a strangled cry. '*Niese! Ne acwellað min cynn!*'

Ronan laughed. 'Oh, don't worry, Edwin, I won't kill

your family. Why would I, when living slaves are so much more useful?' He lifted his hand, ready to write more fire runes in the air.

Leo couldn't bear it any more. He stepped forward, putting one arm on to Ronan's outstretched hand, pushing it down. 'Please, you don't have to do this, Ronan. Please stop. For me.'

Ronan seized Leo's hand and sighed. When he looked up, Leo could see the desire in his eyes. All these months, and he still wanted Leo. He still wanted him to stand willingly by his side. 'I would. I would stop all of this, Leo. I'd stop enslaving people in this way, using the power of the shadow realm to control them. If only you would accept me as I am, I'd…' he faltered, 'I'd find another way to convince these people to obey me. A less destructive way of ensuring their loyalty. But I can't do it on my own. I can't…' He moved closer, slipping both arms round Leo's waist. Leo let him, knowing that his own safety and that of the boy rested on his cooperation. 'I know I could do better, be a more merciful ruler, more… compassionate, if only you were by my side. If you were to pledge yourself to me, once and for all, I promise you, Leo: I would stop all this unnecessary suffering.'

Leo began to tremble. His mind was screaming at him

to push Ronan away, to run. But he needed to buy time. So he leant in, bringing his arms round Ronan's back, burying his head in Ronan's shoulder. 'I'm tired, Ronan. I'm tired of all this fighting. I'm tired of being left up in this room by myself, day after day. I want to start living again.'

Ronan breathed in sharply and turned to the guards. 'Take the boy back to his family. Let them go.' Leo heard the guards hustle the boy out of the room.

'So… you're finally agreeing, Leo? To commit to me?' Ronan asked quietly. 'To commit to what I'm trying to achieve here? To making a better world for us, and for people like me?'

Leo took a deep breath in. 'Yes. I am. I'm ready.' He let go of Ronan and stepped back. 'What would you have me do?'

Ronan's face was glowing with excitement. 'The binding ceremony. Remember, Leo? I told you about it before. One of the spells I learnt since coming here.' He began pacing up and down, rubbing his hands. 'Once it's done, you'll belong to me completely. Forever.'

Belong? That was the only way Ronan seemed to be able to think about love. As if it was just a more intense form of ownership.

Leo smiled wanly. 'Till death do us part?'

'Not even death.' Ronan laughed again. 'I'm not planning on dying, and I'm going to find a way to keep you alive too. To keep you safe. Nothing will ever separate us, Leo. Nothing, and nobody.'

After he and Ronan had spent some more time talking, discussing their 'future', Leo persuaded Ronan that he needed rest. Ronan seemed eager not to do anything to jeopardise their reconciliation, or to undermine Leo's resolve. Eventually – after professing his love over and over – he left Leo to sleep.

But one thing Ronan insisted on doing before he went was choosing a time for the binding ceremony. A few days were needed to prepare all that was required for the spell. Ronan was also keen to enhance its power by holding it on a magically significant date. He'd settled on the winter solstice.

It was little more than a week away: Leo's stomach churned at the thought of it. He hated the idea of binding himself to someone so evil, so insane. But what choice did he have? He'd hoped that by continually refusing to be in any kind of relationship with Ronan, the other man would be persuaded to let him go, to send him home.

But Ronan hadn't given up. Instead, he'd isolated Leo and locked him away in this tower in an attempt to forcibly change his mind. And Ronan's patience – Leo could tell – had worn thin.

This was his only hope now: that after the ceremony, Ronan would let his guard down. That there would be an opportunity, at some moment when Ronan was relaxed and undefended – was asleep, perhaps – for Leo to kill him.

Leo knew that *he* probably wouldn't survive, either. Most likely, even if he managed to kill Ronan, he'd die with him. He suspected the binding ceremony would somehow tie his life to Ronan's. He'd seen that kind of magic before: Gwydion had tied Jack's life to his, as a form of protection. But even if by some miracle Leo did survive, he'd still have no way to get home.

Maybe Ronan's grip on this world would weaken with his death, and maybe the worst of the nightmarish creatures that served him would disappear. But Ronan had ordinary human supporters too. If Leo ran, they would almost certainly hunt him down, wouldn't they?

May as well let them find me.

If he was lucky, they would kill him quickly. Better that than spend the rest of his life trapped in this place.

Sighing, he swung his legs out of bed and crossed over to the small wooden table that stood in the centre of his room. He picked up the crude charcoal drawing he'd sketched earlier that day. It was a picture of his home, and of the old willow tree, with its slender, drooping branches, that stood next to the garage. He'd even included his battered Peugeot parked in the driveway. It was one of many pictures he'd tried to make over the past few months. He wanted to set things down on paper as much as he could, to have some tangible record of what his life had been. He didn't have his phone any more, or any photos. All he had left was what was inside his head. And he'd been determined to hold on to that for as long as possible. But now… what was the point? What did it matter whether he forgot his home, his friends and his family? If he had no future, it seemed futile, to try to hold on to the past.

Taking the drawing, Leo held it over a candle and watched as the flame began to eat into it, making the paper blacken and curl.

FOUR

MERRY WAS STIFF, and she could feel hard ground beneath her. She thought about moving. But she was also pleasantly warm. It was almost like she was snuggled up against someone…

Her eyes shot open. The witch fire she'd conjured last night was still flaming away against the roof of the cave, and the embers of the fire were flickering, but there was something else too: a faint gleam coming from the cave entrance. Daylight. Finn's arm was draped across her waist, and he was lying right behind her, breathing softly. She turned her head, peering over her shoulder.

'Finn?'

He muttered something in his sleep.

'Finn, wake up.' Merry nudged him with her elbow.

'Huh? Merry?' He squinted at her and pulled her closer.

'Finn – no. It's morning. We should find Jack.'

'Jack?' Finn rolled away from her with a groan. 'I thought – I thought it was a nightmare. But it's not, is it?' He covered his face with his hands. 'This is real.'

Merry sat up. 'Depends on your definition of real. I'm not even sure we're in a real place. Jack was telling me last night about—'

'Yeah,' Finn interrupted, 'I heard. Elves, dragons, mermaids, et cetera.' He pushed himself up on to his elbows. 'Maybe he's making it up. Or he's insane.'

'I don't think so. But my point is, this place *is* crazy. It's not normal, even for Anglo-Saxon England. So maybe the crazy is affecting you, and once we get home again you'll be fine.'

'Maybe. But that still doesn't explain why *you* haven't lost your power.' He sat up properly, wincing and rubbing his arm.

'Well, perhaps I will. My power's always been a bit weird; perhaps I'm just more resistant than you to whatever's happening. Or –' Merry fished a hairband out of her pocket and tied her hair back – 'maybe your family wasn't actually magical back in the Dark Ages?'

'No, it wasn't. Our family line only dates from 1483, apparently. That's when Richard Lombard murdered all the other wizards operating in his territory and founded the very first Kin House.' Finn smiled ruefully. 'Right bunch of ruthless bastards, the Lombards used to be. Still are, some would say.'

Merry grimaced. 'Nice. But my point is, if your family weren't magical back in whatever year we're supposed to be in, perhaps that's why you've no power here. Right now, in this place, all the Lombards who exist are plebs.'

Finn blew out his breath slowly, considering. 'I hope you're right. Cos this is up there with the day my brother fell into a coma for how much fun I'm not having. It's like some part of me has been cut away.' He sniffed and glanced sideways at her. 'What if my magic doesn't return? What if I have to feel like this every day for the rest of my life?'

Merry pushed away the alarm building in her chest.

'You won't. We're going to find Leo and get out of here. And then you'll be fine.' Finn didn't look convinced.

But he should be. Because that's what's going to happen. I'm going to make sure of it.

Merry disentangled her legs from the blanket and stood up. 'I'll go and find Jack. Back in a minute.'

After the dim interior of the inner cave, the daylight nearer the entrance made her squint. And then she pushed past the curtain of ivy and had to shield her eyes with her hand. A red sun was rising, making the snow sparkle. Jack was a little distance from the cave; he'd taken Sorrel's saddle off and was rubbing a cloth over the horse's back. He turned and watched Merry approach.

'Did you sleep well enough?'

'Yes. But you should have woken me. Have you been up all night?'

'I've become used to not sleeping much, over the last few months. Although...' Jack picked up a comb and began running it through Sorrel's mane.

'Although what?' Merry prompted.

'I may have slumbered a little while. I think I dreamt of you.'

'Of me?'

'It was dark. We were sitting on a blanket next to a lake, and I was wearing...' Jack's fingers moved to touch his shoulder, 'a brooch of some strange design. And you had been weeping, because I could see the traces of tears still on your face. And then –' he raised his hand as though he were about to brush imaginary tears from Merry's cheek, before dropping his arm abruptly and turning away. 'I don't remember any more.'

Merry froze to the spot. What Jack was describing wasn't a dream – it was a memory. She remembered the exact evening he was talking about. It was the first evening she'd spent at the Black Lake alone with him. It was the first time she and Jack had kissed. But this man standing in front of her now – this different Jack – hadn't been caught by Gwydion or possessed by the King of Hearts. He hadn't been forced to cut out people's hearts for Gwydion to use in his dark magic. And he'd never held her in his arms as she'd cried about her life falling apart. So how could he be remembering it?

The anxiety was back, twisting her guts. She moved further away from Sorrel; horses made her nervous. 'So, what's the plan? Did you think of anyone who might be able to tell us where Ronan is, or who might have seen Leo?'

'There is – or was – a large settlement a few hours' ride from here. The local lord is a good warrior and has led ambushes against Ronan's followers. I will go and see him. I hope he will have some news.' His eyes narrowed as his gaze slid past Merry's shoulder.

She turned to see Finn walking towards them.

'What's going on?' He looked from Jack to her.

'Jack's going to find the local lord – he might know where Ronan is.'

'OK. I just need a minute to repack my bag—'

'No.' Jack shook his head. 'I can travel faster alone. Stay and rest; I'll be back by tomorrow morning.'

Merry could see the muscles in the side of Finn's jaw twitching. He obviously didn't trust Jack. And she wasn't entirely comfortable with just waiting around for Jack to return, either. This Jack seemed like a decent guy, but if there was a chance for him to save the king, his blood father, by turning her and Finn over to Ronan, was she absolutely certain he wouldn't take it?

Perhaps Jack sensed her doubt. He clapped a hand on her shoulder before mounting his horse. 'I promise, I will return. I owe you my life, remember? We South Saxons do not dishonour blood-debts.' He unhooked a bag from the saddle and tossed it to Finn. 'There is extra food in there. Merry, protect the cave, but do not use your power more than you must. Each spell twists and taints the air, or so I'm told, and I fear there are already watchful eyes drawn towards you.' With a twitch of the reins Jack urged Sorrel into a trot; a minute later he emerged from the fold of land around the cave on to the higher ground of the surrounding plain, and disappeared from her sight.

Merry frowned up at the sky. There were black dots, high in the clear air. Birds, or something more sinister? She shivered and caught hold of Finn's hand.

'Come on. We should probably collect some more firewood before we get inside.'

Protecting the cave was straightforward enough. Merry decided to use the same spell she'd cast before to weave a shimmering, silver net of filaments across the entrance, strong enough to resist magical or physical attacks. She made one amendment, though, waving her hand to make the net transparent, just in case anyone (or anything) was spying on them. More of a problem was what exactly she and Finn should do with themselves for the next twenty-four hours. It was the most amount of time they'd ever spent together. And there were literally no external distractions. Even going for a walk seemed like a bad idea given Jack's dire warnings. After a few attempts at conversation they slipped into an awkward silence, Merry hunched on the floor near the rebuilt fire, Finn leaning against the wall nearer the mouth of the cave, hands in his pockets, staring at the dreary landscape.

In the dim half-light it was difficult to keep any sense of time. As she listened to the crackling of the fire, Merry's eyelids began to droop. Despite her efforts to stay awake, she drifted towards sleep, her head nodding.

'Hey.' Finn's voice, loud in the stillness of the cave, made her jump. 'Sorry. I didn't mean to startle you. But I think we should get some fresh air.' He gestured at the pall of woodsmoke; the cave was large and high-ceilinged, but still it hung in the air like a cloudbank.

'Oh, yeah.' Merry waved a hand to extinguish the fire, then pushed herself up, coughing a little. They both walked towards the cave mouth. From the very slight shimmer she could tell that the net was still in place. It didn't seem to be blocking the airflow, and it was pleasant to be able to see the outside world, even if it was just the gully outside the cave. Merry leant as close as she could to the net, peering upwards. 'Looks like lunchtime.'

'That's what I thought.' Finn had the bag of food and one of the blankets in his hands; spreading the blanket on the floor, he sat down and began rummaging around inside the bag, opening packets and wrinkling his nose at the contents. There were streaks of dirt on his neck and face, stark in contrast with his pale skin, dark circles under his eyes. His words at the Black Lake came back to her: how many people *was* she willing to risk for Leo's sake? Finn had chosen to come here with her, but if he'd known what it might cost him…

He glanced up at her. 'What?' A smile ghosted across his features. 'Checking me out again?'

Merry smiled in return. 'Obviously. And…' she hesitated, 'I was thinking that maybe you should go back. That I should try to send you back.'

'Send me back home?' Finn sat up straighter, his knuckles tightening round the apple he was holding. 'Why? Because I've lost my power I'm suddenly a – a liability?'

She recoiled from his burst of anger. 'No, of course not. It's just—'

'Or maybe you don't want me around now you've got Jack back again.' His face hardened. 'Is that it? You don't want me getting in the way?'

'Don't be ridiculous.' To her own irritation, Merry felt herself blush. 'I'm worried about you, that's all. Clearly, I shouldn't be.' She sat down, facing the cave mouth instead of Finn, wrapping her arms round her bent legs and hunching her shoulders. She was just trying to help him, and all he could do was snap and sulk – well, two could play at that game.

Silence.

Then, she heard Finn sigh.

'Merry?'

'Shut up. I'm not talking to you.'

'Um… at the risk of being overly literal, you did just talk to me.'

Merry gritted her teeth, swinging round. 'You are so bloody irritating sometimes.'

'I know. But *lovably* irritating.' There was an unspoken plea at the back of his grey eyes. 'Right?'

'Huh.'

Finn's shoulders sagged. 'I'm sorry. Honestly. It's just…' He dragged a hand through his hair. 'I slept badly. And I need something to do. Waiting around like this, I can't stop thinking about Cillian.'

Merry's heart contracted in sympathy. Cillian, Finn's poor, non-magical brother, had died only a few days ago, not long before Finn had followed her through the point of intersection at the Black Lake. But he'd been in a coma for nearly a year before that: either persuaded or compelled by Ronan, he'd swallowed some unidentified magical potion, and had never woken up. At least she still had a chance of getting Leo back.

Finn had picked up a pebble from the floor of the cave and was turning it over and over between his fingers. 'Do you think this is what it was like for Cillian? This…' His fingers brushed the centre of his chest. 'This constant ache of longing for something you can't have?'

There was fear in Finn's eyes. She moved to sit next to him, taking his hand in hers. 'No. Cillian never had any power. It must have been hard for him, growing up in a Kin House family, surrounded by people like us, but I don't think he would have felt how you do now. His power wasn't ripped from him. He couldn't have missed it in the same way.'

'I hope you're right.' Finn's mouth turned down and he bowed his head, and Merry thought about how badly he must miss his brother, how heavily the guilt and grief must be weighing on him. She slipped one arm round his waist, resting her head on his shoulder. He sighed into her hair, hugging her back tightly. 'Talk to me,' he murmured. 'Tell me everything about you that I don't already know.'

'Everything? It's mostly pretty boring. Apart from the bits where every now and then some magic-wielding nutter is trying to kill me, and you know about that stuff.'

'I don't care. I need a distraction.'

So, Merry talked. She described her early childhood with Leo, their dad leaving them, their mum growing more and more distant. She told Finn about Gran testing her at twelve years old to see if she could be a witch, how excited she'd been to start training, and how painfully disappointed she'd felt when Mum had forbidden it. She talked about how Leo had struggled with coming out. About school and netball and fencing and how she used to dream about being an Olympic athlete. She even told him about Alex, the boy at school who had fallen in love with her, and how she'd messed him up by casting spells on him that she had no idea how to reverse.

'…and when I pulled him out of the river I got the credit for saving him, but I was the reason he was in there in the first place.' Merry sighed. 'He's never forgiven me. Or I don't think he has: he hasn't spoken to me for ages. And I don't blame him. Some things just aren't forgivable.'

They were lying shoulder to shoulder on the blanket. Merry glanced sideways, wondering how Finn was reacting to what she'd just said. Would he think it was terrible, what she'd done to Alex? Or would he not care, because Alex was just a pleb, and he'd been taught to think that plebs weren't that important, anyway?

But Finn was asleep, his mouth open a little, breathing softly.

Probably just as well.

Turning to lie on her side, Merry studied his face for a bit, noticing the length of his eyelashes, the sprinkle of pale freckles across the bridge of his nose, the shadowing of coppery stubble along his jawline. Her eyelids began to grow heavy again, and this time she didn't resist the lure of sleep.

It was dark outside when Merry woke. Finn was still asleep next to her, but she was too cold and stiff to lie there any longer. Her throat was sore as well – all the talking, and the smoke from the fire, probably. Wincing at the ache in her shoulders, she pushed herself to her feet and summoned a ball of witch fire into life in her fingers. Finn muttered in his sleep, frowning. Merry pulled the bit of blanket she'd been lying on across his body and stumbled towards the spring at the back of the cave.

The bubbling water was ice-cold, but she still gulped it down as fast as she could, floating the globe of witch fire next to her head so she could use both hands. When she paused, she noticed the small wooden bowl that she'd used the previous night to see Leo – it was still sitting on the rock next to the spring. She picked it up, hesitating. Jack had told her not to use magic, but would it really matter if she did just the one spell? The longing to see her brother again was so strong it made her chest ache. Quickly, she plunged the bowl into the small pool beneath the spring, scooping up the water and leaning over it. In the violet glow of the witch fire she could see her reflection. The colours were wrong, though: her hair, slipping out of the ponytail, looked dark brown, not auburn. Her eyes looked green instead of hazel.

She didn't look like herself at all.

Merry saw her reflection's eyes widen with realisation.

I look like my ancestor. Like Meredith.

She stared at herself for a bit longer. And then, setting the bowl down, she ran to her bag and pulled everything out until she reached the seven-sided wooden trinket box stashed away at the bottom.

Sitting back on her heels, the box in her hands, Merry traced one finger over the intricate design carved into the box's lid. Interlocking figures of eight, inlaid with flint, rippled along the edges, interspersed with Celtic knots at each corner. And at the centre, a flint disc etched with the crescent moon. Six months or so had passed since the night she and Leo found the box in the attic – six months of her time, at least. It felt like longer.

Inside the box were the key, the braid of hair and the manuscript. She left the key and the braid where they were. The hair was Queen Edith's, and the key... Merry wasn't exactly sure of its provenance, but since it was the key to Gwydion's tower it was unlikely that Meredith had made it. The manuscript, however...

She flipped through the pages. They were still blank, as they had been ever since Gwydion died. Meredith had made the manuscript fifteen hundred years ago as a way of guiding whichever of her descendants ended up having to deal with Gwydion. And it had worked, sort of. The manuscript had 'woken up' when Jack and Gwydion woke up from their enchanted sleep under the lake. It had answered Merry's questions about Jack and advised her what to do, although often in annoyingly vague terms.

Perhaps she'd be able to wake it up again.

Merry thought back to the blood magic she'd performed – with Finn's help – a few weeks ago. Because she and Gran were linked by blood, she'd been able to use blood magic to reveal the location of the cave where Ronan had left Gran to die. She and Meredith were linked by blood too. Doubly linked, in fact: by ordinary genetics, and because of the oath. The oath that Meredith had sworn, which meant that a part of her had continued through each of her descendants, allowing Meredith herself to be present at Gwydion's final defeat.

So much in magic seemed to come down to blood.

Of course, blood magic was dangerous. Merry smiled briefly as she remembered Leo's childhood obsession with *Star Wars*. In her world, it was blood magic that led to the dark side: it could so easily be used for black spells, to control or hurt or kill. That's what Gwydion had used it for. And every use of blood magic drew the evil energies of the shadow realm towards the spell caster, like pins to a magnet, looking for a crack in the caster's defences, looking for a way in. But Merry hadn't suffered any side effects from using it. Nothing demonic had possessed her. No fallen angels had shown up at the foot of her bed to drag her into the darkness.

At least, not yet.

And my intentions are good. Surely that must count for something?

She would just have to hope so. Fishing Gran's obsidian knife out of the side pocket of the bag, Merry held her right hand out above the manuscript and pressed the point of the blade into the soft flesh between her thumb and forefinger. Her blood began to drip on to the manuscript, soaking into the parchment. She started to sing, combining bits from various spells: the hydromancy she used to see Leo, the charm for finding lost things, a memory spell. Making it up as she went along; it seemed to be what she was best at.

After she'd sung everything she could think of, she waited. The blood had spread in splodges across the parchment, but nothing seemed to be happening. No writing appeared on the page, no helpful map. Merry swore and drove the knife into the ground. She opened the trinket box to shove the manuscript back inside –

The blood stains had vanished. In their place was the same spiky writing she'd seen before. The same word of greeting.

Eala.

She blinked and swallowed hard.

The manuscript prompted her again for a response.

Eala.

'Um… Hello, again. Do you remember me? I need your help. I need to find Meredith, the person who created you. Can you tell me where she is?'

Yes.

Merry held her breath, waiting.

Meredith is in the woods near the cottage.

'Oh, for…' She took a deep breath. 'OK. But can you tell me how to get to the cottage?'

There was another pause. Finally, another word bloomed on the page.

Yes.

Excitement fizzed through her veins. If anyone in this place could help her find Leo, it would be Meredith and her sisters. Hurriedly, Merry rolled up the manuscript and began repacking the trinket box and everything else.

She was nearly finished, when the sound of raised voices came from the other end of the cave. Someone was trying to get inside.

FIVE

FINN WAS LEANING against the wall by the mouth of the cave, his arms crossed. On the other side of the invisible net, silhouetted by the faint grey light of dawn, stood Jack. Merry conjured more globes of witch fire; now she could see he was frowning angrily, one hand gripping the hilt of his sword. There was a bloody gash on his forehead.

'What happened?'

'Jack tried to walk through the barrier you created and got thrown several metres away.' Finn smirked. 'I think he's a bit cross.'

Merry quickly murmured the words to dissolve the

net. A gust of cold air swept in, raising swirls of dust from the floor and making her shiver.

'Come in, Jack – it's safe now. Finn, can you go and get Gran's healing ointment from my bag?'

Finn rolled his eyes, but he did as she asked. Jack stomped into the cave and glared at the wizard's retreating back.

'He laughed at me. I know he's your friend, but…' His mouth snapped shut, flattening into a narrow line.

'I understand.' Merry patted Jack's arm. 'I didn't like him either when I first met him. So… did you find out where Ronan is?' Her stomach tensed. 'Or my brother?'

'No. I'm sorry. There have been more attacks not far from here, more villages destroyed. But none of the people I spoke to know where Ronan is hiding. They've lent me another horse, though, and there is another encampment we could try.'

Merry shook her head. 'I've come up with an alternative plan.'

Finn was back. He held out the pot of ointment to Jack. 'And what is this plan?'

'Well,' Merry glanced at Jack, 'I've found a way of reaching the friend that I mentioned. Meredith.' Finn's eyes widened slightly, but he didn't say anything. 'I think she'll be able to help us. Jack, you've already done so much, but would you mind lending us this other horse? I'll try to find a way to send it back to you once we've reached Meredith.'

'There will be no need,' Jack replied. 'I'm coming with you.'

Finn groaned, and Jack's lips twitched as if he was trying to suppress a grin. 'This will be my kingdom one day. I need to make sure what's left of it isn't destroyed by your quest. I brought some fresh supplies back with me; we should eat before we leave.'

Once Jack had left the cave, Finn turned to Merry. 'Meredith – she's your ancestor, right? The witch who put Jack and Gwydion to sleep?' When Merry nodded, he continued: 'So how did you find her?'

'I haven't precisely found her. Not yet. But I have this manuscript that she made. I used some blood magic to reawaken it and—'

'Blood magic? Again? That's the third time in…' Finn knitted his brows, 'I don't know exactly, but it can't be more than three weeks. It's not safe.'

'Seriously?' Merry put her hands on her hips. 'Weren't you the one *encouraging* me to use blood magic before? The first time I tried it, you said I should go for it. Those were your *exact* words, as far as I remember.'

'Yes, but I didn't mean for you to get hooked on it. You of all people should know that using blood magic is risky.' Finn looked nervously out of the cave, as if he expected something monstrous to suddenly materialise, intent on raining down magical retribution upon them both.

'I am not hooked on blood magic, and I'm not using it to hurt anyone. I'm not Gwydion.' Merry took a deep breath, swearing softly. 'Look, the only thing I care about right now is getting Leo back. And I'll do anything it takes to make sure I do. There's no need to be all... judgy.'

'I'm not judging you, Merry.' She could hear the exasperation in his voice. 'Honestly, I'm not.' He ran his hand down her arm, entwining her fingers in his. 'But I am trying to look after you.'

Jack was back, carrying a woollen sack plus a larger bundle.

'Here is the food.' He passed the sack to Merry and set the bundle down on the floor. As he opened it, the fragrance of lavender spilt out into the air. 'And here are some clothes.'

'Clothes?' Merry echoed.

'If you are to journey through the kingdom, it would be as well if the pair of you looked less...' He shrugged slightly. 'Outlandish.'

'Oh.' Merry glanced down at her jeans and jumper, both covered in dried mud and bits of dead vegetation. 'You think we need to blend in more.'

Jack nodded. 'The customs of Northumberland are strange to us here.' There was a slightly odd expression in his eyes. As Merry reached into the bundle he caught hold of her arm. 'Though indeed, I have never seen such fine weaving, even on the queen's robes.' He lifted the fabric of her sleeve to examine it more closely, grazing her skin with his fingertips as he did so.

Merry drew her breath in sharply as Jack touched her. She couldn't help it. The solidity of him, after so many months of grief and dreams, was a shock. The fact that he was warm and breathing, instead of lying cold and dead underneath the Black Lake. Every time she remembered, it hurt her like a plaster being ripped away too early from a partly healed wound.

Jack had let go of her arm and was holding out a pile of folded clothes. 'Get changed.'

Merry grabbed the clothes and swung away from him.

Finn was frowning at her, clutching his own stack of clothes to his chest like a shield. Before she could say anything, he stalked outside.

She sighed.

At least the new clothes were warm. There was a long linen shift, a bit like a nightie; a blue, long-sleeved woollen dress over the top of that, and then a green sleeveless over-dress fastened at the shoulders with round brooches and at the waist with a woven belt. It was all a lot more colourful than Merry had expected. The brooches looked like silver, ornately carved into tiny, flowing animal shapes. There was a hooded, fur-lined cloak too.

When Merry returned to the cave entrance, Finn was already there. He looked older in his new outfit, more of a man and less of a boy. There was a sword belt slung round his hips, Leo's sword in the scabbard. As Finn waited, one hand resting on the hilt, Merry couldn't help remembering all the fairy stories she'd read as a child, where the handsome prince rescues the princess from a life spent doing housework, or stuck in a glass coffin. 'You look... nice.'

'Thanks,' Finn said stiffly. He bent and picked up an apple and a hunk of cheese. 'I'm going to stretch my legs.'

Merry didn't have much of an appetite. She forced down a couple of handfuls of dried fruit, then went to repack her bag and refill the water bottles. It didn't take long; after slipping the cloak round her shoulders and extinguishing the last globe of witch fire floating in the dark interior of the cave, she was ready to leave.

Jack appeared, mounted on Sorrel and leading a huge grey stallion that apparently answered to the name of Blossom. The horse neighed when it saw her, tossing its head and straining against the rope Jack had in his hand. To Merry's disgust, Finn didn't seem remotely concerned. He patted the horse on its neck and pulled himself on to its back quite easily. Then he held his hand out to her. 'Shall we?'

There wasn't really any choice. After a couple of undignified minutes spent being dragged up on to the horse by Finn, she was settled in front of him, gripping Blossom's mane and clinging on with her knees while Finn held the reins.

'Now,' Jack glanced at Merry, 'you must guide us.'

Merry opened the manuscript. 'Please, take us to Meredith.'

The spiky writing appeared instantly.

Your way lies through the courts of the dead.

Whatever was speaking to her through the manuscript still seemed to have a thing for being cryptic. She read the instruction out to Jack. 'Does that mean anything to you?'

He frowned for a minute or two before his face cleared. 'It means the barrows. Obviously.'

'Huh?'

'The graves of the dead kings. This way.' Jack set his horse walking.

Finn urged his horse forward too. 'Ooh, the dead kings,' he muttered into Merry's ear. 'Look at me, I know everything.'

'He's just trying to help. And we need him. We don't know our way around here.'

'I know, I know. But still, he's really, *really* irritating.'

Merry couldn't help it. She snapped back, 'But in a lovable way, right?'

Finn straightened up and jerked the reins so the horse lurched forward, forcing Merry to hang on to Blossom's neck.

Merry sighed, and wondered how many days it would take to reach Meredith.

The next three days were uneventful. The lands they rode through seemed empty of life, though every so often they passed the charred remains of wooden houses, blackened timbers sticking up out of the snow. In the sky above one ruined village Merry noticed large, reddish-brown birds of prey riding the wind.

Jack followed her gaze. 'Kites,' he murmured eventually. 'Crows aren't the only birds that eat the flesh of the dead.'

Merry looked away.

On the third night, they stopped near some ruins, the tumbled masonry and broken pillars hinting at a monumental past. After a quick meal, Jack lay down and went straight to sleep. Finn was sitting next to Merry, staring into the fire, his chin propped on one hand.

'What are you thinking about?'

'My family,' Finn replied, not shifting his gaze from the flames. 'Wondering how my dad's going to take it, when he finds out that his only remaining son and heir is now a pleb.'

Guilt whispered in the back of Merry's mind. 'But he loves you, doesn't he?'

'Oh yes. He loves me,' Finn replied softly.

'Then… is he really going to care? Even if this turns out to be permanent, surely the most important thing will be that you're back home again, and safe.'

'You don't understand,' Finn was shaking his head. 'My dad's whole identity is bound up in his *position*, in magical society. Our family have been at the top of the pile for hundreds of years. If that ends on his watch, because of his sons, he's going to feel like he's failed. Like he's let down every single generation since our house started. That's why he—' Finn broke off.

'Why he what?'

'Nothing.' He winced and rubbed the centre of his chest.

'Does it still hurt?' Merry asked. 'Where your magic used to be?'

'It aches, the whole time. Kind of like… when you feel really starving hungry. But more painful. Makes me feel a bit sorry for Ronan.'

'Seriously? But why?'

'Because the magic he was born with didn't last. So he has to steal magic from other people, but that never lasts, either. Don't you think that he must feel like this the whole time?'

Merry frowned into the flames. Finn was probably right. And she did pity Ronan. Sort of. But when she thought about everything he'd done, all the people he'd hurt…

Some things just aren't forgivable.

'Can I ask you a question?' Finn's voice jerked her back to the present.

'Sure.'

'Are you still in love with Jack?'

'What?' Merry sat up straighter.

'You heard me.'

'Um…' Was she still in love with him? 'It's complicated.'

89

'Right.' Finn's tone was scornful.

'But it is.' Merry glanced at Jack's sleeping form. 'I did love him; I told you that. I loved him enough to free him from Gwydion's curse by allowing him to die. And now he's here, and as far as he's concerned, none of what we went through together ever happened.' She shivered, pulling her cloak more tightly about her. 'This isn't the Jack I knew. But he still looks more or less the same, and he still sounds the same and sometimes...' The knots of tension in her stomach got worse. 'I mean, how would you feel if Cillian came back to life, but he didn't recognise you? If he looked at you like you were a stranger?'

Finn's face sort of... shut down.

Merry wished she knew a spell to unsay what she'd just said.

'You knew Jack for how long?' Finn demanded. 'A few weeks? A few months at most. And you're comparing his death to me losing my brother?'

'Honestly, I didn't mean to—'

Finn threw up a hand, silencing her. 'Just don't, Merry. Don't say any more. I need some sleep.' He lay down, facing away from her, and pulled the hood of his cloak over his head.

Merry stared at his back, willing him to turn round.

'Finn?'

He didn't answer.

'I'm sorry. I wasn't thinking. But grief… it isn't rational or – or – *measurable*. And Jack's not the only person I've lost.' Finn still hadn't moved, or given any sign that he'd heard her. A gust of cold wind stung her eyes. She got to her feet and went to find some more firewood.

Just after dawn, Jack shook her awake. Finn was standing next to Blossom, waiting for her to mount, but he didn't speak to her. They rode for what felt like hours through another forest before he finally leant forward to whisper to her, his lips brushing her ear.

'I didn't mean that my grief was somehow worth more than yours. I just… I miss my brother. That's all.'

'Of course. It's OK.'

'No, it isn't. I came here to help you, Merry, to try to make up for what I did at the Black Lake. You mean a lot to me. But you don't owe me anything. And I have no right to be jealous of Jack. Jealous of the feelings you had for him. Or have for him.'

'I don't *have* any feelings for him, so there's no reason for you to be jealous. That was what I was trying to explain yesterday. Very badly.' Merry gazed at Jack, riding a few metres in front of her. 'Seeing him alive has brought back the memories of the person I loved. But I can't be in a relationship with a ghost. If we survive this mess, you're the one I want to bring home to meet my mother, so to speak.' She twisted round so she could look at Finn. 'You. Not Jack.'

For a moment, Finn stared at her, his grey eyes wide. Then he slid one hand round her waist, pulled her against him and kissed the back of her neck gently. 'Thank God. I thought I was going to have to challenge Jack to a duel.' He laughed softly. 'And I'm not one hundred per cent certain that I'd win.'

Merry smiled and rested her head back against Finn's shoulder. They rode on for a while in a comfortable silence.

Jack, still a little way ahead of them, seemed to be getting slower and slower. He kept turning his head, scanning the woodland on either side of the path, riding with one hand on the hilt of his sword.

'Jack,' Merry called, 'is anything wrong?'

'I do not like this forest.'

Merry looked around. To her, the forest seemed like most of the other woods they'd been through since she arrived here. Damp – chilly – the trees crammed so closely together that, even in their leafless winter state, there was hardly any light filtering down to the track they were following. The still air, heavy with dust, reminded her of something. The forgotten corner of a museum, or an abandoned church. A crypt. She shivered and rubbed her hands together.

Jack slowed his horse until he was riding next to them. 'I know I haven't been here before. Yet somehow, if I close my eyes, I remember riding this path, a group of mail-clad knights around me, until we were attacked...'

A long, low growl coming from the trees off to the left made the hair on the back of Merry's neck stand up. Both horses snorted nervously.

'What was that?' Finn was craning his neck, peering into the undergrowth.

'A wolf.' Jack drew his sword. 'Can you ride faster? We must escape this wood before it is too late.'

'It's already too late.' Merry pointed ahead. Not just one wolf, but many — too many for her to count — were stalking through the trees towards them. The animals were advancing purposefully, evenly spread out, almost in ranks. The horses were terrified. Jack still had Sorrel under control — just — but Blossom seemed to be trying to back away and sideways at the same time, tossing his head and rolling his eyes. Finn was leaning forward, gripping the reins and swearing but it didn't seem to be helping. 'Let me down,' Merry insisted.

'Are you crazy? You can't – dammit –'

She didn't waste time in arguing. Squishing her right leg up in front of her and cursing her long skirts, she twisted and slid underneath Finn's arms and off the horse.

The wolves were only a few metres away now, almost encircling them. Merry realised a shielding spell wouldn't be enough. She would have to drive them off.

Clenching her hands into fists, she began to sing. A stinging hex, basically. But Merry added more. She wove into the hex the words of a spell to control lightning, keeping the power coiled within her fingertips until the pain of it almost took her breath away.

As if responding to a signal, the wolves attacked.

Merry threw up her hands, releasing the spell. Behind her she could hear the horses screaming and Jack and Finn yelling, but she ignored them, concentrating on the magic coursing through her outstretched arms. She had to spin and duck, aiming the spell, making sure it hit every wolf hard, hard enough that the animal was no longer a threat.

And it was working. The wolves were howling, writhing on the forest floor. Some of them managed to escape, limping away as fast as they could, melting back into the shadows. More of them didn't. Merry kept going, out of breath, murmuring the spell now rather than singing it. But almost all the wolves had fled or collapsed and she was nearly done, nearly—

'Merry!'

She swung round to see a huge blond wolf leaping at her, brought up her hands—

Jack's sword flew past her head and buried itself in the wolf's chest. The animal crashed to the ground.

Merry let the spell fade and lowered her arms, breathing heavily, grimacing: the air stank of burnt fur.

'Are you hurt?' Jack, still leading Sorrel, wrenched the sword out of the dead wolf. He had bloody claw marks along one arm. 'Merry?'

'No. Just tired.' She flexed her aching fingers and looked around. 'Where's Finn?'

'Blossom bolted. I'll find him.' He jumped on to Sorrel's back and rode into the forest.

Left alone, Merry crossed her arms and looked around her at the ring of dead wolves. The snow was stained with blood. When Ronan had killed a wolf back in the woods near Tillingham, she'd buried it – covered it with a mound of roses. But there were no roses here. And far too many bodies…

But what else could I have done?

One of the bodies was twitching; she moved closer to investigate. This wolf was alive. It gasped for air, trying feebly to get back up on its feet. And then Merry saw one of its paws, and froze.

It was a human foot. The top part of the wolf's leg was as it should be, but the bottom half of the leg, and the foot... Merry clapped one hand to her mouth. The wolf whined again, scrabbling at the ground with its front paws.

I could try to help it – him – but...

Revulsion and fear and exhaustion coalesced into something hard, sitting in the centre of Merry's chest. Whatever Ronan had been doing here, whatever he was still doing, nothing and no one was going to stand between her and her brother. She didn't have time for pity.

Raising one hand, Merry murmured one line of the spell she'd been singing. The wolf collapsed. It didn't move again.

'Merry!' Jack was returning through the trees. And next to him was Finn, still on Blossom's back. He was covered in tiny scratches, but otherwise seemed unharmed. When he got closer, in answer to Merry's raised eyebrows, he shrugged and said:

'Brambles. Lots of them. But at least they stopped the

damn horse before he threw me in the river.' His eyes widened as he took in the pile of dead animals. 'Bloody hell. You OK, Merry?'

'Yes. I'm fine.' Merry went to her bag, found the pot of Gran's ointment and tossed it to Jack. 'Put some of that on your arm. We need to keep going.' She got the manuscript out from the pouch on her belt and checked the instructions. 'Nothing's changed. We just keep heading through the forest.'

'Actually, I think we're nearly at the end,' Finn said, as he pulled her up on to the horse. 'The land slopes downwards further on, and I could just see the trees start to thin out…'

'Then let's get out of here.'

They rode fast now, not speaking other than to urge the horses to a quicker pace. Finally, after another couple of hours, Merry could see what she'd been straining her eyes for: a cottage, tucked into the edge of the forest, a wisp of smoke rising from the roof. And then the details came into view: a thatched roof, shutters over the windows, a stream winding past the front of the building.

Finn drew the horse to a halt.

'Why have we stopped?'

He pointed. There, coming through the trees from the

left, were three young women. One tall and blonde, one black-haired and pale, one with vivid green eyes. Merry recognised them from the dreams and visions she'd been having for the last six months: Carys, Nia and Meredith. Carys and Meredith appeared much as Merry remembered, but Nia, the middle sister... she looked terrible. Gaunt and sickly.

The sisters became aware of the newcomers. Meredith ran towards Jack as he dismounted. 'Jack, I thought I might never see you again...'

They knew each other?

Before Merry could react, Nia had wandered over to them. She stared up at Finn. 'You do not belong here.'

'Well,' Finn slid down from Blossom's back. 'We're not exactly from around here...'

But Nia wasn't listening. She was gazing at Merry, and the curiosity on her face gave way to horror. She stumbled backwards. 'No! Why have you come back out of my dreams? That path was never followed.' Shaking her head, she raised her hands as if to cast a spell. 'You cannot exist! You cannot—'

Finn caught her as she collapsed.

SIX

CARYS CAST A suspicious look at Merry before turning to Jack. 'Quickly, take her inside.'

Jack lifted Nia out of Finn's arms and hurried into the cottage with Meredith and Carys. Merry left Finn to deal with the horses and followed them. The interior of the witches' home was almost exactly as Merry remembered seeing it in the dreams she'd had earlier in the year. One large room open to the roof, with a central hearth and three shuttered windows. Sweet-smelling rushes spread across the floor. At the far end, a door into a smaller room, all in shadow – a bedroom of some sort, Merry assumed.

A tripod, with a flat metal plate dangling beneath it, was set over the fire, while a chair, a bench and a couple of wooden stools were drawn up nearby. Jack carried Nia into the smaller room; after grabbing a couple of storage jars from a shelf, Carys followed them.

Merry turned to Meredith. 'I'm sorry I startled her.'

Before Meredith could respond, Jack returned. Merry couldn't help herself: 'So you do know each other? But when I mentioned Meredith to you, you didn't say anything…'

Jack and Meredith looked at each other. Merry's throat tightened.

Luckily, Finn came in at that moment and asked Jack the question that Merry wanted to ask. 'Does this mean you could have brought us straight here? That we've wasted all this time?'

'No,' Meredith replied. 'He's never been here. I would not allow him to know where we lived, for his protection and our own.'

Jack nodded. 'She's speaking the truth. And when you and I first met in the forest, I did not know you. I owe Meredith a blood-debt too; surely you would not have had me betray her?' He took one of Meredith's hands in his and kissed it.

Merry turned away, avoiding Finn's gaze, concealing her confusion by taking off her cloak and folding it up. 'I suppose not.' She had known that *her* Jack had been in love with Meredith, and that Meredith had loved him back. The fact that he was in love with her in this reality too really shouldn't have come as a shock. 'You saved his life?'

'They all did,' Jack answered. 'She and Carys and Nia. They came to our village, just before it was destroyed by Ronan. Told us we were in danger.' He glanced at Meredith, and Merry saw the warmth in his eyes blaze again. 'Told me who I really was. Many more would have died without their help.'

'We did what we could.' Meredith crossed her arms. 'So, Jack I know. But who are you?'

'This is Finn, and I'm Merry. I'm a witch too.' On impulse, she added, 'Merry is short for Meredith.'

The other witch's frown deepened.

Merry pressed on. 'We thought you might be able to help us find Ronan. Or that you might even know where he is. Because I'm sure he has my brother confined somewhere. I saw him sitting at a table, but the spell didn't reveal where.'

'That's why you think he's alive?' Meredith sat down,

gesturing that the others should sit too. 'Are you certain? Too often magic will show us merely what we wish to see.'

'No. I'd know if Leo was dead. I'd—' The enormity of what she was saying, of even using the word 'dead' in the same sentence as her brother's name... it crushed the breath out of her. Finn reached across and let his hand rest lightly on her back. His touch steadied her. 'He's alive. You'll just have to take my word for it.'

Meredith nodded. 'And do you know anything else that might help us find him? Why Ronan is keeping him alive?'

Merry wasn't about to repeat Ronan's lie about loving Leo; it was too monstrous a claim. Instead, she said: 'He used him to transport something from where we live to here. A thing from the shadow realm. I've heard it called a... a King of Hearts.'

The other witch drew back. 'Do you have dealings with the shadow realm? Is that why Nia fears you so? She clearly knows you, at least from her dreams. And what she knows does not appear to be good.'

Jack's hand strayed towards the hilt of his sword. 'Was I wrong to trust you, Merry?'

'No. Of course not.'

'But you're not being truthful with us. Tell me, why do

you believe you and I have met before? That we have loved each other? And what did you mean last night, when you said the only way to save me was to let me die?'

Merry swore under her breath, her cheeks reddening. How could she have been so careless? 'I thought you were asleep. But you were listening to us the whole time...'

'Yes.' He shrugged. 'I want to trust you, Merry. You saved my life. But in times such as these I do not easily trust those I do not know. And really, I do not know you.'

Merry turned away, struggling to overcome the horrible mixture of hurt and shame that was churning up her stomach. She swallowed hard and took a deep breath.

'Very well. I'll tell you the truth.' She looked squarely at Meredith. 'All of the truth. Unfortunately, by the end of the story, you may wish you'd never met me. And I wouldn't blame you.'

Meredith pulled her shawl more tightly round her shoulders. 'How does it start, this story?'

Merry switched her gaze to the hearth and the bright, dancing flames, and tried to work out how to answer that question. Did it begin with her and Leo under the lake, and her failure to realise that the King of Hearts still needed to be dealt with? Or did it start with Meredith's oath, after Gwydion killed her sisters? Or even further back, when Gwydion convinced himself that Edith loved him, and decided that through her he could gain the crown?

'Oh – of course.' She grabbed her bag from underneath the bench. 'The story begins the night that my brother and I heard a strange noise coming from the attic, and we went upstairs, and we found this.' She drew out the trinket box and passed it to Meredith.

The other witch ran her fingers over the carved surface. 'There is magic in this.'

'Yes. That's because you made it.'

They talked for hours. At one point, they paused briefly while Meredith prepared some food. The fire burnt low. Carys came in every so often with questions of her own – she could hear Merry well enough from the small bedroom where she was tending Nia – but she would not leave her sister for long. Finn dozed off. Fair enough, since most of the story didn't concern him. And it made it easier to talk to Meredith about how he had lost his power; Finn wouldn't have wanted to see her pity. Bits of the story had to be repeated so Meredith and Jack could get it all clear in their heads. Or they asked for more details. And that was OK, apart from when Merry had to describe how Jack had died in her arms. How she'd found Flo's body. How Gran had been drained of her magic by Ronan.

At least Meredith seemed to accept that this time Merry was telling the truth. She could speak calmly about the fact that – in Merry's version of history – Carys and Nia were killed by Gwydion.

Jack, however, raged.

'I would not, though! I would never cut out someone's heart, whatever Gwydion did to me.' He was pacing up and down the room, smacking his fist against the palm of his other hand. 'I should refuse. I would die first.'

'But you weren't able to kill yourself. And you weren't able to refuse.' Merry sighed; they'd been over and over this. 'The thing inside you, the King of Hearts, it took control of you. You had no choice.'

Jack groaned, dragging his hands through his hair and sinking down on to a stool next to Meredith. She reached out to grip his shoulder. 'There's no cause to grieve over something that never happened, Jack. Whatever might have been, you have a choice now: you can choose to give in to Ronan, or you can choose to keep fighting, and regain your kingdom.'

'We can start fighting now,' Merry added. 'Right now.' She turned to Meredith. 'There must be some spell you can cast, something you can do to help me find Ronan. If we find him, we'll find my brother.'

'And we will,' Meredith said. 'Tomorrow—'

'No – not tomorrow. I've wasted too much time already. We've been here five – no, six days, and I have no idea what's happening to Leo—'

'Merry, calm yourself.' Meredith caught hold of Merry's hand. 'It's late, and you've been fighting as well as travelling. You need to rest.'

'But—'

'And, there is much we must still understand, about what your presence here, and Ronan's presence, may mean. How you may be affecting us and our land.'

'You think we're changing the past?'

'It's more than that.' Meredith's forehead wrinkled. 'You say there are no elves in your world. No unicorns, or other magical creatures. I am not sure that we are your past.'

'There never have been any of those things. Only in stories.' Merry thought for a moment, remembering all the wisdom books and knowledge books that the coven had accumulated: centuries' worth of information. 'I think

Finn and I would know, if they'd just died out. People like us, we'd remember.'

'And then,' Meredith continued, 'there is Gwydion.'

'He must be dead,' Jack interrupted. 'He did not come to claim me.'

Meredith shook her head impatiently.

'He has not shown himself for many years. He did not carry out the threat made at your christening. But neither of those things prove he is dead.'

'The wolves that attacked us yesterday – they weren't normal. One of them had a human foot on one of its back legs.' Merry shuddered as she remembered the deformity. 'And Jack told me – my Jack, I mean – that Gwydion used to turn people into wolves. And other things.'

All three fell silent. Finn was fast asleep now, lying on the floor with his head on his bag, one arm flung up across his face. Meredith picked up a blanket and spread it over him. 'It's late. Let's rest now, and hope that sleep will bring counsel.' She yawned. 'There are more blankets and fleeces in the chest beneath the window there.'

'Thank you.'

Meredith picked up her rushlight and went into the smaller room, closing the door behind her.

Jack still had his head in his hands. Merry knelt in

front of him. 'Really, you tried as hard as you could to resist Gwydion. You were so brave. Brave, and kind, and gentle…'

'You said you tried to save me. And that you mourned me, afterwards.' He looked up at her. 'Did we truly care for one another?'

Merry brushed a lock of Jack's hair back from his shoulder.

'What you heard me say to Finn was the truth: in another time and place, I loved you. And you cared for me. Loved me, even. Though I think your heart always belonged to Meredith. I just reminded you of her.'

Jack stared at her, his eyes slightly narrowed as if he was trying to trace Meredith's features in Merry's face. 'I hope you find someone who loves you only for yourself.' He glanced at Finn and pulled a face. 'And if he is your choice, I hope he deserves you.'

Merry smiled. 'Finn has his issues. And I don't know exactly where we're heading; all our time together so far has been spent dealing with various magic-related crises. But I do know you're not seeing him at his best.' She stood up. 'He's a decent person, Jack. Perhaps you can give him a chance? You might like him if you got to know him.'

Jack didn't reply. But he did help Merry get out a pile

of fleeces and woven blankets. It wasn't the most comfortable bed, but she was asleep in minutes.

Merry woke with a start, her heart hammering in her chest. 'Leo…' Her voice was raspy; Jack and Finn were both sleeping nearby, but neither of them stirred. There was no sound from the small bedroom, either. Merry wanted to yell, to wake everyone up, to demand that they should start helping her find Leo right now – but making all her companions angry probably wasn't a smart move. The cottage was smoggy and gloomy; maybe fresh air would improve her mood. Merry pushed herself upright – wincing as the muscles in her back pinged with discomfort – put on her cloak and slipped outside.

The sun wasn't yet up, as far as she could tell. There was a small area of cleared land surrounding the cottage; nearby was something that looked like an enclosed vegetable garden, and then a small outbuilding with logs piled up beneath its eaves. Everything was hushed, apart from the soft plashing of the stream gurgling along its narrow course. She strode across to the outbuilding; a goat emerged from the dim interior and bleated at her, nuzzling her hand curiously. By the entrance to the building was a trough of water.

Merry pushed the goat away and waved her hand across the water's surface.

Show me my brother…

The water darkened. When it cleared, she was looking at Leo. He was standing this time, and there seemed to be other people round him. Someone's hand was in view, painting runes on his forehead and cheeks in black ink. Someone else was placing a golden circlet on his head. There was already a thick gold torc round his neck. But Leo was taking no notice of them. Instead he was staring out at her, his face set, as if he was in some other place entirely. It wasn't the cold blankness that seemed to signify possession by the King of Hearts. Instead, he looked…

Hopeless. Almost as if, in his head, he was already dead. Or wished that he was.

'Merry?'

Merry flinched and hurriedly dismissed the vision in the water. Finn was standing nearby.

'I saw you were gone when I woke up. Is everything OK?' He squinted at her. 'You've gone really white.'

'It's Leo. Something's happening. They're doing something awful to him…' Merry's voice sounded high and breathless in her own ears. 'I have to help him.'

'Well…'

Someone shrieked. Merry began to run back to the cottage, Finn at her heels.

When they got inside, everyone – Jack included – was crowded round Nia. The youngest sister looked even worse than she had last night. Her eyes were wild, and there were bloody scratches across the backs of her hands and down the sides of her face, stark against the sallow flesh. Carys was pressing a cup to her lips as Jack supported her.

'Just a little now, Nia, love,' Meredith urged. 'It will help, I promise…'

Nia took a few sips and sank back, her eyes closed. They all waited. The cottage was silent apart from the crackle of the fire and the caw of a distant crow. Finally, some colour came back into Nia's cheeks.

'What happened?' Merry edged forward a little; it felt like she and Finn shouldn't be here, witnessing this family crisis.

Jack wrapped a blanket round Nia's shoulders and straightened up. 'She had a vision. She says that she—'

'I will tell her.' Nia opened her eyes. 'A dream, or a vision, I cannot tell.' She took another sip from the cup that Carys was still holding. 'I dreamt of a dark tower in the woods. Meredith and Jack were there, and Jack was sitting on a chair carved all over with…' She raised a hand, as if reaching out to touch some invisible object.

'With what?' Merry murmured. She was almost holding her breath, trying not to touch the ball of panic building in her stomach.

'Dark things. Symbols, and faces.' Nia snatched her fingers back into her fist. 'But then it wasn't Meredith any more. It was you,' she pointed at Merry, 'and there was someone else on the chair. I couldn't see his face.'

Leo.

'I saw him, just now. My brother. They're doing something to him, they're – they're preparing him for something—'

'Merry,' Finn interrupted, 'you don't know what you saw exactly, and neither does Nia—'

Carys cut across him. 'What did you see?'

Merry told her about the runes and the crown. 'Do you know what it means?'

'No.' Carys glanced at Meredith. 'But, if Ronan is planning to use him in some sort of magical ceremony, then it would make sense for it to be happening tonight. It is the solstice.'

Merry pressed the heels of her hands against her eyes.

I've arrived too late. Leo thinks I've abandoned him. And now I have no time left.

But the tower, and the carved chair… She looked up at the other witches. 'I know where Leo is. I think Gwydion's got him. And I'm going after him right now.'

SEVEN

MERRY TURNED TO look for her bag. 'I've got to get to the lake. I mean, where the lake is going to be.'

Jack reached for his sword belt. 'How far is this lake?'

'No idea. But I'm not going on horseback.' Now she knew where she was going, she could get there by using a 'broomstick spell' – the unofficial name for a type of shifting spell that some witches used to magically transport themselves from place to place. Not that she would aim to get inside Gwydion's tower directly: she didn't feel confident about trying to materialise inside a room, and then there was the risk of coming face to face with Gwydion. Or Ronan. But the edge of the lake would be close enough. 'And I can't take you with me—'

'Merry, stop.' Finn was in front of her. 'Hold on for a minute.'

'No, Finn – it's too dangerous.' She tried to push past him, ignoring the voices of Carys and Meredith in the background. But he got in her way again.

'Will you listen, just for once?' He put his hands lightly on her shoulders. 'You can't just go marching in there like this. You don't know what you're up against. Seriously. You need a plan.'

Merry looked up at him. Finn had told her that once before: the night she'd found out about Ronan, the night Finn had used a spell to get her to the lake. He'd asked her then to wait, so they could figure out what to do together. Instead, she'd kneed him in the groin and run off to deal with Ronan on her own...

'OK.' She put her bag down. 'Let's make a plan.'

An hour or so later, they had the bare bones of a strategy. Meredith had suggested – and Merry had eventually, reluctantly, agreed – that the attempt should be delayed until sunset at the earliest. It made sense: harpies and birds would see through a concealment charm, so if Ronan was using them as spies, dusk would give better protection. And hopefully the witches and wizards who followed Ronan would be too busy celebrating the solstice to be as vigilant as they might otherwise be. What they hadn't agreed so far was who – if anyone – would go with her.

'I still think I should go alone,' Merry tried again. 'I'm going to go in, get my brother out and come back here. I'm not going to risk Leo's life by trying to deal with Ronan at the same time. There's no need for anyone else to risk his or her life, either.'

Finn turned away to look out of the window, muttering something under his breath. Merry didn't catch the words, but the depth of frustration radiating from the wizard was unmistakable. She watched him for a moment, noting the stiffness of his stance and the way the tendons were standing out on his hands as he gripped the windowsill, until her attention was reclaimed by Carys.

'You may be powerful, Merry, but there is much that you do not know. This is not your time. This is not your world. Meredith should travel with you.'

Merry opened her mouth to argue, but Meredith leant forward.

'You care for your brother. So why increase the danger to him by refusing our help?'

'But… what about Nia?'

'Carys will stay with her. And Jack—'

'I'm going.' Jack's face was grim. 'Remember, this will be my kingdom one day.'

Merry dragged her hands through her hair. 'All right. I'll go with Meredith, and Jack, and…' she glanced at Finn.

'I'm not staying here.' Finn threw his hands in the air. 'Face it, Merry: without you, I'm stuck in this world. As a pleb.' He coloured, and nodded at Jack. 'No offence. But I'm going wherever you go. If you survive, I survive. And if you don't…' He shrugged.

Merry sighed. 'Fine. Carys will stay here with Nia. The rest of us will use the broomstick spell to go to Gwydion's tower at sunset. Everyone happy?' The sarcasm in her voice didn't really translate into Old English. But Finn rolled his eyes at her and stalked outside.

There were still about six hours to go before sunset, Meredith had told her. It was possible the hours would fly by, but somehow Merry doubted it.

Eventually, though, the sun did begin to dip below the horizon. Merry had spent most of the intervening time practising shifting spells, moving Gran's obsidian knife to different places within the cottage. Now she and Finn were waiting, cloaks on, while Meredith was saying goodbye to Nia.

'I'll be back soon, I promise. Try not to worry.' Meredith had one hand on Nia's cheek, her head tilted to make sure her sister was paying attention; it was hard to remember that Meredith, and not Nia, was actually the youngest of the three sisters.

Carys and Jack were outside, talking in low voices; Merry could see them from where she was standing. Jack said something and Carys laughed, then he gripped her shoulders like he was telling her something important. That he was going to look after Meredith, probably. That she shouldn't worry. It was the sort of thing a brother would say. The sort of thing Leo would say.

'Merry?' Finn touched her hand. 'Leo's going to be OK. I'm sure of it.'

'Thank you.' Her voice sounded tremulous; she tried again. 'I mean, I know he will.' Smiling, she wound her fingers into Finn's. 'I'm glad you're coming with me.'

Surprise flashed across Finn's face. But then he smiled back at her and straightened up a little. 'Of course you are. Even without my power, I'm still pretty impressive.

I'm still a Lombard, after all.' It was the closest he'd come to sounding like his old self since they'd arrived here.

Jack and Carys came back into the cottage and Meredith dropped a kiss on Nia's forehead. 'Well,' she said, 'we're ready.'

'So, we're just going to use the broomstick spell to get there.' Merry bit her bottom lip. 'Meredith, I know where I'm going – more or less – but you don't. Should I try to take all three of you, or—'

'No. The less familiar you are with a place, the more magic the broomstick spell requires. You mustn't spread yourself too thinly.' Meredith pursed her lips for a moment. 'Do you know any gifting spells? If you can plant a picture of this lake in my head, I may take Jack, and you can take Finn.'

Merry thought back to her lessons with Gran, and the various knowledge books she'd ploughed through. She'd read some gifting spells, though she hadn't tried any; they were firmly in the advanced magic section. Not at all complicated in themselves – only one line long – but Gran had muttered darkly about costs and consequences. There'd been spells for gifting a day of one's life, for gifting health, for gifting power – she glanced at Finn, wondering whether it would be worth trying that one on him – for gifting thoughts.

That one could be used as a curse. But it might be just what I need here...

The thought in her case would basically be a memory of one of the times she'd been at the lake. Merry took a deep breath. She was going to have to be very careful, and very specific.

'I'm ready.'

Meredith took Merry's hands and laid them on her own temples. Merry closed her eyes and summoned up an image from about a month ago, from the evening that she'd watched Leo and Ronan sitting together by the edge of the lake. She put in all the details she could remember: the water, stagnant due to the drought, the rotten smell of the exposed and dying vegetation, the dried-up grass, the first stars emerging as the blue-black night crept in from the east. It had been around sunset then too...

'*Ic giefe ðe ða weorðan giefe...*'

'I see it,' Meredith murmured.

Merry gasped, clutching at her own head. There was – not pain, not exactly. But an intense, sudden cold, right in the top of her skull. Like being stabbed with an icicle.

'It is the price.' Carys was watching her from the other

side of the room, concern in her eyes. 'The image in your mind, you have gifted it to Meredith. So, it can no longer be yours.'

She was right. Merry could still remember the evening she'd been thinking about. She could remember what had happened before she'd stood at the edge of the lake, and she could remember what had happened later. But between those times, there was a gap. A grey space, empty apart from a dull sense of loss.

Merry held out a hand to Finn. 'Ready?'

He nodded, squeezing her fingers tightly. Meredith was still staring ahead, as if she could no longer see anything but the image Merry had put into her head. Jack took both her hands in his.

The broomstick spell, as Merry had learnt it, was in modern English; as she began singing the charm, Meredith started to sing too. Different words, but the same melody. Merry could feel the magic prickling across her skin, raising the hair on her arms, vibrating invisibly across the space between them. But as she concentrated on another evening at the lake, envisaging the water and the grassy shoreline, the painful stretch of the spell enveloped her, rushing in to drown every other sensation...

★

Someone was groaning. Merry was certain – well, almost certain – that it wasn't her. Not that she didn't feel like groaning; it just seemed like far too much effort, right at that moment.

She risked opening her eyes. Jack was sitting on a fallen tree trunk, sipping something from a leather bottle. Meredith seemed to be fine: she was staring at a stand of trees nearby. Finn, however, was kneeling on the ground, clutching his stomach. The strangulated groans were coming from him.

Meredith took the bottle from Jack and passed it to Merry. 'Metheglin. Cold, but it still helps.'

Merry took a cautious sip. The liquid was slightly grainy and tasted of thyme, a little bitter but not unpleasant. The ache in the pit of her stomach faded.

'Better?'

'Yes, thank you.' As Meredith took the cordial to Finn, Merry walked nearer to the trees. The fading light had deceived her: what she'd initially taken to be the edge of a forest was actually the curve of an enormous hedge. She could see it now, stretching away in either direction.

Black holly. It had to be: the hedge that Jack had mentioned once, the hedge that had been there before the Black Lake. Just as well she hadn't imagined appearing right at the edge of the water.

'It is spreading everywhere.' Meredith was at her side. 'Black holly used to be rare, but now… the trees send out shoots beneath the ground and strangle any other plants in their path. They grow faster than we can destroy them.'

Merry shivered. 'It's like a virus.' Meredith looked blank. 'I mean, a sickness.'

'Ah.' The other witch nodded. 'Yes. The land is ailing. And we do not know how to heal it.' Meredith's sorrow enveloped Merry like a mist, setting a lump in her throat.

Finn and Jack joined them.

'Are you feeling better?' Merry asked hesitantly. Even in the dusky light, Finn looked rather green.

'I'd rather not talk about it.' He pulled a face. 'Tell me what that is, instead.'

'A hedge of black holly. Whatever you do, don't touch it.'

'Do we have to go through it? Or is there a—'

'Speak lower!' Jack interrupted. 'I see no guards, but that does not mean we are not being watched.'

Merry glanced upwards. There were black specks circling in the sky high above them; birds of some sort. Perhaps just ordinary birds doing ordinary, bird-type things. But perhaps not.

Meredith was watching the birds too. She nudged Merry's elbow. 'A concealment charm?'

'Good idea.' Merry began singing softly: a charm to shield the singer and those around her from unfriendly eyes for as long as she wished not to be seen. Meredith was singing too, and even though Merry didn't recognise the words or the tune she could feel, deep in her core, that it was the same sort of magic. Both songs came to an end.

'I don't feel any different.' Finn was staring at his hand as if he expected it to suddenly be transparent. 'Has it worked?'

'You're a wizard,' Merry muttered. 'What do you think?'

'Fine. I suppose we won't know for sure until we run into one of Ronan's minions.'

'Come along, wizard.' Jack grinned and swung his bag on to his shoulder. 'It's too late to back out now.'

Finn glared at Jack's back, picked up his bag and hurried after him. But Meredith was still staring up at the circling birds.

'Meredith? What's wrong?'

There was a moment of silence before she answered; just a heartbeat's worth of space, but enough for doubt to flower along Merry's spine.

Meredith dropped her gaze and shook her head.

'Nothing. Nothing is wrong. Let's hurry.' She strode off in the direction of the hedge.

Up close, the black holly hedge was a lot worse than Merry had expected. She'd seen it once before in a dream, and she and Leo had walked among the petrified remnants, underneath the Black Lake in Tillingham. But shadows and husks were no preparation for seeing the living trees as they were now in front of her. The black branches were as thick as her waist, the twigs that bore the sharply pointed leaves, each the width of her wrist. The leaves themselves looked as though they were coated in dark green enamel. Claw-like, silver-tipped spines curved out from their edges.

'Surely there's a gate somewhere?' Finn asked, craning his head back to see the top of the hedge.

Merry concentrated, frowning, trying to remember everything she'd ever learnt about black holly. 'Maybe not. In the story Gran told us, Gwydion had to learn how to use some special type of rune to get through the hedge.'

Finn started to draw his sword, but Meredith stopped him.

'No. You'll merely dull the blade or break it. An obsidian knife might work, but it would be dangerous, and slow.'

Merry pulled Gran's obsidian knife out from her bag and weighed it in her hand. Perhaps she could cut through the hedge with it, but the knife was small, and what she didn't have was time: twilight was now deepening into darkness. Whatever was supposed to happen to Leo tonight could start at any moment. She shivered. The temperature was dropping, and the wind was making her ears ache. She pulled up the hood of her cloak as she glared at the hedge. The idea of setting the whole thing on fire was so tempting; her fingernails tingled in anticipation. But using magic to open the hedge? She may as well send up a flare, telling Ronan: I AM HERE.

No, she couldn't use magic on the hedge.

Her glance strayed down to the knife, still in her hand. And she smiled.

The enlarging spell was simple: junior grade stuff. But Merry added in a few improvements as they occurred to her. By the time she'd finished singing, the obsidian knife had become an obsidian axe.

Even Finn seemed to be impressed.

He was less impressed when she passed the axe to Jack. 'I could do that. I'm just as capable as he is.'

'I'm sure you are. But he's a trained carpenter.' At least, he was in her world – she raised an eyebrow at Jack.

To her relief, he nodded. 'I know how to handle an axe.'

Finn gave Merry a look that clearly said *whatever*, but he stopped arguing.

Meredith cast a charm for sharpness across the blade, just to be sure, then Jack adjusted his stance and lifted the axe above his shoulders. 'Everyone stand back.' He sliced the dark blade carefully downwards. The axe cut through the thick black branches like an oar going through water. Jack smiled grimly. 'This will not take too long.'

While Meredith and Merry both sang a spell to shield him from any flying bits of debris, Jack worked his way cautiously through the hedge as the temperature continued to drop. Eventually, he succeeded in opening up a narrow tunnel. Merry peered through it; the darkness at the end was less dense, somehow, than the tangled shadow between the trees. Jack brought the axe back, and she returned it to its original size and shape.

Meredith conjured a ball of witch fire, and she and Jack started to edge their way through the tunnel.

Finn hung back. 'That was pretty clever, changing the knife like that.' He squinted up at the now dark sky. 'And

I agree that Jack did a better job with the axe than I would have done. Probably.'

'That's very… generous…' Merry's teeth were chattering.

'Um, maybe you should cast a spell to warm yourself up?'

Merry thought for a minute, realised she didn't actually know any spell like that (other than ones for setting things on fire, which would probably be overkill) and shook her head.

'OK. Well…' Finn gently wrapped his arms round her and drew his cloak round both of them. Merry rested her head against his chest, feeling her cramped muscles relax as the warmth of his body seeped into hers. Whatever lay beyond the hedge wasn't going anywhere. Just for a moment, Merry wanted to stay where she was, and listen to Finn's heartbeat.

The other side of the hedge was… different. There was no snow here, for a start. And the darkness was dispelled by globes of witch fire, floating at intervals round the perimeter. Merry had expected an empty space between the hedge and the tower. But there were lots of buildings: some that looked like dormitories or barracks, others that were clearly furnaces, judging by the piles of weapons and the anvils visible through the doorways. But the fires were banked; no one was working this evening.

'Where is everybody?' Finn asked.

Meredith pointed across the clearing. 'There, I would guess.'

Merry followed her direction. There was the tower, the stone tower that Jack had described to her. Less than five months ago she'd left him dead there, beneath its flooded remains. But beyond the tower, joined to it by a sort of rampart, was another building. A huge wooden hall, with ornately carved and gilded pillars bracing the walls. Firelight shone through tall windows, rich with stained glass.

'Bloody hell.' Finn slipped a hand into hers. 'He's built himself a fantasy mead hall.'

'There will be slave quarters and guardrooms beneath.' Jack observed. 'See? There is a staircase to one side.'

Suddenly, a concealment charm didn't seem like much protection. Merry glanced back at the others. 'Let's keep moving.'

They circled away from the hall before walking further towards the tower. Merry was hoping to find the tall wooden doors that were – in modern Tillingham – beneath the lake. She had the key from the trinket box that would hopefully still open them, and if Leo was tied to the horrible, throne-like chair, as Jack had been, then he would be somewhere down there, in the bowels of the tower.

Unless they've moved him. Unless he's already in that hall, and Ronan is doing something terrible to him…

Perhaps she *would* have to get into the hall, to fight and kill everyone and everything inside. A vision floated into her mind: herself, walking towards Leo across a floor slick with blood. She flexed her fingers, feeling the power prickling just beneath her skin.

I will do it, if I must…

She pushed the thought away as Meredith touched her hand and pointed wordlessly. Ahead was an avenue of black holly trees, leading up to the base of the tower, lit from above by more globes of witch fire. But walking towards them, from round the other side of the tower, were two…

Guards? They had spears in their hands, the tips dull red in the witchlight, and long knives belted round their waists. But somehow, it was obvious that they weren't human. They didn't move properly. They stalked, rather than walked, their heads darting from one side to the other. The skin on Merry's scalp crawled, and she edged closer to Finn.

The creatures came nearer. Merry could hear them talking to each other now, their speech soft and sibilant. Their faces were the faces of men, sort of. Eyes and nose and mouth were in the correct place, and correctly proportioned; handsome, even. But the details were wrong. The tips of their ears were pointed. So were their teeth, the canines slightly elongated. The pupils of their eyes were vertical ovals. And their fingers, wrapped round the spear shafts, ended in claws, not nails. She held her breath as they passed, forcing herself to stand still, even though every muscle in her body was screaming at her to curl up in a ball on the ground. Finn was trembling next to her.

The concealment charm worked: the creatures moved away towards the hall, oblivious. Merry began breathing again.

'What the hell were they?' Finn's voice was raspy. 'And why did I suddenly feel crazed with terror?' He paused and rubbed a hand over his face. 'I mean, that wasn't just me, was it?'

'Elves,' Meredith muttered. 'It is their aura. When they wish to, they can use magic to create fear in the minds of those around them, to amplify the dread that they arouse in the minds of all humans. They used to dwell in dark places, in barrows and hillsides. But now, the whole world is dark.'

Jack put his arm round her shoulder. 'Come. The moon is rising.' He led the way towards the avenue of trees.

Merry lingered for a moment, looking after the dwindling figures of the elves.

'Not exactly Legolas and Elrond, were they?' Finn murmured. To her surprise, he sounded faintly amused.

'No. Definitely nothing *Lord of the Rings* about them.' She turned to look at him, her eyebrows raised.

He shrugged. 'Well, I figure our time here is coming to an end. Either we get Leo and escape, or you kill everybody and we escape, or Ronan kills us. Whatever happens, I won't have to be like this for much longer.'

'Would it really be so bad? Living as a pleb?'

Finn gave a sort of laugh, but there was no amusement in his voice any more. 'You don't know my family.' He bowed and gestured for her to go ahead of him. 'Shall we?'

Meredith and Jack were halfway along the avenue of black holly trees. The path sloped downwards in between sheer walls of earth, higher than Merry's head. But there, at the end of the slope, were the doors. Within two minutes they were there, at the entrance to the tower.

Merry's heart leapt as she lifted her hand to the carved doors. She could feel the power thrumming through them now, and wondered briefly why she hadn't noticed it in her own time, the night she and Leo had followed Jack beneath the lake.

Still, she'd broken into this fortress once before, and she could do it again. The key from the trinket box was in the side pocket of her bag. She got it out and held it against the pitted surface of the wood. For a moment both doors were outlined in soft orange light, before swinging silently open.

'What, no menacing creak?' Finn murmured.

'Guess Gwydion and Ronan skipped the "Evil Villainy for Beginners" class. Let's go.' They were faced with the five corridors again. But otherwise, Merry hardly recognised the place. The entrance hall was hung with tapestries that she'd only seen in shreds, but which were now whole and bright with colour. They stirred slightly in the breeze from the windows set high above the doors. Each corridor was lit with torches, set at intervals along the walls, smudges of light fading into the distance.

'Which way?' Meredith and Jack were peering down the corridors.

Merry hesitated. Last time, they'd followed Jack's footprints in the dust, but which corridor had they taken? The floor was clean now. If Leo was where she feared, they needed to find a way down. A broomstick spell was too risky here – far too many walls, and the room itself might be different, but—

A faint but long-drawn-out wail came from the right-most corridor.

'This way.'

The others followed. The corridor twisted and turned, but it kept descending, through gradual slopes and sudden short flights of steps. Past storage rooms and other spaces that were obviously cells: there were people slumped within the shadows, some of them crying softly.

'Merry!'

Finn's hiss made her look up. Just in time: a pair of elvish guards had appeared from a side corridor. She pressed herself quickly against the wall. The guards were speaking in their own tongue, but as they opened one of the cells they switched into English.

'Come now, human.' One of them went into the cell and dragged out an elderly man. The prisoner looked half starved: he could barely stand. 'They want some sport, up in the hall.' The old man began to cry and beg for mercy, but the elves just laughed their musical, chiming laughs and hauled him away, back along the same corridor they'd come from. Finn started to run after them, but Jack grabbed his arm.

'Don't. Fighting will alert them to our presence.'

'But there has to be something we can do.' Finn smacked a fist into the wall. 'We can't leave these people like this…' He broke off, shaking his head.

Merry took his hand. 'I don't like it any more than you do, but Jack is right. We can't fix this, not now.' Besides, she wouldn't risk Leo for anyone. 'Let's go.'

The four of them hurried along the corridor, leaving the block of cells behind. There were more side-corridors and more doorways, but Merry ignored all of them, sticking to the main path. And soon enough the corridor ended at a door. There was no handle or lock visible, but Merry pressed her key to the wood and it quickly swung open. The room on the other side of the door was almost as she remembered it: a long trench down the centre of the floor with a fire burning in it, and shelves covering the wall at the far end. The throne-like chair was there too, and there was someone sitting in it, tied fast – barely conscious, by the look of it.

Merry recognised his face, despite the bruises that mottled his cheekbones and had swollen shut one of his eyes. Despite the dried blood matting his hair and staining his neck. Beneath the bruises and the blood his skin had an oily, unhealthy sheen. But still, his features were so familiar. Not surprising, since they had haunted her dreams for months.

Not Leo.

Gwydion.

EIGHT

BILE ROSE IN Merry's throat. Her heart pummelled her ribcage as the shock of seeing Gwydion alive – and in the very same room where she'd pierced his chest with a sword not five months ago – took her breath away. She staggered and grabbed hold of Finn's arm.

'What's the matter, Merry? Who is this?'

Meredith answered. 'It is Gwydion, the wizard.'

'I was wrong, then,' Jack murmured. 'He is still alive.'

Merry gritted her teeth, as anger fuelled the magic building within her. 'Everything that's happened, he started it. This is all his fault.' Her hands were trembling, aching, sparks of power sizzling from the edges of the nails. She'd killed Gwydion before, in her own world. She could do it here too. She raised her arms.

'Hold on.' Finn took hold of one of her wrists. 'What's Ronan doing with him?'

Pausing, she forced herself to study the man she hated. He was slumped in the chair, bound to it with the same vicious restraints he'd used on Jack in her world. Clearly, he was no longer the master here; Ronan was. Still, Gwydion deserved whatever Ronan had done to him. He deserved all of it.

Gwydion shifted in his bonds. He opened his eyes and looked at her, but there was no sign of recognition. When he saw Jack, however, his eyes widened in fear. He struggled uselessly against the leather cords.

'Jack… He made me do it. I had no choice.' Gwydion's voice was weak and rasping. He winced at every in-breath. 'I swear. I wanted to hurt her, to have my revenge. But not like that. Never like that—' He broke off as a convulsion shook his body. 'I loved her, once. More deeply than any man should.'

Edith. He's talking about the queen. About Jack's birth mother.

Merry shook off Finn's grip and raised her hands again,

but Jack was quicker. He ran past her, shoving Finn out of the way and pulling out his knife.

'Jack, wait!'

Ignoring Meredith's plea, Jack held the knife against Gwydion's throat.

'What did you do to her?'

Gwydion jerked back into consciousness. 'It wasn't me, it was him. Ronan. He killed my Edith. But then…' Gwydion moaned, shaking his head from side to side.

'Then what?' Jack demanded.

'No, I don't want to…'

'My mother is dead. So what did you do? What could you possibly have done?' Jack brought his arm back and struck Gwydion hard across the face. 'Tell me!'

'He made me eat…' Gwydion's voice came out in a broken, pitiful sob. 'He made me eat her heart.'

Jack let go of the wizard, a look of horror on his face. He staggered backwards, dropping his knife, and fell to his knees. Meredith ran to crouch next to him. She wrapped her arms round him, murmuring in his ear, stroking his hair while he clung to her. Eventually, she looked up at Finn and Merry.

'We've lingered here too long: every minute, we risk discovery. As soon as Jack is able, we must leave.'

'Wait,' Gwydion cried. 'Kill me, I beg you. Ronan—'

The leather cords fastened to the top of the throne, which had up until now been hanging unused, sprang to life, wrapping themselves round Gwydion's head and face like so many tentacles, criss-crossing his eyes and mouth, silencing him.

Finn and Merry both jumped back.

'What the hell is that thing he's sitting on?' Finn took a cautious step towards the throne. 'Ronan what? Are you trying to tell us something?'

But Gwydion was pinned into complete immobility.

Finn glanced back at Merry. 'Can you break him out of there?'

'No. I won't risk alerting Ronan to our presence.'

'Perhaps we should kill him, then?'

Meredith nodded. 'I agree. If Ronan has kept him alive, it is for some purpose. We cannot allow him to fulfil that purpose. We must end the wizard's life and we must do so quickly. And quietly.'

'No.' Merry stepped further away, holding her hands behind her back. 'No way. Forget it.'

Finn raised an eyebrow. 'Why? I get that it's… unpalatable, deliberately taking a life. But five seconds ago, it looked like you were all for killing the bastard.'

Finn was right. But Merry didn't want to kill Gwydion any more. What she wanted was worse: she wanted him to suffer. Killing him in his current state would be merciful. And the last thing Gwydion deserved was mercy. She shook her head. 'No. He's half dead already: Ronan's clearly got what he needs from him. I'm sure Gwydion *wants* us to kill him: Ronan's probably planning to torture him to death, or something. But to be honest, I'm fine with that. Killing him won't help me get Leo back, and that's the only thing I'm interested in right now.'

'You're not thinking clearly,' Meredith replied. 'There is more at stake here than simply rescuing your brother—'

Merry cut her off with a wave of her hand. 'Not for me there isn't. I did everything you asked of me, Meredith. I did everything that you, and that manuscript you created, told me to do. I killed Gwydion, and I broke the curse, and still the bad guys won.'

'I understand that, but—'

'No, you don't.' Merry sighed. 'I've lost too much already. Too many people I love have suffered and died because of Gwydion and his King of Hearts. Too many people are still suffering. So let him stay here and rot. I'm going to find my brother.'

'Just wait a minute, Merry.' Finn started forward, frowning.

'Forget about what Gwydion deserves: wouldn't killing him be a good thing for the people who live here? He's evil and Ronan's evil…' He rubbed his eyes. 'I mean, getting Gwydion out of the way could be a helpful thing to do.'

Merry groaned. 'Finn. We don't have time for this.'

'I agree.' Jack pushed himself to his feet, his face set hard. He stared at Gwydion for one long moment before abruptly turning his back on him. 'Leave the wizard to his fate: we've wasted enough time on him. Merry, your brother is not here. Where should we search for him next?'

Merry could see Finn bristling beside her, but thankfully he didn't protest any further. She bit her lip. She'd been so certain that Leo would be confined in the same place Jack had been. Where else did crazed witches like Ronan keep their prisoners, if not in the dungeons?

An image floated into her mind, a picture from a children's book: Rapunzel, leaning out of her prison at the top of a tall tower…

Why not? Ronan knows the old stories as well as I do. He'd probably think it was funny.

She gripped Finn's hand. 'We go up. Up to the highest point in the tower.'

Jack nodded, turned and strode towards the door, without so much as a glance in Gwydion's direction.

Meredith sighed and shook her head. But she followed him.

★ ★ ★

Leo was ready.

As ready as he could be, given what lay ahead. That night he was to participate in a binding ceremony, and pledge his undying loyalty to Ronan. The ceremony itself was born of dark magic; once he'd gone through with it, he would be tied to Ronan's will. It was preferable to being drafted into Ronan's army of enslaved souls: he wasn't going to have to endure the sheer horror of having the King of Hearts inhabit his mind and body again. And he would still be able to make his own choices, when Ronan allowed it. But the binding ceremony would give Ronan the power to rule Leo, by speaking a certain magical word.

Of course, Ronan swore he wouldn't use the word. He claimed it was enough for him that Leo had agreed to be bound in this way. And maybe Ronan truly believed that he could be so... self-restrained.

Leo didn't.

'Stand straight, human.' One of the elves who was preparing him for the ceremony breathed its stinking breath into Leo's face, making him gag. At least the creature had discarded its aura for now – that was the only reason Leo could stand to be this close to it. 'You have to be marked.' The modern English words sounded strange in the creature's mouth. Taking up a brush, the elf began to paint symbols and runes all over Leo's chest and face with some dark, strange-smelling liquid. Leo braced himself, but there was no pain this time. Not like the night at the lake, when Ronan had burnt a rune into Leo's skin to summon the King of Hearts. He shuddered slightly, remembering the agony, remembering how he'd screamed as the rune had dissolved his skin like acid.

He closed his eyes and took a few calming breaths. He had to stay focused on his task; getting rid of Ronan was all that mattered now. His mouth went dry at the thought of it. A few nights ago, he'd pulled a loose flint from the wall of his room, and had been using its sharp edge to work a piece of wooden kindling into a blade of sorts. It wasn't as good as a metal knife, but stuck into the right place, into the right organ, or perhaps Ronan's throat, it might do the job. He just hoped he'd live long enough to see the bastard die.

'Hold up your arms.' The elf dropped a linen shirt over Leo's head, followed by a long, embroidered tunic. Its assistant set a heavy gold torc round Leo's neck, and a gold belt round his waist. Finally, the elf that had painted the runes placed a jewel-studded circlet on Leo's head. It stood back and nodded to itself, admiring its handiwork. 'We are finished.' The assistant picked up the bowl of dark liquid and hurried out of the room. 'Follow me down to the Great Hall now. Our master waits. It is time.' It grinned, revealing sharp, pointed teeth; *just like a shark*, Leo thought. 'You are lucky to be selected for such an honour.'

'If you say so.' He hadn't had a chance to conceal his makeshift blade yet. 'I just need a minute or so alone, to make sure my mind is… clear.'

The elf arched one eyebrow, tilting its head. 'You hope to escape? There is no way out. Nothing you can do.'

Leo shrugged, trying to keep his voice level, confident. 'I don't wish to escape. In fact, I'm looking forward to – to joining with Ronan. To taking my place at his side. This is a big moment for me, that's all.'

The elf didn't move.

Leo decided to try another tack. He was Ronan's favourite, after all. 'You can stand outside the room and wait for me. Now move, before I tell your master that you were—'

The elf leapt forward, pinning Leo against the wall, its

claws so tight round his throat that he could hardly breathe. 'No, human. It is time. We leave now.'

Voices, outside the room – the elf looked over its shoulder, loosening its grip slightly, and Leo shoved it hard in the chest. The elf staggered backwards and drew a knife from its belt, switching on its aura again so that Leo cringed away, terror paralysing his limbs, paralysing his tongue, even though all he could think of was trying to beg for mercy—

'Leo!'

It was his sister…

He rubbed his eyes: his sister was there, standing in the doorway, breathing hard, sparks leaping from her fingertips. The elf snarled and flew at her. But Merry was ready: she chanted some words Leo didn't understand, moving her hands quickly. The air shimmered brightly and the elf dropped to the floor, hitting the ground hard, clawing at its neck. Leo watched as the creature thrashed about, choking, its face turning black. Finally, its eyes rolled back in its head, and it lay motionless upon the floor.

'Leo?' Merry was on her knees next to him.

She was dressed like someone from this world; was this just another dream? He lifted his hand and touched her face. 'Merry? Are you… real?'

'Yes, Leo. Yes, I'm real.' There were tears running down her cheeks.

'You came back for me.'

She smiled through the tears. 'Of course I did.'

And as Merry wrapped her arms round him, he realised he was crying too.

Finally, Merry let him go, and Leo saw that they weren't alone. There was another girl, a bit older than Merry. She looked vaguely familiar, although Leo had no idea who she was. As he watched, she touched Merry on the shoulder and spoke to Leo in Old English. Something about going, he thought, but...

He shook his head. 'I don't understand.'

Merry pressed one fingertip to his forehead, just like she'd done under the lake when they'd been eavesdropping on Gwydion. Something inside his mind... shifted.

'I said,' the girl smiled at him, 'that we should leave now, if you are well enough.'

'Yes, I'm well—' Leo stopped short: he could hear that the words were coming out in Old English, even though he was thinking in modern English. 'Um, thank you...'

'Meredith.'

'Thank you, Meredith.'

Merry stood up. 'Finn, can you see what Jack's doing?' The tall, red-haired boy – who'd been staring at Leo with a mixture of relief and embarrassment – nodded and turned away. So Finn was here too; did that mean that he and Merry were officially together, as Ronan had claimed? The last few weeks of Leo's life in Tillingham, before Ronan had brought him here, everything had become blurred at the edges. It was the same kind of feeling he used to get when he was ill, and running a fever: he'd been aware, but at the same time strangely detached from what had been going on around him. He'd probably never find out exactly what Ronan had been doing to him…

Finn came back into the room, dragging the body of one of Ronan's human guards. The other end of the body was carried by a man with long, blond hair, tied back in a ponytail.

Jack…

Leo had wondered sometimes whether Jack could be alive in this other world, but he'd never seriously expected to see him again. He couldn't help himself: jumping up, he pulled Jack fiercely into a bear hug. The other boy didn't seem to recognise him: he resisted at first, then stood stiffly while Leo embraced him. But Leo didn't care. Eventually he stepped back. 'It's good to see you, Jack.'

Merry put her hand on Leo's shoulder. 'Come on, big brother. It's time to get out of here.'

'Bloody hell. I don't understand.'

Leo opened his eyes to find himself standing in exactly the same spot as before.

Merry swore again, her hands on her hips. 'Why are we still in the tower?'

The plan had been to use the broomstick spell to transport them all out of the tower and directly back to the woods where Meredith and her sisters lived. Merry and Meredith had cast the spell together. But clearly, it hadn't worked.

'Something is wrong,' murmured Meredith. 'Can you not feel it? The dark magic is strong here, stronger than elsewhere in this place.' She flattened one hand against the wall beside her and closed her eyes. When she opened them again, Leo could see the fear there. 'A spell has been cast round the tower, to counteract our own magic.' Her voice trembled slightly. 'To prevent us from leaving.'

Merry shook her head. 'You can't be right. Because that would mean—'

'That Ronan knew you were coming.' Leo's stomach churned. Had his sister and the others walked straight into a trap? Had Ronan used him as bait, once again?

'But he might not know we're already here,' said Finn. 'Let's go back the way we came. We can still fight if we have to.' He drew the sword from the scabbard at his waist. 'Here, Leo: this belongs to you.' He handed Leo the sword, and took the dead guard's weapon for himself. Jack drew his sword too.

Leo stared at the hilt in his hand. It had come from the trinket box; so many months ago, now. A different lifetime, almost...

'Merry, what about the key? The one from the trinket box. Do you remember how it guided us before, when we were running away from Gwydion?'

His sister gasped. 'Of course. Did you tell Ronan about it?'

'I don't think so.'

Merry stuck her hand into her bag, pulled out the key and held it up in front of her. 'Show us the way out.' The key seemed to spring to life, vibrating slightly and jerking Merry forward. 'Brilliant, Leo.' She flashed him a tight smile. 'Come on.'

Following the key, Merry began to lead them down

the wide spiral staircase that ran along the inside of the tower. It was dark, despite the globes of witch fire she and Meredith had conjured to light their way. Leo pressed as close as he could to the wall; there was no banister and a long drop on the other side of the steps. At least no one seemed to be pursuing them. About halfway down the key veered off and took them along a corridor that eventually ended in a sort of landing. There was light here: a soft glow. Merry extinguished her witch fire and crept forward carefully. Leo followed.

They were on a balcony, set above a huge hall. Leo peeked over the edge of the wall. The hall had clearly been set up for the binding ceremony. There was a circle drawn on the stone floor, surrounded with strange symbols and candles. More candles were set on spikes sticking out from the walls above. Blood-red roses were growing in profusion, twisted round the pillars, scenting the air with their heavy perfume. A vast banqueting table, laden with food and drink, was pushed against a side wall. But there was no one in sight. Leo frowned.

What's Ronan playing at? Where the hell is he?

His sister was nudging him: the key was vibrating in her hand. It took them towards an opening on the far side of the balcony, and beyond that, down a long flight of stairs that led to a sort of alcove off the main hall. But at the bottom of the stairs, Merry hesitated.

Opposite them, set into another alcove on the far side of the hall, was a set of doors. And they were open. Leo could see the dark shapes of buildings and trees. And above them, stars, glowing in the night sky. The promise of freedom only metres away.

But to get to the doors, they would have to cross the open expanse of the hall.

'Let's make a dash for it,' Merry whispered. 'Ready?'

They were off, running, Leo's heart thudding in his ears. He gripped Merry's free hand tightly. Finn was keeping pace with Merry, hovering protectively by her side. Jack was slightly ahead, pulling Meredith along with him, and Leo could see they were nearly at the doors now, a few more steps and Jack would be through.

We're going to make it, we're going to—

The doors slammed shut, hurling Jack and Meredith to the floor. Finn dragged Meredith upright as Jack scrambled back on to his feet, and Merry sped up, holding the key out in front of her –

The candles in the great hall suddenly seemed to swell in brightness, illuminating every corner of the room.

And someone was laughing.

Leo forced himself to turn round...

It was Ronan. He was sitting on one of the thrones at the far end of the hall. And surrounding him, crowded into the large space, were dozens and dozens of his followers: free humans, enslaved humans, elves, other creatures that Leo didn't recognise.

They were trapped.

NINE

'**Y**OU! YOU KILLED my mother!' Jack yelled at Ronan, changing the grip on his sword and raising it above his shoulder like a spear. Ronan waved one hand lazily in the air and Jack cried out in pain, dropping the weapon and clutching his wrist. The hilt of the abandoned sword was glowing red.

Ronan stood up, grinning. 'Ah, Merry. And Finn too. It's grand of you to drop by.'

Merry walked forward, placing herself deliberately in front of Leo. She held her head up high, but Leo could tell she was shaking. From fear, or anger, he could only guess. But when she spoke, her voice was calm. 'We're leaving, Ronan. Don't get in our way.'

'Or what?' Ronan cocked his head to one side, smirking. There were sniggers and snatches of laughter from among his followers. 'I'm not entirely sure you appreciate the gravity of your situation, Merry.'

'Oh, please.' Merry's voice was scornful. 'You're nothing more than a thief, Ronan. And all you have is stolen magic and parlour tricks. That won't be enough to stop me this time.' Slowly she raised her hands in front of her. Leo could see the magic, no longer just sparking from her fingertips but forming a solid arc of silvery energy, dancing between her hands, lighting up her face. The power was rolling off her in waves, distorting the air around her, making Leo's hair stand up on end. 'And I'm not alone.'

Meredith walked past him and stood next to Merry, her hands raised in a similar fashion.

Ronan jumped up from his seat, but he didn't come any closer. A vein in his temple was pulsing slightly.

'How dare you challenge me.' He spat the words out, his jaw clenched. 'Have you forgotten what I took from under the lake? Do you not see what I've built here? Have your friends not told you who controls this kingdom now?' Taking a deep breath, he raised his hands, mimicking

Merry's stance. But the light that began to arc across his hands was red, not white. 'Leo is mine. And to make sure he understands that, I'm going to destroy you. Just like I destroyed Flo, and your grandmother —'

The tall windows behind Ronan exploded inwards.

As the hall erupted with screams and shouts Leo ducked, covering his head, waiting for the storm of splinters to hit him. But nothing did. He straightened up and saw glass fragments flying everywhere, heard them shattering as they hit the walls and floor — but he and the others were protected. The fragments dropped out of the air and fell abruptly to the ground in front of Merry and Meredith, as if there were an invisible barrier round them: Meredith was singing a shielding spell.

Before Leo could wonder any further, two enormous branches of black holly snaked through the broken windows, blocking them. The branches thrashed about blindly, like the tentacles of a giant octopus, smashing into the walls, sending chunks of masonry flying. Ronan's people scattered, desperately trying to avoid the poisonous, silver-tipped thorns soaring towards them.

Merry's hands were moving quickly, leaving an echo of silvery light behind them: Leo realised that his sister was the one controlling the black holly, directing it. His breath caught in his chest: since when had she been able to wield this sort of power? He watched in dazed fascination as one of the branches wove past him, punching a massive hole in the wooden doors they'd tried to get through before. Both branches were sending out side shoots now, putting out more and more silver-tipped leaves, trapping Ronan's supporters in a tangle of green and black vegetation. Ronan himself was standing on a table, writing fire runes in the air as fast as he could, burning all the holly within his reach. But he wasn't quick enough: the scything tendrils forced him backwards. Ronan flung his hands up, magic still spilling from his fingertips, before falling. The black branches finally overwhelmed him, and he disappeared from Leo's view. The hall grew dark as more holly wrapped itself round the outside of the building. An ominous creaking from the wooden roof above snapped Leo out of his stupor and sent his heart racing.

Merry was yelling. 'Get outside! Finn, get Leo out!' Finn grabbed Leo's hand and they ran together towards the wooden doors. There were more branches now, coming in from outside the hall, blocking up the doorway. Finn sped up, dragging Leo across the threshold with a last burst of speed.

They were outside. Jack and Meredith were there too,

both gasping for air. But where was Merry? Leo turned back to the hall…

But it wasn't there. There was just a mass of black holly, spreading inwards from the hedge, and it was growing as more and more branches shot up through the sky and arched towards the place where the hall had been. Finn pulled him backwards, away from the reach of the thorns. Leo tried to resist, but horror had snatched away his voice and drained the strength from his legs. He stumbled, unable to tear his gaze away from the dark tendrils that were sealing up the last exit from the hall, sealing his sister inside –

Merry flung herself through the last chink in the holly. Leo could hear Ronan howling in rage and pain, screaming his name –

The gap closed, and there was silence.

'Come on.' Merry pulled Leo and Finn into a circle. 'Hold hands.' She began to sing, her voice trembling, breathless. Somewhere behind them, Meredith was singing too.

Another spell. The world pitched and swirled and melted into darkness.

★   ★   ★

Merry was shaking. She was vaguely aware of Finn putting his arms round her, leading her into the cottage. Of Carys pressing a cup of hot liquid into her aching hands.

'Leo?'

'Drink the cordial. I'll tend to your brother.'

Merry sank gratefully on to a stool, inhaling the thyme-scented steam of the metheglin deeply, letting it clear her head before she took a sip. The muscles in her back cramped, making her wince. Leo was free. She'd rescued her brother from Ronan. But it wasn't over, not yet.

'Carys,' she raised her voice, 'is Leo well enough to be moved? Can you take us to the nearest point of intersection? We have to get home.'

Meredith looked up from where she was sitting by the fire. 'Tonight, you need to rest. All of us do. And Carys has already given Leo a draft, to help him sleep and recover. Tomorrow is early enough to be thinking of going to the gateway.'

Merry considered arguing. But she was exhausted: she felt as fragile as hoar frost after using so much magic. Finn was yawning. And Jack – Jack was already snoring, lying on the floor with a blanket pulled over him.

'OK. I suppose we can wait a few more hours.' She drained her cup. 'Thank you, everyone.' Carys was still busy with Leo, but Meredith smiled back at her. Wrapping herself in her cloak, Merry lay down with her head on her bag and fell instantly asleep.

Voices woke her: Meredith and Carys, arguing quietly. Merry forced her eyelids open, squinting against the daylight pouring through the tiny windows. Yesterday's magic had left the skin on her hands prickling with discomfort, as though someone had taken sandpaper to her nerve endings. Gingerly, she pushed herself up on to her elbows.

'Meredith? What's the matter?'

'Nothing,' Meredith said quickly. 'Are you hungry? Carys has made some honey cakes.'

Merry got to her feet, grimacing as tendrils of pain shot up and down her spine – she was so over sleeping on the floor – and limped across to the fire. The cakes were still hot. But she was starving; despite her sore palms, she picked one up, flipping it from hand to hand, blowing on it. 'Is Leo awake?' She could see Jack and Finn, both sleeping at the far end of the room, but Leo was in the small bedroom the three sisters shared.

'No, but he is well enough. Though there is much enchantment still hanging on him.'

'Ronan's been putting spells on him for months.' Merry's hunger vanished. 'He will get better eventually, though, won't he?'

'We think so. He needs rest, time away from magic. Ordinary folk weaken under too much enchantment. They begin to…' Meredith tapped her fingers on her knee, 'fade, I suppose.'

That didn't sound good. 'Then the sooner I get him home the better.' Merry glanced out of the window. The woods surrounding the cottage seemed ordinary enough, but this whole world was far more magical than the one she'd grown up in.

The sisters were glaring at each other.

'What?'

Meredith began pleating the fabric of her dress. 'I think you should go home, today if possible. But Carys…'

'I think you should stay.' Carys crossed her arms and lifted her chin as if issuing a challenge. 'We need to make sure this is properly ended. We need to make sure Ronan and Gwydion are both dead.'

'Of course they're dead.' Merry turned to Meredith. 'You were there. You saw what I did with the holly. Do you really think anyone could get out of that? And Gwydion was almost dead already.'

'I agree it's unlikely,' Carys began, 'but...'

Merry took the silver bracelet off her wrist and threw it in the cauldron of water sitting by the edge of the fire, hurrying through the words of the hydromancy spell. 'Show me Ronan.'

The water turned an inky black. But no image of Ronan appeared.

'See?' Merry waved her hand again to end the charm. 'He's dead.'

'Perhaps,' Carys muttered. 'Or perhaps he shields himself from your sight. We have no proof.'

'Can't we go back and check?' It was Finn, yawning and rubbing his head. 'I mean, I don't mind staying a little longer.'

Merry raised an eyebrow. 'I thought you were desperate to get home?'

He shrugged. 'The pain isn't going away, but it isn't getting any worse.' He brushed his fingers across the centre of his chest. 'I can hold on, if we have stuff to do here.'

'No.' Meredith stood up. 'You must leave, because of what is outside.' She walked across to where Jack lay, still sleeping, and nudged him with her foot. 'Jack, wake up. There is something you should see.' Once Jack had staggered to his feet, Meredith led them out of the cottage and a little way into the woods. 'Look.'

Merry glanced in the direction Meredith was pointing. 'What the…' She rubbed her eyes and looked again, but it was still there.

A lamppost. A modern lamp post, casting a pale sodium-yellow glow across the snow, despite the daylight. Despite the lack of any obvious source of electricity.

Finn walked up to the lamp post and knocked on it with one fist; it made a hollow metallic sound. 'Please, someone tell me that we're not in Narnia.'

Merry put her hands on her hips. 'We're not in Narnia, Finn.' But the lamp post worried her. It could have come straight from her world. Straight from twenty-first century Tillingham.

'This is why they must leave, Carys. And it's not just this: Jack has told me of dreams he's had, images in his head from a life that he hasn't lived.' Meredith turned her back on the lamp post. 'I think their presence is damaging our world. And I believe Ronan is dead. There's nothing more for Merry to do here.'

'She's right,' Jack commented. 'Our land, our people – they have been through enough. We can deal with the remnants of Ronan's force, now he is gone. But to risk further damage…' He put one hand on Merry's shoulder. 'You stopped Ronan. We will be forever in your debt. And I will miss you – all of you,' he nodded at Finn, 'but I think you should return to your own world.'

Carys swore and kicked a chunk out of an old tree stump. 'Have you all run mad? You didn't witness Ronan's death. You didn't return with his body. We cannot be certain he is gone.' She dragged her hands through her loose hair, frowning down at the forest floor. 'I will see if Nia is awake. She may have seen something that will guide us.'

Carys hurried back into the cottage, and the rest of them followed her. It wasn't long before she reappeared in the main room, having spoken to her sister.

'Nia agrees with you.' Carys shrugged and turned to Merry. 'She thinks you should be allowed to go.'

Merry's shoulders un-hunched, and she tried not to smile too widely. 'Can we go now?'

'Shortly. There is a gateway not far from here. An ancient standing stone. Rightly, there should be days of preparation to use the gateway as you wish to use it: spells should be cast to protect the world you are leaving, and the world you travel to. Charms, to strengthen the gateway itself. Incantations to balance the forces within the gateway.'

'But—' Merry burst out.

'But, there is a quicker way.' Carys pulled a disapproving face. 'Since you are going back to where you truly belong, you might be able to use blood magic to open the gateway. To bend it to your will. I can teach you the right spell, if you insist.'

'Yes, please.' Merry jumped up. And then she realised: going home meant leaving here. She'd have to say goodbye to Meredith and her sisters. She'd have to say goodbye to Jack. Again. A strand of sorrow mingled with her happiness, clouding it like ink dropped through water.

Learning the spell didn't take long, but the other preparations Carys insisted on making – chanting incantations over Merry's obsidian knife, for instance – were more time-consuming. It was late afternoon when they were finally ready to leave, and colour was bleeding out of the forest as the daylight faded.

Jack was waiting outside the cottage, holding the two horses. He was leaving too, riding to give news of Ronan's defeat to the remnants of the king's council. He held out his hand to Leo. 'I wish we had been given more time to know each other.'

'Me too,' Leo replied. 'We were friends, before. I'd like to think we could have been friends again.'

'We would have been, I am sure of it.' Jack nodded to Finn. 'Good luck, wizard. I hope you recover your magic.'

'Thanks.' Finn clapped him on the shoulder. 'Take care of yourself.'

And then it was Merry's turn. 'It was good to see you again, Jack.' She looked up into his eyes; it was sad, saying goodbye, but it wasn't like losing him again. This Jack was a different person; she found she was able to let him go. 'Take care of Meredith and the others. I hope you get your kingdom back.'

'All will be well, Merry, I'm sure of it.' He put his hands on her shoulders and kissed her lightly on the forehead. 'Remember me; a week ago I didn't know you, but now I will never forget what you've done for us.'

He stepped away from her and leapt on to Sorrel's back. And then he was gone, swallowed up by the forest.

Merry stared after him. Someone touched her arm: it was Finn, his eyes more blue than grey in the gathering shadows.

'It's time to go.' His voice was sympathetic. 'If you're ready.'

'Of course.' She shrugged her bag on to her back, checking again that the obsidian knife was safely in the side pocket, and turned to say goodbye to Nia.

The middle sister's eyes were large and bright; too bright. Nia put her hands on either side of Merry's face. 'Are you listening?'

'Yes, I'm listening.'

'Time is not like a spear. Many pasts may lead into the present moment, and many futures may follow on from it.' She frowned. 'Do you understand?'

'Um…'

Nia obviously took that as a yes, because she carried on. 'Time is a lake, not a river. And a magical event is… It is like a stone, in a lake. The ripples. It changes everything, do you see? The past. The future. Everything.' Nia's breath was coming in short gasps, but she was staring intently into Merry's eyes, as if she could force some epiphany from the weight of her gaze.

Merry didn't want to disappoint her. 'Of course.' She nodded. 'That makes sense. I understand.'

Nia's shoulders relaxed. 'I knew you would.' She frowned. 'I wish I understood why he was using him, but I don't know yet.' She smiled and kissed Merry on the cheek, backing away. 'I will tell you, next time you visit.'

'But I won't—'

It was too late. Nia had already darted back inside the cottage, leaving Merry none the wiser.

'Nia grows worse again.' Carys had appeared at Merry's side, her voice toneless.

'I'm sorry.'

'It is the way of things, for those cursed with the sight.' She sighed, almost imperceptibly. 'Come.'

Only Carys was going with them to the stone; at the last minute, Merry clung on to Meredith, a sudden sense of loss twisting her insides.

Meredith hugged her back, whispering in her ear. 'Don't weep, my friend. Part of me will always be with you. And who knows: perhaps one day we will meet again, in another world.'

Merry took Leo's hand and left Meredith and the cottage behind. She didn't allow herself to look back.

By the time they'd walked for an hour or so, Merry could see the edge of the wood. She couldn't yet see the stone. But she didn't need to: she could feel its power. Her own magic hummed through her veins in response.

They had reached the gateway.

TEN

THE STONE WAS as wide as it was tall, a massive granite slab, somehow standing upright at the edge of the wood. Merry rested her hand against the rough surface. Despite the low clouds and freezing air, the stone was warm. And there was something else too: a whisper, on the very edge of hearing. Trying to make out what the voice was saying, Merry leant closer…

'Echoes, from other worlds,' Carys commented. 'It happens sometimes, when the alignment within the gateway is right.'

Merry nodded. She could feel the energy surrounding the stone; it was an ancient magic, tied to and born of the land. And she knew she could do this, knew that she could get them all back to modern-day Tillingham again. She smiled to herself. The power of the land seemed to be hers to bend to her own will: almost as simple as clicking a pair of ruby slippers together and whispering, '*There's no place like home.*'

Leo gasped and Merry swung round.

'What's the matter?'

'Nothing. It's OK. I thought I saw something, that's all.' He trailed off, still staring into the trees as if he expected Ronan to suddenly appear from the shadows.

It was definitely time to go.

'Carys, thank you.' Merry stepped forward and gave the other witch a quick hug. 'I'm glad we met. And I hope… I hope your story is a happy one in the end. I hope you and the others will be able to defeat the rest of Ronan's forces.'

Carys smiled slightly. 'They are weakened, for the time being at least. And if Ronan does live…' She shrugged. 'He cannot kill us all. Even if my sisters and I do not survive, others will live through this darkness, and will see the dawn. Remember that, if darkness comes for you. Remember, and hold on to hope.' She held her hands out wide. 'Blessings be upon you, my sister.'

Merry bowed – it felt like the right thing to do.

Nodding to Finn and Leo, Carys turned away and ran back into the woods. Within a few seconds, she was lost from view.

'Right.' Merry retrieved Gran's obsidian knife from the bottom of her bag. 'Let's go home.' Drawing the tip of the knife along the inside of her arm, she used her blood to draw part of the rune Carys had shown her on the standing stone. She repeated the process with Finn and Leo, completing the pattern. As the last stroke was put in place, the surface of the stone seemed to ripple. 'OK. Everybody hold on.' When Finn and Leo had put their hands on the hilt of the knife, Merry guided it forward so the point of the blade was touching the stone. Longing for her home, sudden and crushing as a hammer blow, made her chest ache with sadness.

I need to get back. Back to my family, back to my land. Back to my own world.

As she began to sing the spell Carys had taught her, she closed her eyes, tightened her grip, and thrust the knife into the stone...

Merry was lying on her back. But...

There was grass beneath her fingertips, not snow. And it was warm.

She opened her eyes. Blue sky above. A plane, vapour trails streaming out behind it. The hum of traffic in the distance, and the chug of a heavy diesel vehicle – a tractor? – nearer by.

Home.

The stone – unchanged – was looming above her. She pushed herself up on to her elbows. They seemed to be at the edge of a field full of green, cabbage-type things. There was Finn, leaning against the stone, his eyes still shut. And there was Leo, standing and gazing around him. He was crying.

Merry scrambled upright.

'Leo, what's the matter?'

'Nothing. I'm fine, I'm… You brought me home.' Giving up on words, he threw his arms round her, squeezing her tightly. 'I don't know how to thank you.'

'You don't have to thank me. You and me,' Merry's voice wobbled, 'we're a team, remember? Besides, I'm a witch – I should have realised sooner what Ronan was…'

A flicker of sadness, or regret, crossed Leo's face. 'Don't be daft. The way I was feeling I wouldn't have listened to you, even if you'd told me he was the devil incarnate.' He sniffed, drying his eyes on his sleeve. 'There was probably a part of me that doubted him, deep down. But I wanted my happy ending, Merry. I wanted it so badly that I ignored the warning signs.'

'Don't you dare blame yourself. Ronan manipulated you. Emotionally, and with magic – you were under his spell. Literally.'

'Until you saved me.'

'We're family, Leo.' Merry took a deep breath and wiped a tear from her face. 'We save each other: that's what family does. I wouldn't even be here without you. Gwydion would have killed me, if you hadn't been with me under the lake that night.' She stepped back. Finn was watching them, an odd expression on his face. Merry tried to sense what he was feeling, but her ability to pick up on people's emotions didn't seem to have returned. Still, she could hazard a guess. Her brother was back. But Finn's brother was dead. He hadn't been able to save him.

Leo stretched out his hand.

'Thank you too, Finn. For coming back for me. And helping my sister.'

Surprise displaced whatever else Finn had been feeling. He grasped Leo's hand. 'You're welcome. And about before: I'm really—'

Leo cut him off. 'It's fine, honestly. It was all quite a long time ago, from my point of view.'

Merry touched the centre of Finn's chest. 'Do you feel anything? Has your power come back?'

'I feel something. More than I did.' He chewed on his bottom lip for a moment. 'I guess I should try a spell.'

'Here.' Merry plucked a dandelion clock from amidst the grass and held it out to him. 'D'you remember, sitting in our garden? You made the little seed things float away.'

Finn took the stem, held it between his fingers and closed his eyes.

Nothing happened.

Merry's heart sank. She opened her mouth to say, *Don't worry, give it time,* but before she could force the words out, the seeds rose upwards in the same double helix pattern that she remembered.

'Yes!' She punched the air, grinning at him. 'I told you so. I told you it would come back. I was right – your magic was affected by being in the other world, that's all.'

Finn beamed at Merry and grabbed her round the waist, spinning her in a circle and laughing. 'I'm finally me again, Merry.' He glanced at Leo. 'Wiser as well as older, hopefully.'

Leo smiled. But his smile faded quickly. 'Look: someone's there.'

Merry followed his gaze. There was a man standing on the other side of the field. He was staring at them, shielding his eyes with one hand. In the other he held a shotgun. As Merry watched, he began striding towards them.

'We should get out of his field,' Finn murmured. 'This,' he gestured to the Anglo-Saxon clothes they were all wearing, 'is going to be difficult to explain.'

Together they hurried round to the far side of the standing stone, out of view of the farmer.

Merry linked hands with Leo and Finn. 'Time for a broomstick spell again.' They could hear the farmer shouting. He wasn't far from the stone. 'Hold on tight...'

Merry wasn't sure what she had expected when she got home, but it hadn't been this: that everything would look exactly the same. Or almost exactly. The tree in the front garden seemed a bit different – lopsided, sort of – although she couldn't exactly work out why.

Mind you, the four months or so Leo spent in the other world passed in just four days here. Perhaps I should be expecting everything to be the same...

She frowned at the tree a bit more.

'Hey.' Finn pointed at Leo. Her brother was shaking. 'Think he's in shock.'

Merry took Leo's hand again.

'I thought... I thought I'd never see it again.' He couldn't take his eyes off the house.

'I know. But you're home now. You're safe. Come on, let's go and find Mum.'

They crossed the road and walked up to the front door. Merry was about to ring the doorbell (one thing she'd forgotten to take with her was a key) when Finn grabbed her arm.

'Wait...' He stared down at the doorstep, tapping it with the toe of one foot. 'The last time I saw your mum was just after I'd stopped you killing Ronan.' He peeked up at Leo, who was still gazing at the house. 'After I got in the way. She might not want to see me.'

'Of course she will. That was—' Merry stopped. How long ago was it? They had no idea how much time had passed here. 'So, you messed up. But you helped fix it too. Of course she'll want to see you. Come on.'

Merry pressed the button for the doorbell. She heard footsteps from inside – someone coming down the stairs – and the door opened.

Mum's jaw dropped.

Leo stumbled forward into his mother's arms.

★

After seeing Mum and Gran, and crying, and hugging, and crying some more, getting out of their dirty Anglo-Saxon clothes and getting clean had been the priority. Standing beneath a jet of hot water again was blissful. Merry lathered the shampoo into her hair, trying to force the tense muscles in her body to relax. It was hard; her mind was too restless, reeling from the change in time and place, buzzing with the information she'd gleaned from a brief conversation with Mum. Apparently, she'd been gone for almost three weeks, though however many times she counted she didn't see how she and Finn could have spent more than eight nights in the other world. She'd missed the first day of school, so Mum had told her teachers and friends that she had glandular fever. On the plus side, Gran's power had started to return. Only a little, and no one knew how much better it would get, but still. It was more than anyone had hoped for.

Reluctantly, Merry got out of the shower, dried off and wrapped a towel round herself. She knew Finn was on the landing, waiting for his turn.

Downstairs, it looked like Mum had taken the food out of every cupboard and piled it all on to the kitchen table. She was also making platefuls of sandwiches.

'I'm sure you must all be hungry. There's cheese, cheese

and pickle, ham – and I'm just making some chicken ones – and there's some soup and—'

'Mum, that's plenty. Leave the sandwiches and come and sit down. Actually, what I really want is some tea. Lots and lots of tea.' Merry filled the kettle up, then sat down next to her mother. 'Is Gran OK? It wasn't too much of a shock for her?'

'No. She started improving a couple of days ago. And she already looks better after seeing you. I left Leo up there with her. Is Finn…?'

'In the shower. I expect he'll be down soon.'

Mum shook her head. 'I had no idea he was with you. After what happened at the lake when you…'

When I completely lost it, and attacked him and broke his leg.

'Yeah. Well, he wanted to help. He showed up as I was leaving.' Mum looked like she was about to ask a lot of other Finn-related questions. 'So, what else has been happening here? I guess not much.'

Mum jumped up and started getting mugs out of the cupboard. 'Tea or coffee? Though we should probably all be drinking brandy for the shock. I'm sure I've got a bottle somewhere—'

'Mum? What's happened?'

Mum stopped, staring down at the packet of tea in her hands. 'There have been some... odd things going on while you've been away. That's all.'

Inwardly, Merry groaned. 'Huh. I guess by odd you mean magical?'

Mum nodded, still apparently engrossed by the tea. 'The cherry tree in front of the house – one of its branches turned to glass. We had to take it off.'

That would explain the lopsidedness Merry had noticed.

'And down by the lake we found...'

'What?'

'Well, I'm not sure. But Sophia Knox says it's a black holly tree.'

Sophia Knox was one of the most experienced witches in Gran's coven. If she said the tree was black holly, she was probably right.

'But how could a black holly tree show up here? They don't exist in our world any more.'

'We don't know. Someone suggested it was...' Mum cleared her throat. 'That it might possibly be to do with what Ronan did. And what you did. They think that perhaps there was some damage to the point of intersection near the lake. Because of the type of magic you used.'

Merry bit her lip, remembering the lamp post she'd seen at the cottage yesterday. Meredith had said that it was to do with Merry and Finn and Leo being there, in the wrong world. The black holly must be here for the same reason. But there was no need to panic Mum by mentioning the lamp post to her. Now they were back, everything was bound to sort itself out.

Probably.

Mum put the tea down, like she'd forgotten what she was doing with it in the first place. 'It's going to be fine, the coven will fix it. I don't want you to worry.'

The last time Merry had seen any of the coven members was after Leo had been snatched by Ronan. They'd questioned her about what Ronan had done, about how she'd fought him. And then…

And then, they'd expressly forbidden her from trying to rescue her brother. They'd thought that Leo would be dead. And if he wasn't dead… Well, Merry was supposed to abandon him to whatever torment Ronan had planned.

She didn't have a lot of time for the coven.

Just then, she noticed Finn hovering in the doorway.

'Oh, Finn, come in and sit down. I was just –' Mum gazed around the kitchen distractedly – 'I was just going to make some tea. Are you hungry?'

'Starving.' He grabbed a plate, piled on some sandwiches and sat down next to Merry. 'I've let my parents know I'm still alive. And talked to them about going home.'

Merry slumped in her chair as disappointment washed over her. It made sense: there was no reason for Finn to stay permanently in Tillingham now. And with magic, they could see each other whenever they wanted. Still.

'When are you leaving?'

'Well,' Finn flushed a little, 'my dad actually wondered if I could stay here tonight and leave tomorrow. I've told him it's not convenient—'

'Of course you can stay.' Mum seemed almost outraged that Finn was considering going home.

'He's worried, you see – about me transporting myself home, after what happened to my magic in the other world. He wants to come and fetch me himself.' He glanced at Merry. 'And he wants to meet you.'

Mum patted Finn's shoulder as she put a mug of tea down in front of him. 'There's no need to explain.'

But the wizard still seemed embarrassed. Angry, even. He was glaring at the food in front of him as if it had offended him somehow. Merry remembered what she'd learnt from Finn about the Kin Houses: their innate sense of superiority, their pride, their disdain for other wizards and (especially) witches. She wondered what his dad had said to upset him.

Is he more cross about his son putting himself in danger? Or about his son getting involved with a witch?

Of course, that was assuming Finn had told his dad that he and Merry were… involved.

'I'm sorry.' Finn ran one hand through his hair. 'I'm just not feeling quite right. To be back here, alive, after everything that's happened…' He smiled at her. But it was a tense sort of smile, and Merry wished again that she could sense what he was feeling. He was right, though: everything was weird. It was weird sitting in the kitchen eating lunch as if this was a normal day. Weird, wearing regular clothes again and being back home three weeks later when (from her perspective) she'd only spent a few days away. And then there was this whole thing about the black holly growing near the lake…

Mum was crying.

Merry sighed. Perhaps nothing would be normal ever again.

The rest of the day was pretty much the same. The strange sense of unreality was affecting almost everyone. Only Gran seemed to be immune. She told Merry that their return was no surprise to her. She knew Merry would go after Leo, and she knew she would bring him home again. Still, despite Gran's confidence in her, Merry was relieved when it got late enough to go to bed. Finn was sleeping on the sofa since Gran was using the spare room. When Merry went in to say goodnight to him he was stretched out, still in his clothes, staring up at the ceiling.

'Hey.'

'Hey.' Finn swung his legs off the sofa. 'You OK?'

'Yeah. I'm going to bed in a minute.' She sat down next to him, picked up the book he'd left on the floor and began thumbing the pages.

'So, I—'

'I was thinking—'

They both stopped. Finn said: 'After you.'

'Oh, nothing really.' Merry thumbed the book some more, watching the words and letters flick past. 'I was just going to say, I think I've got dimension-lag. Like jet lag, but...'

Finn smiled. 'I know what you mean.'

'It's almost like – like the stuff in the other world didn't really happen.'

'Yeah.' Finn fell silent, drumming his fingers on his knee.

Merry was still fiddling with the book; it was hypnotic. 'Well, I guess...'

Finn leant across and pulled the book out of her hands. 'Look, I know this is awkward.' He stared down at the book as if studying the back cover. 'We've been through all these adventures together in the other world, but now we're back here and it's like nothing's really changed.'

Merry understood. There was unfinished business between them. Finn had lied to her about Ronan. His actions had made it possible for Ronan to snatch Leo.

'You're right.'

Finn dropped his head into his hands.

'But,' Merry continued, 'what you did was for your brother. I understand: you've seen what I was willing to risk for Leo. What I was willing to do. And you helped me do it. You were brave, and—'

'I had no power – I was useless.'

'No, you weren't. You were there for me, Finn. When I needed you the most. And that… counts for something. It really does.' Merry put a hand on his arm. 'Besides, as a witch, I like you despite the fact that you're a wizard.'

Finn grinned reluctantly. 'Is that so?'

'Of course. I like you because you're kind, and funny, and thoughtful – most of the time – and you're a really good kisser…'

The next minute they *were* kissing, lips mashed together,

entangled in each other's arms. Merry leant back against the sofa, twisting her fingers into Finn's hair, and Finn ran his hand down the length of her body, hooking her leg and drawing her knee up towards his hip—

There was a knock at the door.

'Merry?' It was Leo.

Damn.

They broke apart quickly. Finn cleared his throat. 'Come in.'

Leo stuck his head round the door. 'Sorry. Can I ask you something, Merry?'

'Sure. I'm coming up now.' She stood. 'Night Finn. And don't worry about that other stuff, OK? I meant what I said.'

Finn nodded. 'Thanks, Merry. And sleep well.'

Merry followed Leo upstairs to his room. 'What did you want to ask?'

'Um…' Leo rubbed the heel of one hand against his eyes. 'Ronan made a mark on my chest, when he took me.'

Merry remembered: Ronan had burnt a rune into Leo's skin. Not one she'd recognised.

'Well,' Leo continued. 'It had disappeared completely. But now…' He took off his T-shirt. There were faint red blotches in the centre of his chest, almost like a pattern of tiny blisters. Merry touched one with her fingertip and Leo flinched. 'Why have they come back, Merry? What does it mean?' His voice was strained. 'Was Carys right? Is Ronan still alive? Is the King of Hearts still stuck inside me?'

ELEVEN

'**N**O, I'M SURE it's nothing like that.' Merry squinted at the marks some more, trying to work out if the pattern was really a pattern, and if so whether it was the same as the burn that Ronan had inflicted. 'It's probably because of the shift in dimensions. We've kind of gone back in time, compared to the other world. Maybe the wound is trying to… un-heal.'

'I suppose.' Leo sounded doubtful.

'It's not Ronan, Leo. He's not here any more.' Her brother didn't answer. 'I'll go and get some of Gran's salve from the kitchen. That'll do the trick.'

Merry hurried down to the kitchen and found the box with Gran's various potions inside. She helped Leo spread some ointment on the blisters and said goodnight to him. Leo had got into bed with all the lights still on, and she didn't blame him: if she'd been through what he had, she wasn't sure she'd ever sleep in the dark again.

She brushed her teeth and went into her own room. It seemed a little airless; maybe not surprising, since she'd spent the last few nights sleeping in rooms with no glass in the windows. Merry unlatched the casement. The moon was almost full, and she stood for a while, gazing at the silver strip of road that ran in front of the house, and the light-flooded fields beyond. There was no wind to speak of; everything was hushed, peaceful, still. Apart from a horse, trotting along a field edge in the direction of the house.

It was the most beautiful horse Merry had ever seen: tall, gleaming white, its mane rippling like silk. She watched as the horse broke into a gallop, tossing its head, and changed direction to speed across the field...

There was something on the horse's forehead. Something that caught the light as the horse turned – something long and sharp and twisted.

Merry rubbed her eyes and squinted, leaning half out

of the window. But whatever it was had galloped too far. Another minute more, and all she could see was a patch of white that soon disappeared into the shadows beneath the trees.

She hesitated.

Unicorns were real, in the other world.

But now she was back home. So, whatever she'd just seen, it obviously wasn't a unicorn.

Because it couldn't have been. Unicorns don't exist. Not here.

Her fingers brushed against something: the Algiz rune she'd carved into the windowsill, more than two months ago now. It was a little faded and singed round the edges; she thought briefly about finding her knife and cutting the rune afresh. But it was late, and now she really was tired.

Besides, there's nothing out there more dangerous than me.

She shut the window again and got into bed.

★　★　★

Leo lay as still as possible. He was having such a wonderful dream. Dreaming that Merry had rescued him, that he was back home in his room. And it was so vivid. There were all his things, half-shadowed in the early morning light that filtered through the curtains: the battered pine wardrobe with the handle of his cricket bat sticking out from on top, the old Crystal Palace FC posters on the wall. He could hardly bear the thought of waking up. Even the mattress beneath him felt soft…

He sat bolt upright in the bed, breathing hard.

It's real.

Ronan's gone and I'm home, I think…

He pinched himself, and it hurt. Jumped out of bed and pulled back the curtains: there was the garden, the yellowed grass of autumn, honeysuckle running riot over the back hedge. He ran and opened the bedroom door to check the rest of the house was there, that this wasn't all a mirage…

Leo's heart rate finally began to subside. He sank back on to his bed and lay there for a while, savouring the freedom. Eventually he heard movement in the rest of the house. The gurgle of water in the pipes, faint music from the radio in the kitchen, the rattle of cutlery as someone unloaded the dishwasher. Ordinary, twenty-first century noises, every one of which made his heart leap with happiness.

When Leo got downstairs, he found the kitchen crowded. Mum, Merry and Finn were all in there, though nobody seemed particularly chatty. Merry was reading, and Finn was mixing something up in a large bowl.

'Morning, love.' Mum hugged him like she was also trying to do a reality check. 'How're you feeling?'

'Good. Glad to be back. And alive. Where's Gran?'

'Still in her room. She'll be down later. There's a coven meeting here.' Mum glanced at Merry, a slight frown wrinkling her forehead, but his sister didn't react – just carried on flicking through the magazine in front of her. 'Finn's going to make some pancakes. Would you mind taking your grandmother a cup of tea first?'

'Sure.'

Gran was sitting up in bed. There was a book open in her hands, though she was staring out of the window, not reading. She smiled at Leo, but she looked so frail compared to how she had been before Ronan had drained her magic, as if she'd aged five years in the two weeks that Ronan had held her captive. He hadn't really noticed it yesterday. Guilt flooded his core, making him squirm.

'I'm sorry, Gran.'

'What for, darling?'

'For getting involved with Ronan. If I'd stayed away from him you'd never have ended up like this.'

'Nonsense. You're not to blame for Ronan's actions. Neither is Merry.' She took a sip of her tea. 'How is your sister this morning?'

'Oh, all right, I think. She's downstairs, reading a magazine.'

'And you? If you want to talk about anything…'

'No, thanks. I feel… good. Glad to be back.'

'Hmm.' Gran peered at him over her glasses. 'And that young wizard is still here?'

'Yes,' Leo said. Gran pursed her lips, looking thoughtful, so he added, 'But I guess he'll go today. He said his dad is coming over to fetch him.'

'Well, I think I'll have my tea and then take a rest.'

Leo left Gran to it and went back downstairs. Merry met him on the bottom step.

'The pancakes are ready. How are those spots on your chest?'

Leo peeled back the dressing under his T-shirt and took a peek. 'Um, they look the same. No worse, but no better.'

'Oh.' Merry frowned. 'I thought they'd be gone. I wonder if—'

'Let's worry about it later.' All Leo wanted to do was forget about Ronan and about everything to do with him. 'I want to see if Finn's pancakes are any good.'

After breakfast Leo decided to binge-watch some TV. Any TV – he didn't particularly care, so long as it didn't involve any magic, fantasy or history. In the end, he settled on *Die Hard*. He made it through the first film, and had watched twenty minutes of *Die Hard 2: Die Harder* when the doorbell rang.

The man waiting on the doorstep was obviously Finn's dad. He was an older, slightly shorter version of the wizard – the same red hair, though peppered with grey, the same grey-blue eyes. There was another, younger man standing behind him.

'Hi.' Leo opened the door wider. 'Come in. I'm Leo.'

'Of course.' The man's expression was bland. 'I'm Edward Lombard. And this,' he nodded his head in the direction of the younger guy, 'is one of my nephews.'

Does he not have a name? Leo wondered. The nephew glared at his uncle's back. But then he grinned and held out his hand to Leo.

'Cormac.' There was no family resemblance here: Cormac was about the same age as Finn, tall but gangly, with a shock of wavy, light brown hair, round glasses and a messenger bag slung across his body. 'Great to meet you.' He sounded like he meant it. Leo smiled back.

Mum hurried into the hallway. 'Oh, Edward, I'm so sorry. I was in the garden.'

'My dear Bronwen.' Edward took Mum's hand and

bowed over it – unbelievably, she blushed. 'I'm so delighted to see you again.'

'So am I. I mean, to see you. And… I'm so sorry for your loss.' Leo had almost forgotten that Finn's brother had died – only a few weeks ago in this world. Nothing in Edward Lombard's face had betrayed any sign of grief. 'What you and Marie-Louise must be going through is just…' She stopped, shaking her head.

For a moment, the wizard's mask slipped. His features sort of convulsed, and the anguish in his eyes was unmistakable. But just as quickly, the moment passed.

'Thank you, Bronwen. My wife and I are coping. And it was a mercy, really.'

Finn appeared in time to catch the end of this sentence. Leo could see his jaw clench, and his hands form into fists. But Merry was next to him, and Mum immediately introduced her to Edward. By the time the older wizard got round to greeting his son, Finn's face was just as impassive as his father's.

'Dad.' Finn nodded his head. 'I'm glad to see you again.'

Cormac caught Leo's eye, his expression full of amusement, before stepping forward to pull Finn into a hug.

'Cormac!' Finn seemed pleased to see his cousin at least. 'What are you doing here?'

'I've come to check you over, make sure you're fighting fit before we drag you back home.' He bowed to Merry. 'And I'm at your service too, should you have any magical ailments that need attention.'

'Cormac is a healer,' Edward added. 'I thought he might be useful. I understand Eleanor is… indisposed, following recent events.'

Mum flushed again, but this time with irritation.

'Well, yes. Thank you. There's a coven meeting in a little while, which Merry will need to attend, but why don't we go through to the garden for now? My mother is waiting there…'

Leo hung back as the others started to follow Mum: he doubted Edward Lombard would be interested in talking to a pleb, and he didn't want to spend any more time around the wizard than he had to. But as he turned to go back into the living room Merry caught hold of his arm.

'Why don't we ask Finn's cousin to look at those blisters on your chest? I'd feel better if an actual healer checked them out.'

'No, Merry, forget it. He seems nice enough, but I don't want some bloke I've never met before—'

'Please, Leo? You remember what Jack said, about how

Gwydion linked their lives together using the puppet hearts? Jack had marks on his chest, from where the spell had been worked…' She shivered, and fell silent.

'Is that what you think this is? That Ronan's somehow…' Leo took a deep breath. 'That I'm joined to him?' Panic tightened his chest. 'But I can't be. You got me out before the binding ceremony. And Carys washed away the runes he'd had painted on me.'

'No.' Merry gripped his upper arms, looking up at him. 'I really don't think this is the same as with Jack. But I don't want to have to worry about it. I want everything to be normal again.' Her face was drawn.

Leo sighed. 'Fine. He can have a look, if he wants. I'll be watching TV.' Privately, Leo doubted the guy would come and find him. Finn had – he admitted to himself, somewhat grudgingly – turned out to be OK. Mostly. He was probably an exception, though.

But Leo had barely got through another scene of the film when Cormac turned up.

'Can I come in?'

'Oh, sure.' Leo hit the pause button.

'*Die Harder?* I like the first one, and the fourth. But this one…' He tilted his hand from side to side.

'Yeah. It's not great. But I haven't watched anything for

months so…' Leo trailed off, uncertain how much Merry would have revealed.

'I know.' Cormac's voice was sympathetic. 'I can't imagine why you're not curled up in a ball with the shock of it all.'

'I'm not sure, either.' Leo stared down at his hands. He was meant to be starting a degree in medicine at the end of September – only a couple of weeks away – but right now even the thought of walking to the local shops sent his heart rate rocketing.

'So, shall I take a look?'

'Um, sure.' Leo pulled his T-shirt over his head and peeled off the dressing Merry had stuck over the tiny blisters. 'Is a healer the same as a doctor, then?'

'Sort of.' Cormac pulled a magnifying glass out of his bag. 'Though without the white coat or title. The spells and potions are easy enough if you've the knack for it. I wanted to train as a doctor, but you probably know how the Kin Houses feel about too much interaction with normal people. Still, I've sneaked into a fair few medical lectures, with the help of an invisibility spell. Does this hurt?' He made a sign in the air just in front of Leo's chest.

'Ow, yes!'

'Sorry.' Cormac frowned for a moment. 'Um, you can put your top back on. But leave off the dressing.' He began rummaging in his bag, extracting various strange-looking things and dumping them on the sofa.

'Why normal?'

'Hmm?'

'You said "normal people". Not "plebs".'

'I hate the term "pleb". And whatever else wizards and witches are, we aren't normal.' Cormac held up a small glass vial with an exclamation of relief. 'I'd like to give you some of this, if that's OK with you. Two drops under your tongue twice a day. The next step is a cleansing spell, but I'd rather try this first.'

'What is it?'

'It's herbal. Mostly. No eye of newt or anything like that.'

The vial was filled with a clear purple liquid. As Leo opened it a warm scent, something like cinnamon, filled the room. He sucked some of the liquid up into the dropper, opened his mouth and squeezed twice.

Oh.

The medicine had a pleasant lemon flavour. Not at all what he had expected.

'Not bad, huh?' Cormac smiled.

'No. But…' Leo hesitated, not sure he wanted to know the answer, 'what's causing these spots?'

The wizard took off his glasses and began cleaning them. 'Honestly, I've not seen anything quite like it before. The most likely explanation is that the healing spell used in the other world relied somehow on something *in* that world. And now you're back here…'

Leo's shoulders sagged with relief. Nothing to do with Ronan, then. Just a… side effect of being back home. 'OK. Two drops twice a day.'

'Yeah. And I'll check on you again tomorrow.' Cormac reddened slightly. 'I mean, if you want me to.'

'Won't you have to go? If your uncle and Finn leave?'

'Even if I do, I can always pop back. My uncle may be able to force Finn to do whatever he wants, but—' He broke off, waving a hand as if to erase his words. 'Sorry.' He sighed. 'Family drama.'

'Don't worry. We've had plenty of that over the last few months.' The sound of voices floated through from the hallway: the other witches, arriving for the coven meeting.

Cormac finished jamming everything back in his bag. 'Are you going to go out and say hello to them?'

'No way. The coven isn't keen on outsiders. Guess they've got too many secrets.'

Cormac was staring into space, fiddling with the fastening on his bag, popping and unpopping the press stud.

On impulse, Leo asked, 'D'you want to stay and watch some TV? I don't mind skipping straight to *Die Hard 4.0*.'

Surprise flashed across the wizard's face, but then he grinned. 'Sure. I'd like that.'

★   ★   ★

The coven was assembled – or crammed, if Merry was being honest – in the dining room. Gran was sitting at the head of the table: pale, gaunt, but upright. Roshni, Gran's deputy, was next to her, and the other witches had arranged themselves as best they could, some sitting, some standing round the edges of the room. Most of them had greeted Merry as they arrived: there was relief that she had returned, but more than that – surprise. Merry herself slipped in last of all, shutting the door behind her.

'Welcome, sisters,' Gran began. 'As you can see, my granddaughter has returned. And she has brought her brother back with her.' The room erupted with questions. Gran gazed at her fellow witches, one eyebrow raised, and the noise subsided. 'Thank you. Merry?'

Merry took a deep breath.

It's a coven meeting, that's all. I'll just tell them what happened. Most of what happened.

She stepped forward.

'Hi, everyone. So, you'll remember, when I last spoke to you all, that Ronan had used power drawn from the King of Hearts to force open the point of intersection and escape. He had taken my brother with him. Well, this is what happened next...'

She spoke for nearly an hour, dealing with various questions along the way. The witches wanted to know all about the other world, what Ronan was doing there, how Meredith and her sisters lived, and about the magic Merry had used. Even without the ability she used to have to read people's feelings, Merry could sense the disquiet in the room. Not just because of what she'd done, but because she couldn't definitively prove that Ronan was dead. She began to wish she'd gone back to the tower and got his body, and brought it home with her.

Mrs Knox raised her hand. 'Would it be worth us trying to seal off this end of the – what did you say Meredith and her sisters called the points of intersection?'

'Gateways,' repeated Merry.

'I like it. Much less of a mouthful. Anyway, should we seal up the gateway by the lake?'

Roshni shook her head. 'It's too dangerous. It could destabilise the whole area. And there would be nothing to stop Ronan finding another way in. *If* he is still alive, and *if* he has the ability and the desire to replicate what Merry did. We have no evidence that this is so. Given what Merry has told us of her use of the black holly, I cannot see how he could have survived.'

Merry could have hugged Roshni right then.

'Quite.' Gran peered at the notebook in front of her. 'But what about the strange tree that has appeared by the lake? Lysandra?'

A young witch Merry didn't know edged forward. 'Lysandra Blackheart. I've just moved here from the Petworth Coven.' She gave Merry a little wave. 'The tree continues to grow rapidly. I've checked Behn's Arboreal, and it does appear to be black holly, as Sophia suggested.'

Mrs Knox inclined her head.

'Apparently, it spreads through underground suckers. So, I recommend we remove the tree and use *mortiferis* on the land around it.'

'Agreed.' Gran looked away as if she was going to call on someone else, but Lysandra hadn't finished.

'Also, when I was in the woods yesterday afternoon, I found another small shrub that had been, um...' She glanced uncertainly at Merry. 'Turned to glass. It was a normal plant the day before.'

Merry felt the blood rush into her cheeks as twenty-plus pairs of eyes turned towards her. Of course, a lot of the witches in the room would have seen the yew tree that she'd inadvertently turned to glass the same day she'd found Flo's body. Those who hadn't seen it would definitely have heard about it. 'Honestly, this is nothing to do with me. I only got back here yesterday. And I didn't leave the house all day.'

Silence. Until Denise, Flo's mum, pushed her way forward. 'There's dark magic at work. Unleashed by that monster Ronan, or by someone else.' The glance she gave Merry was full of hatred. 'I said this when my Flo was murdered, and I'll say it again: we should turn this over to the Stewards.'

Merry was shocked into silence, unable to believe what Denise had just said. The Stewards were like a supreme court for the covens. She remembered the paragraph she'd read in one of her wisdom books over the summer. Covens pretty much governed themselves, but the Stewards oversaw the archives of historical and prohibited magic, and mediated if there was a serious dispute between witches. They also had the power to deal with witches who'd gone rogue: who ignored the oaths they'd taken to protect non-magical people and use their powers for good. In the most serious cases, where a witch was using dark magic to harm or kill, the Stewards had authority to magically strip out that witch's power, to turn her into an ordinary person. But Merry hadn't hurt anyone; the Stewards wouldn't be interested in what she'd done.

Would they?

The other witches were arguing loudly about Denise's suggestion when Roshni slapped her hand on the table.

'That's enough!' The voices subsided. 'There is no reason for involving the Stewards. No oaths have been broken. And Merry hasn't even taken the oath, so she is technically not subject to the Stewards.'

'Oh, *technically*.' Denise's tone was scathing. She pointed at Merry. 'Roshni told you not to follow Ronan, but you did, and now—'

'Denise, please.' Gran's voice was gentle, but Denise stopped talking. 'Roshni is right: there is no reason for us to involve the Stewards. We need to find out what is causing these... disturbances round the Black Lake, and to deal with it. Anything else is a distraction. Are we agreed?'

There was a general murmur of consent round the table

– apart from Denise, who had her lips clamped together in a tight line. Roshni and Mrs Knox began debating the technical merits of two different spells for testing the area round the lake, and Merry took the opportunity to slip out.

Mum and Edward Lombard were sitting in the kitchen; they seemed to be reminiscing about their misspent youth, or something like that. Mum looked up as Merry walked in.

'Has the meeting ended?'

'Not yet. But I needed a break. Denise tried to blame me for everything that's going on and said they should call in the Stewards.'

The colour drained from Mum's face. 'That woman is such a—'

'Don't worry: Gran shut her down. And Roshni said I wasn't technically subject to the Stewards in any case.' If anything, Mum seemed even more concerned. Edward Lombard, in contrast, looked kind of…

Smug? Happy? Smugly happy?

Merry gave up trying to figure out his expression. He was probably just overjoyed to have another reason to look down on witches. She left them to it and went into the garden.

Finn was lying on his stomach on a picnic blanket, reading a book. Merry stretched out next to him.

'I think Denise wishes I was dead. Instead of Flo.'

Finn shut his book. 'Does she still think you were responsible?' Finn had been with Merry in the woods when they'd found Flo's body. He'd witnessed Denise's grief, and how she'd blamed Merry for what Ronan had done.

'Yep. She wants to turn me over to the Stewards. Get them to take away my power.' She paused, remembering she was talking to a wizard and not a fellow witch. 'Do you know about the Stewards? They're like—'

'Yeah.' Finn frowned, just like Mum had done, and glanced back towards the house. 'I've heard of them.'

Merry smacked him on the arm.

'Hey, this is supposed to be the part where you tell me that I haven't done anything wrong. That everything's going to be OK.'

'Sorry.' He shifted position so he was on one elbow next to her, looking down into her face. 'Everything's going to be OK, Merry.' Tracing the line of her jaw with one finger, he tilted her chin up a little. 'I promise.'

Merry lifted her mouth as Finn bent to kiss her, the heat and slow passion of it radiating through her body, soothing her. Her hand drifted up, sliding beneath his T-shirt on to his warm, bare skin. She pulled him closer.

He whispered in her ear, 'Shall we get out of here?'

It was so tempting. They could use the broomstick spell and be miles away in a matter of seconds…

But she couldn't. She couldn't leave Leo and Mum and Gran after she'd only just got back. And there was still the question of why black holly was growing by the lake, and what it was that she'd seen in the fields last night…

'I have to stay. I need to know for definite that I haven't screwed up.'

'You haven't.' Finn rested his fingertips on her cheek and kissed her once more, gently, before rolling on to his back. 'You had to save your brother. You did the right thing. You always do.' She heard him sigh. 'Can I ask you something?'

'Sure.'

'Yesterday evening, you said you understood what I had done at the lake, why I stopped you from killing Ronan before he could open the point of intersection and disappear.'

'Yes.'

'So… does that mean you've forgiven me?'

Merry stared up at the wisps of white cloud floating high above her.

'Well, it's the same thing, isn't it?' It wasn't; she knew that. Rationally, she accepted that Finn had acted as he did to try to help his brother. But if he asked her to swear that she no longer felt any resentment about what he'd done…

I'm not sure I could.

But Finn seemed to accept what she'd said. When Mum called them a couple of minutes later they linked hands and wandered back into the house. The dining room was empty; the coven meeting must have finished. Mum and Edward were standing in the hallway.

'Ah, there you both are.' There was something a little overeager about the wizard's greeting. 'Merry, I was hoping to see you before we left. Marie-Louise and I were wondering whether you'd like to come and stay with us for a while. We'd love to have you. Finn can show you the estate.'

Merry blinked, too surprised to reply. Beside her, she was aware that Finn had stiffened up, even as he let go of her hand. Edward added, 'Given the current situation with the coven, and the threat that the Stewards might become involved, it could be the perfect solution.' He turned to Mum. 'She'd be safe with us, and she can visit for as long as she likes.'

Mum opened her mouth to reply, but Finn got there first.

'I don't think that's a good idea, Dad.' He was shaking his head, and there was a definite edge to his voice. 'I can stay here if Merry wants. But I don't think she should come to Ireland.' Perhaps he felt Merry's confusion, because he added, 'I mean, she'd be really bored. And… and she's got school.'

Edward waved a hand dismissively. 'Oh, pleb school is hardly any reason for—'

'Thank you for the invitation.' Merry bowed her head; it seemed appropriate, given the fuss Gran had always made about the right 'etiquette' when dealing with wizards. 'But school is important, as far as I'm concerned. And I'd rather not be away from my family right now.'

There was a flicker of what almost looked like vexation in Edward's face. But he merely said, 'Of course. I understand. But the offer is still there, should you change your mind.'

'Thank you.'

'Well, we should get out of your way. I've booked us into a hotel in town.'

Now it was Mum's turn to raise her eyebrows. 'I thought you'd be going home.'

'I have some business in London, and it seems a shame to separate the young people when they're getting on so well. I know Finn will be pleased to stay a little longer. I'll find Cormac.'

Finn didn't look pleased. Annoyed, angry even, but not pleased.

Edward reappeared, Cormac in tow, and made for the front door.

'I'd better go.' Finn was definitely gritting his teeth. 'I'll see you tomorrow, Merry.' He left without another glance.

Merry hurried upstairs to the bathroom and splashed some cold water on her face. Perhaps Roshni had been right. Perhaps she should stay away from Finn – from wizards in general – and find a nice, normal, uncomplicated boyfriend. One with normal, uncomplicated parents.

But after everything Finn had done for her, not to mention the way he made her feel when he kissed her.

I wonder if one of my knowledge books has an anti-love spell, in case this all gets too complicated? Or a spell that would make me want to be sick whenever I look at Finn, instead of wanting to…

She swore. Exercise, that was what she needed. A good long run through the woods, listening to her music, breathing fresh air. There, she could forget about Finn, and Denise, and the damn Stewards. She ran up to her room and began rooting through her drawers for a clean sports bra.

That evening, Mum, Gran and Leo carefully avoided talking about the coven meeting, or any of the weird stuff that had been happening. Nobody mentioned the Lombards, either. When Merry got upstairs to bed she fell asleep quickly and didn't stir once until the house phone woke her from a deep sleep. She squinted blearily at the clock on her bedside table. Not quite six o'clock – it wasn't even light yet. The ringing stopped. Merry turned over and was about to go back to sleep when she heard footsteps go past her door, followed by Mum's voice. She was talking to Gran, and she sounded worried.

Merry argued with herself for a minute, then got up and padded out on to the landing.

'Mum? What's going on?'

Mum hesitated.

'Bronwen,' Gran called out, 'you may as well tell her.'

'Fine.' Mum wrapped her arms round her torso. 'That was Sophia Knox. Our contact in the police just called her. They've found a body in the woods. A man.'

Merry clutched the doorframe.

'Finn?'

'No, of course not. An ordinary person. But, it looks like he's been gored to death.'

'You mean stabbed?'

'No, I mean gored.' Mum grimaced. 'By an animal.'

'Ugh. But there aren't any boar in the woods round here.' Merry paused. 'Are there?'

'No. But Sophia says…' Mum glanced towards Gran. 'She says she saw something else in the trees near her house last night. She claims she saw a unicorn.'

TWELVE

'**B**UT, SOPHIA, ARE you sure it wasn't a deer?' Roshni asked, for about the fifth time. She was walking through the woods ahead of Merry and four other witches, talking to Mrs Knox.

'Absolutely sure,' Mrs Knox snapped back. 'Not senile, you know. Know a bloody unicorn when I see one.'

Merry edged forward. 'I thought unicorns were supposed to be peaceful and noble and all that?'

'Just myth. Truth is, no one knows what a unicorn is like, because myth is all they've been in our world.' Mrs

Knox sighed. 'But I know horses, and that thing I saw last night was like a horse that's gone bad. I reckon—'

Roshni held up a hand and the witches fell silent. Ahead of them through the trees lay the Black Lake; Merry could see two uniformed police officers, one in the distance peering at the ground by the edge of the water, the other nearby.

'OK, everyone,' Roshni whispered, 'spread out. On my signal we'll use *sistite* to immobilise them. 'Merry, are you with us?'

Merry nodded as the witches near her moved silently away, forming a line parallel to the edge of the clearing. This was the first time she'd cast a spell with other members of the coven; despite everything she'd done, there was a knot of nerves in the centre of her stomach as she waited for the signal. She wished Gran was there with her; but Mum had said – rightly – that Gran wasn't strong enough. For once, Gran hadn't argued.

Roshni raised one arm, a ball of witch fire hovering at her fingertips. When she brought her arm down, Merry and the other witches all began singing the first phrase of the spell.

The nearest police officer stopped what he was doing and looked around, trying to locate the source of the music. When he spotted Merry he strode towards her.

'Hey, what the hell are you doing?'

Merry kept singing, raising her hands to direct the spell, feeling the mingled power of the other witches flowing through her.

The policeman's hand went to the yellow Taser on his belt. But even as he wrapped his fingers round the weapon his movements slowed – stopped –

Both policemen were frozen out of time: not seeing, not hearing, not breathing.

The singing faded, and the witches gathered round Roshni.

'Good work, everyone.' Her gaze lingered on Merry. 'Nicely done. Now let's find out what's going on here.'

Roshni led the way over to the dead man. There were murmurs of dismay and horror from many of the witches. Merry had seen corpses before: Jack, Gwydion, Flo. But this…

There was so much blood. It was everywhere, splashed across the ferns and brambles, staining the blanket of old leaves that covered the forest floor. She gagged and turned away.

Roshni was assigning tasks. Merry and Lysandra were

given the job of sweeping for spells. Lysandra looked slightly green; by silent agreement they went to start work at the furthest edge of the clearing.

'So, I guess we could use *unbindan*?'

'Sure,' Lysandra nodded, crossing her arms tightly in front of her body. Merry wondered what the other witch had been told or had heard about her.

For the next ten minutes, they worked slowly and carefully. The enchantment they were weaving revealed no spells but the ones other witches were casting around them. Merry was relieved.

No wizards or male witches involved this time, hopefully…

She and Lysandra moved to a new section and began singing again.

'*Unbinde ða diegol ðaes aeðmes—*' Merry broke off. There was something there. It looked almost like a strand of grey, pearlescent mist, hovering about a metre and a half from the ground. Mrs Knox hurried over.

'Well.' Mrs Knox walked round to the other side of the mist. 'Definitely not a spell. What do you think?'

'Hold on…' Lysandra pulled a battered book out of her backpack and flicked through the pages. 'Um, in her *The Energy of Enchantment*, which is really the seminal work in this area, Stowell suggests that a purely magical being would, in theory, leave an elemental trace imprint. But of course, no one's even seen one…'

Merry took a deep breath. It was too early in the morning to be dealing with this. 'Hold on. What's an elemental trace imprint?'

'Just another type of signature, really. Like a spell signature. Stowell believed that animals like unicorns, if they had existed, and being in nature pure magic, would leave an imprint behind that would show up in contrast to the underlying non-magical reality. In fact, she predicted—' Mrs Knox coughed loudly and Lysandra blushed. 'Sorry. I've done quite a lot of reading on this. It's kind of a hobby.'

Merry walked closer to the body and cast another revealing spell. The lines of mist appeared again, lots of them here. Lysandra joined her and they kept going, until there were strands of mist leading right back to the lake. Right back to the point of intersection. The other witches were now casting revealing spells in different parts of the clearing, trying to find out where the unicorn had gone next.

Merry stared at the lake; it seemed to be tugging at her, claiming her –

'Do you feel it?' Lysandra asked

'Yes. I feel like… like I'm an iron filing, and the lake is a magnet. What is it?'

'There's more magic on the other side of the gateway: it's calling to us. Khan theorises that there's a process like osmosis, whereby areas with higher magical concentration will—'

Lysandra broke off with a gasp. Merry spun round, but even before she saw the elf creeping along the edge of the lake, she felt the gut-wrenching terror the creature was projecting. Lysandra, nearest to the elf, was shaking, her eyes scrunched shut.

The elf began to run towards them. It was grinning, and Merry could see its sharply pointed teeth. She forced herself to hang on to the fragment of her will that wasn't telling her to grovel in fear. 'Mirror…' She tried again, gritting her teeth to stop them chattering. 'Mirror, mirror, silver bright, turn the magic cast in spite…' It was an old spell, and not much used any more, but it was all Merry could think of. She chanted the words over and over, and as she did so her fear began, slowly, to ebb away.

The elf had stopped smiling. But it brought up its spear and levelled it at Lysandra, drawing back its arm…

Merry darted forward and grabbed Lysandra as the spear sailed towards her, dragging her out of the way. She brought up one hand, ready to cast a binding spell –

The elf had gone. So had the other policeman, the one

who had been examining the ground at the edge of the lake. The elf had taken him, and they'd both vanished into thin air.

'That poor man…' Lysandra's voice was still shaky. 'He was just here doing his job. And what the hell was that thing?'

'An elf, from the other world. I've seen them before.' Merry took Lysandra's hand and they hurried back to the other witches. 'Roshni—'

'I saw it.' The older witch looked more flustered than Merry had ever seen her. 'Sophia, I need you to alert the neighbouring covens. Tell them…' She pinched the bridge of her nose. 'Tell them we have a serious magic incursion near our local point of intersection. Let's figure out exactly what's happening before we give them more details. Merry, go and fetch your grandmother and—'

'No.' It was Denise. There were bright red spots of colour in her cheeks, and she was breathing heavily. 'She shouldn't be allowed to do any magic. It's her spells that have caused this.'

'Denise,' Roshni began, 'now is not the time—'

'Yes, it is. Don't try to pretend: we all know she's responsible for whatever's happening here.' Denise flung an arm out, pointing at Merry. 'Ignoring orders, and going after that no-good brother of hers.' She spat on the ground. 'She should have left him there to die. That was what she was told to do.'

Merry's heart began to beat harder; she jammed her fingernails into her palms. 'How can you say that? Do you have any idea what Ronan was doing to him? What he would have done?'

'I don't care! You're no true witch. You never have been: you're a freak, you and your brother both. How much dark magic did you have to use to break open the point of intersection like this? What did Ronan promise you?'

'Promise me?' Out of the corner of her eye, Merry could see Mrs Knox creeping closer to Denise. 'He nearly destroyed my entire family!'

'I wish he had!' Denise muttered a spell, forcing a second witch who had been trying to approach her to fall back. 'The whole lot of you together are worth nothing compared to my Flo…'

'Flo was my friend. I miss her too.'

Denise screamed with rage. 'I'm going to make sure the Stewards destroy you, Meredith Cooper. I'm going to watch as they chain you up and strip out your power!' She raised her hands. 'And as for your brother—'

Enough.

It was like someone had switched off the volume: the witch's mouth was still moving, but no sound was coming out. The fury and hatred on her face were replaced by shock, then realisation, then fear. Denise put one hand to her neck, her eyes wide.

Merry walked forward until she was standing in front of Denise. 'Nobody threatens my brother.' Some corner of Merry's brain was amazed at how quiet, how steady her own voice was. 'Nobody is going to hurt him ever again. Do you understand?' Denise seemed to shrink; she stumbled backwards, clutching at her throat and nodding her head. Merry waved her hand; the other witch dropped to her knees, groaning.

Everyone was staring at her.

'Roshni, I'm going home. I'll tell Gran and Mum what's happened. Shall I ask them to meet you at Mrs Knox's house?'

Roshni nodded.

Merry turned on her heel and walked through the trees towards the road. She would have run, but her vision was too blurred by tears.

As soon as she got out of the woods, Merry called her mother and told her what had happened to the policeman.

She didn't say anything about Denise. Her head was aching, and the muscles in her neck and shoulders were painfully tight. Rather than use a broomstick spell she kept walking, pushing herself to move quickly. This wasn't exactly the first time she'd used her magic against another person. She'd fought Gwydion, Ronan – even Finn. So why did this feel different?

I haven't taken any oaths, and I haven't broken any rules.

It was self-defence: Denise was about to attack me.

In any case, she deserved it.

The arguments went round and round in her head until she wanted to scream, but she couldn't shake off the gnawing sense of guilt. Couldn't stop seeing the doubt and fear in the eyes of the other witches. She told herself that she shouldn't – that she *didn't* – care what they thought. But it wasn't true.

When Merry got back to the house she realised Mum and Gran had left; Mum's car was missing from the driveway. Merry reached into her pocket for her keys – tried the other pocket – realised she'd forgotten to take her keys with her, and rang the doorbell instead.

Leo answered the door.

'Hey. Mum told me about the dead guy at the lake. And the elf. I thought I'd seen the last of those things.'

He shuddered, rubbing his hand over his face. 'Are you all right?'

'Not really.' The sound of voices attracted her attention. 'Who's here?'

'Cormac came by to check those marks on my chest, and then Finn showed up, but when I went to make tea they got into an argument about something.' Leo picked up a piece of junk mail from the sideboard and began shredding it into tiny pieces. 'So,' he asked without looking at her, 'do you think what happened at the lake is because of Ronan?'

Tears pricked Merry's eyes again. 'No, I don't. Ronan's dead.' She knew Leo wanted reassurance. He needed her to be the strong one, to comfort him. But she just couldn't. Not right now. All she wanted was to see Finn, to have him put his arms round her and promise her again that everything was going to be OK. Leaving her brother in the hallway, she followed the voices through to the living room. Finn and Cormac were standing on the patio, just the other side of the open doors into the garden, but they didn't seem to see Merry as she paused in the shadows at the other end of the room.

Finn looked terrible. Unshaven, with his hair sticking up in odd tufts, like he hadn't slept well – or hadn't been to bed at all. Suddenly uncertain, Merry listened.

'... whatever your dad says. You're just going to have to ignore him, Finn.' Cormac waved a hand for emphasis. 'Honestly. I'm telling you, now is definitely the wrong time.'

'But when the hell is it going to be the right time?' Finn asked, his voice strained. 'I have to tell her, Cormac. The longer I leave it, the harder it's going to be...'

Cold swept up Merry's body, from her feet to the crown of her head, as if she'd been dropped into a bath full of ice. She struggled to breathe against the sudden tightness in her chest.

'Then don't tell her,' Cormac said. 'After all, it doesn't matter any more.'

'Are you insane? I already said to her, before we went to get Leo, that there was another reason I came to Tillingham. She's bound to ask me about it eventually.' Finn dragged a hand through his hair. 'Even if I don't say anything, she's going to find out somehow.'

Merry heard movement behind her. Leo was hovering by the threshold of the room; she put a finger to her lips and turned her attention back to the two wizards.

'Oh, for...' Cormac was shaking his head. 'So you really think that now, in the middle of everything else she's having to deal with, Merry's going to take it well when you tell her that you were sent here by your nightmare of a father? Because he believes that the Lombards' magic can only be rejuvenated by you making babies with a powerful witch, and she just happens to be the lucky girl who ticks all the boxes on his list? You think she's going to cry for joy and let you send out wedding invitations? Bloody hell, Finn. He even suggested you should put a spell on her to make her fall in love with you…'

Merry gasped.

The handsome prince. Doesn't he always have his own agenda? That was what Ronan had said to her a few weeks ago.

She just hadn't understood it at the time.

Finn and Cormac both swung round, staring back into the sitting room. The colour bled from Finn's face as he saw her. He took a step forward, one hand outstretched.

'Merry, please – I wasn't going to—'

'Shut up.' Her voice was not much more than a whisper, but Finn jerked back as if she'd slapped him. 'How could you do this to me?' The walls seemed to be closing in round her. 'Everything you've said to me, everything you've done… You let me think you cared about me, when all this time—'

Cormac tried to interrupt. 'But, Merry, you have to listen—'

'No, I don't!' Merry backed away from the two wizards. 'I don't have to listen to any more of your lies. You are so dumped, Finn Lombard! I wish I'd never met you. I wish…' The sorrow swelling in her throat choked her. She pushed past Leo and tore up the stairs into her room, slamming the door behind her and sealing it shut with a spell.

Then, the tears came. Her back against the door, she slid down until she was crouched on the carpet, clutching her knees to her chest, fighting against the sobs that seemed to threaten to break her apart. No wonder Edward Lombard had been so keen to get her to Ireland. He didn't care about her safety, or what the Stewards might do. He only wanted to… What? Give Finn more of a chance to persuade her into a long-term relationship? Or get her to his home territory so he could simply keep her there?

It was horrible. Disgusting. Nausea twisted like a knife in Merry's guts.

'Merry…' Leo was on the other side of the bedroom door. 'Can I come in?'

'No.'

A pause.

'They've both gone.' Her brother's voice was closer now; he must have sat down on the landing. 'Finn tried to run after you, but Cormac stopped him. He's taken him back to the hotel they're staying at.'

'I never want to see him again. Never.' She hid her face in her hands, wondering if it was possible to die of humiliation.

'Finn seemed really upset. I thought he was going to hit Cormac with a spell. Or his fists.' Leo paused. 'Maybe... maybe you should let him explain?'

'What is there to explain? You heard what Cormac said. I should never have trusted him.' Roshni had warned her more than once against spending time with Finn. Leo had never liked him. Even Ronan had tried to put her on her guard. How could she have been such an idiot, to believe he'd liked her for who she was? She forced herself to think about how Finn had kissed her over the last couple of months, about how he'd held her, when all the time he'd had this horrible ulterior motive... It made her skin crawl.

The worst thing was, she still wanted him.

'How could I have been so stupid?' Her throat ached with the effort of speaking when all she wanted to do was cry. 'What kind of pathetic excuse for a witch am I, Leo, to be so easily deceived?'

'You're an amazing witch, Merry.' There was a thump, like Leo had smacked his hand against the door. 'You

227

defeated Gwydion. You freed Jack from the curse. You saved me from Ronan. You're a brilliant witch and a brilliant sister. And a bunch of wizards with overinflated egos, and – and a couple of batty witches in the coven doesn't change that.'

From where she was huddled, Merry could see the small pink flowers of the sweet briar plant still blooming on her desk. Finn had given it to her by way of an apology, when he'd got into an argument with Leo. She raised her hands, planning to incinerate it, or make it wither away…

But she couldn't do it.

Her hands dropped.

'Merry? Please, let me in.'

Merry sniffed. 'OK.' Pushing herself to her feet, she removed the sealing spell and opened the door.

Leo hugged her tightly. 'Come on. Let's go downstairs, and I'll make you a hot chocolate. There's a can of whipped cream in the fridge. And I'm sure I saw some marshmallows at the back of the cupboard…'

Dinner was even quieter than the night before. Gran ate in her room; the stress of what was happening had caused a relapse in her recovery. Merry hadn't had a chance to talk to her grandmother, but Roshni had emailed to explain what the coven thought was happening at the lake. The point of intersection between different worlds that existed at the lake also acted as a barrier. But now that barrier seemed to be disintegrating, and the other world – the world from which Merry had just returned – was bulging through the fracture like blood oozing from a wound. Roshni didn't say anything about what might have caused the disintegration. But Merry hadn't forgotten Carys's warning about the spells and incantations Merry *should* have used before travelling home, to protect the worlds on either side of the gateway and to protect the gateway itself.

Mum didn't refer to the fight with Denise, so Merry didn't mention it, either. She wasn't sure whether the other witches had concealed what she'd done, or whether her mother thought it was such a disaster that she couldn't bring herself to talk about it.

By nine p.m. Merry's nagging headache had exploded into a migraine; she took two different lots of medicine (regular-person painkillers plus a witch-made potion) and plodded upstairs to bed. She'd rescued Leo and brought him and Finn home safely. But now, not much more than forty-eight hours later, the joy that had blazed within her was cold as ashes.

★

Two days passed. Merry mostly stayed in her room; she knew Leo must have told Mum something about her breaking up with Finn, but for once her mother decided to be tactful. She didn't mention Finn to Merry, or ask any questions; she just made lots of cups of tea and bought Merry's favourite foods from the supermarket. Every so often Merry checked the coven's Facebook page. There hadn't been any more sightings of creatures from the other world, but the witches were busy trying to conceal what was happening at the lake from their ordinary neighbours, as well as deal with the families of the dead jogger and the missing policeman. More black holly trees were appearing too, so the coven was spread quite thinly. Merry texted Roshni, offering to help, but the older witch told her to stay at home and rest. Perhaps this was code for 'stay at home, because you've already done enough damage', but for once Merry didn't care. All she really wanted to do was lie on her bed, listening to her music, going over and over everything Finn had ever said to her, everything he'd done.

Had it all been lies? Had it all been an act, even helping her rescue Leo? Tricks, to get her to trust him? To fall in love with him? And she'd fallen so easily, in the end. She'd been blinded.

I guess it serves me right. If I'd listened, if I hadn't got involved with him, maybe I'd have noticed what Ronan was up to. I could have stopped him before he found a way to get the King of Hearts out from under the lake. I could have protected Leo better. I wouldn't be in the mess I'm in with the coven.

And it was a mess: she'd attacked one of her sister witches (even if she had been provoked), and at least a couple of coven members seemed to seriously believe she should be investigated by the Stewards. The possibility that someone might try to take her magic away made her break out in a cold sweat. Months ago, she hadn't wanted to be a witch any more. She'd been frightened by her own power. But things had changed. People were frightened of *her* now: she'd seen it, at the lake. And maybe that was a bad thing, but maybe it wasn't, if it stopped them trying to hurt her family.

Because that was what really mattered. She needed to be able to protect Leo, and Mum and Gran, from people like Ronan and Gwydion. Or like Denise, or Edward Lombard. Her power gave her that ability. She couldn't let anyone take it away from her.

There was a knock at the door: Leo.

'How are you feeling today?'

Merry shrugged.

'That's what I figured.' He drew back the curtains,

flooding the room with late afternoon sunshine. 'By the way, you have a visitor.'

Merry's stomach lurched. 'Not Finn? I don't want to—'

'It's not Finn. I texted Ruby.'

Ruby. Merry's best friend for more years than she could remember. Fun-loving, fashion-loving, eerily perceptive. But otherwise normal. Utterly, utterly normal. Merry's eyes filled with tears as she realised how much she'd missed her.

Leo leant nearer, whispering, 'Remember, she thinks you've been ill. That's why you've not been at school and haven't replied to her texts. I'll send her in.'

'Just give me a—'

It was too late. Ruby's head appeared round the edge of the door.

'You look terrible.' She grinned. 'Really terrible. Like "doesn't own a mirror" levels of terrible. Possibly even "doesn't know what a mirror is".' She leant down and hugged Merry tightly.

'I'm happy to see you too.' Merry scrunched up her legs so Ruby could sit on the end of the bed and tried to work out how much time had passed since she'd seen her friend. Three weeks? A month? Whatever: it had been too long. 'It feels like ages. How was St Lucia?'

'Yeah, it was fun. Good to catch up with my cousins.

I missed you, though. Are you feeling better? Was it really horrible?'

'Er… yeah, you know.' Merry knew she was supposed to have had glandular fever, but what the hell were the symptoms? 'I was very… feverish, but I feel much better now.'

'I guess you don't know when you'll be back at school?'

Merry hadn't thought about school at all. She tried to imagine sitting in a history lesson or art class. But it seemed unreal, compared to everything that she'd seen at the lake three days ago – to what might happen, if the coven couldn't repair the point of intersection and the barrier between the dimensions.

Ruby was picking at her nail varnish, a frown creasing her forehead.

'What's the matter?' Merry asked.

'Oh, nothing. I've just been feeling a bit… weird the last few days. Just like,' Ruby forced a laugh and waved her hands above her head, 'impending doom is coming! That sort of thing.'

Merry stared at her friend. She now knew that witches could feel the pull of the other world, just like a disturbance in the Force from *Star Wars*, but was it possible that Ruby could also sense what was happening to the gateway at the lake? 'Don't worry.' Merry tried to sound reassuring, while wondering whether other ordinary people were feeling the same as her friend. 'This is a big year, that's all. The pressure of A levels, and university applications…'

'Yeah, that's true.' Ruby nodded vigorously. 'That's all it is, right?'

Merry knew that Ruby had suspected for a while that Merry wasn't quite normal. She'd dropped hints, suggesting that she'd heard the rumours about Merry and her family, and that she didn't care. But Ruby had never allowed Merry to share the details of her secret life – had actually said, in this very room, that she didn't want to know. That she was better off not knowing.

And now she was looking for reassurance…

Merry nodded too. 'Of course that's all it is. And term's just started: you'll be fine once you get back into it.'

Ruby still looked worried.

Merry considered telling Ruby about Finn. It would certainly distract her friend from whatever else she was feeling. She opened her mouth, trying to say something about how she'd been sort of dating, and now she wasn't –

But what was the point in discussing a relationship that was over? Besides, she didn't want to talk about Finn right now. Even thinking about him, remembering what she'd overheard Cormac saying, made her feel sick and headachey.

She hunched over, massaging her temples with her fingertips. The worry in Ruby's eyes was replaced by concern.

'Here,' she reached for the glass of water on the bedside table, 'you should drink something.' As Merry sipped the water, Ruby plumped up the pillows on the bed and fetched Merry's laptop from the desk. 'Budge up.' She sat next to Merry, leaning back against the pillows, and opened the laptop. 'Time for you to catch up on my YouTube channel. I've got five hundred followers now. Even my mum secretly watches it…'

They ended up watching YouTube videos for nearly two hours. Ruby said she was hungry, so Merry ordered pizza online, sending Ruby down to collect it when the delivery guy arrived. Then they started re-watching old episodes of *Grey's Anatomy*. Ruby didn't mention feeling anxious any more, and Merry almost succeeded in not thinking about Finn, or about unicorns or elves or Stewards.

About ten o'clock, Ruby looked at her phone and groaned. 'It's my dad: he's doing shouty texting. I'd better go.' She got up off the bed and stretched.

'Thanks for coming, Rubes.' Merry squeezed her friend's hand. 'I feel way better now I've seen you.'

'Back to school sometime this week, then?'

Merry considered. What if she did just let the coven get on with stuff? Especially if they had Edward Lombard helping them. 'Yeah, hopefully. And don't worry, OK? Everything's going to be fine.'

After Ruby had gone, Merry got back into bed, repeating the phrase over and over to herself like a spell, like wishing would make it so.

Everything's going to be fine.

Everything's going to be fine.

Everything's going to be fine.

THIRTEEN

MERRY DIDN'T SLEEP that night.

Instead, she read. She went through every wisdom book and knowledge book she had, looking for stories about the points of intersection, seeing if any spells already existed that would give her a clue as to how she might use her power to stop what was happening.

When she wasn't reading, she paced. Up and down across the same stretch of carpet, as the hours wore away.

Was Denise right about everything being her fault? Merry had killed Gwydion, but she hadn't destroyed the King of Hearts, and she hadn't been able to stop Ronan freeing it from beneath the lake. And she'd gone twice through the point of intersection without using the proper spells.

At least she'd killed Ronan in the end.

Hadn't she?

He couldn't have survived in the ruins of the hall, with all that black holly. He couldn't have.

She spotted her favourite silver bracelet sitting accusingly on the dressing table; it was the one she'd used in the hydromancy spell back in Meredith's cottage when she'd tried to see Ronan, and nothing had shown up.

He can't have survived. It's not possible.

Merry glanced at the clock: it was nearly five. She crept across the landing into her brother's room. He was asleep, lying on his back with the covers half kicked off. His face was peaceful enough – still, undreaming – but as for the marks on his chest… Whatever Cormac had given him didn't seem to be working. Not yet, anyway. The blisters were joining up, getting darker and uglier. A police car went by somewhere in the distance, siren blaring; Leo stirred and peered up at her.

'Merry?'

'It's OK. It's early still. Go back to sleep.'

He closed his eyes again. Merry stood there a moment more, debating, before hurrying back to her room to get dressed.

Five minutes later, she materialised in the woods near where the body of the jogger had been found.

Above the trees, the sky had lightened from black to grey, but the darkness within the forest was still impenetrable. Merry conjured a ball of witch fire and set off towards the Black Lake. When she emerged into the open space round the water, it was obvious that something was very wrong.

The lake was still there. But looking at it head on was like looking at one of those fairground mirrors: everything was distorted, blurry and bulging in some patches, distinct but distant in others. And the whole thing was in motion, so that bits of the lake were fading in and out of focus. The brokenness of the gateway made visible jarred her nerve endings like nails scraped down a chalkboard.

Merry took a deep breath, deliberately letting the tension out of her body. She'd done lots of magic over the last six months: there had to be some spell that she'd used or read about that would give her a way to seal the intersection once and for all. Closing her eyes against the distracting vision in front of her, she began running through various types of incantation. Finding spells, growing spells, witch fire, hydromancy. Shifting spells and spells for flight. Hexes and healing charms...

Bones.

Earlier in the summer, Gran had made her learn a charm for knitting bones back together. Merry had got the hang of it, at least in theory. Could she adapt the charm, use it to knit the point of intersection back together?

It would take a lot of power. But she could feel the land around her fighting back, trying to resist the invasion of the other world. It didn't want to be forced into this alternative reality. Perhaps the land itself would help her.

Merry raised her hands, recalling the first words of the spell...

There was a noise behind her. It was Roshni. And next to her, Lysandra.

'Merry,' the older witch asked, 'what are you doing here?'

Merry could feel the blood crimsoning her cheeks. 'I came to fix things. If I can.'

Roshni's eyes narrowed. 'How? You're not planning on going back again?'

'No. I thought about it, but it might just make the

damage worse. I was going to try *be haele*. I thought maybe…'
She paused, swallowing her nerves. 'I think it might heal
the gateway.'

Roshni was still gazing at her. 'But you can't have
worked out a proper adaptation of that spell?'

'No,' Merry admitted. She could hear Denise's voice
in the back of her head: *That girl's not a proper witch…*
'But if I use the spell as direction, and get the intention
clear enough in my own head, I'm hoping that will be
enough.'

The other witches glanced at each other.

Surely, they would allow her to try? 'Roshni, I can feel
my power. It's sitting there, just underneath my skin, like
it's already waiting. I know it's not normal, but…'

Roshni smiled a little. 'Normal may not be what we
need right now.' She looked past Merry, towards the
constantly morphing lake. 'And we need to do something.
We've been through every book and record the coven
possesses, but we've no real clues as to how to deal with
something like this.'

The older witch tucked a stray strand of hair behind
her ear, and Merry noticed the smudges of old eye make-up
beneath her eyes, the unravelling cuffs of the oversized
jumper she was wearing. It surprised her: Roshni was

usually so neat and polished. Even when Gran had been missing, a few weeks ago, she'd never looked anything other than completely put together.

'Roshni, is anything else wrong? I mean,' Merry gestured towards the lake, 'apart from the obvious?'

'Well…' Roshni glanced briefly at Lysandra, 'we weren't going to say anything. But I suppose you should know. Denise has complained to the Stewards about what happened on Saturday.'

Merry felt like all the breath had been knocked out of her.

'You shouldn't worry,' Roshni continued. 'I've told them that Denise threatened you and that she attacked another member of the coven. They may well end up investigating her instead. But…' she shrugged slightly, 'if you could repair the damage to the point of intersection, it would be better. I'd rather not give the Stewards another reason to be snooping around on our patch.'

No pressure, then.

'OK.' Merry breathed out slowly, letting her shoulders drop, trying to force her mind to forget about Denise and the Stewards. 'Will you and Lysandra monitor the gateway to see if it begins to repair itself?'

Roshni nodded, and Merry turned back to the lake

and stretched out her hands again. The point of intersection had no visible form or structure, at least in this world; she had no image to focus on. She would just have to wing it.

'*Ic singe be haele, ic sceal rihtan…*' Merry relaxed her control, allowed her power to flow out of her as it wished, to flow into the fractured gateway along with the words of the spell. The breach tugged at her, hungry for her magic. She let down her barriers even further, drawing up more power from the land and allowing it to spread out from her fingertips like a salve.

Very gradually, the pulsating, disjointed image in front of her began to stabilise, to revert to an ordinary English landscape.

It's working…

She sang faster and louder, imagining the torn edges of the gateway reforming, becoming an impenetrable barrier, something to keep the other world out forever—

'Something's wrong. You have to stop.' Roshni's voice was sharp with stress; she was pointing at the ground, her eyes wide. Merry risked glancing down, away from the lake. The grass beneath her feet looked odd: sort of sparkly, as if there'd been a sudden, heavy frost. But it didn't look dangerous, and the lake wasn't back to normal yet.

So, she kept singing. Somewhere in the back of her mind Merry was aware that Roshni had begun shouting. But she didn't stop. It didn't make any sense to stop, not when she was so close.

It's nearly there, nearly—

Somebody screamed.

Merry's concentration broke. The spell she'd been casting unravelled before her eyes, the lake changing and warping until it looked exactly as it had done when she started.

'No…' Her hands hurt; there was blood oozing from the edges of her nails, where the skin was blistered. But it was all for nothing. 'Why did you scream?' She swung round to face the other witches. 'Why?'

'Why didn't you stop when I told you to?' Roshni retorted. 'Couldn't you see what was happening?' She was kneeling on the ground next to Lysandra, her hands streaked with blood, supporting the younger witch's head. What looked like a large glass spear had pierced Lysandra's shoulder, pinning her to the earth. And above the two witches was an oak tree – or what had once been an oak tree.

Now, it was a tree made of glass. Just like the yew she'd transformed a few weeks ago, Merry could see the shape of the individual branches and leaves – even the acorns

– preserved in transparent perfection. A wide swathe of grass next to the lake had fused into a dimpled, crystalline sheet. A dozen or more glass trees were standing nearby, their leaves chiming gently in the breeze, the glass refracting the rising sun into scattered rainbows. It was beautiful. Until another branch snapped and shattered on the ground.

Roshni moved her hand, swiftly deflecting any more detritus. 'Get over here and help us!'

Stung into motion, Merry hurried across.

'What can I do?'

'Get the branch out. I'll control the bleeding.' Merry automatically grasped the thick glass and yelped: it was intensely cold, cold enough to burn her hands. 'Use magic!' Roshni hissed through gritted teeth.

Quickly, Merry began singing the opening phrase of a levitation spell. Lysandra whimpered as the branch began to shift upwards, pulling against her injured shoulder. Merry struggled to keep the phrasing even and smooth, to keep going as Lysandra began to scream…

Finally, the branch was out. Merry moved it to a safe distance and let it drop. Roshni was crouched over Lysandra now, weaving a spell round the open wound. Eventually she sat back on her heels, panting.

'We need to get her to Sophia's house.' Roshni dragged one hand across her forehead, smearing it with blood. 'Broomstick spell.'

'OK.' Merry knelt so she could hold the other witches' hands. 'Broomstick spell. Hold on…'

Sophia Knox's old ballroom had been virtually empty when they'd materialised: just Mrs Knox (still in her dressing gown) and Mrs Galantini (another long-standing member of the coven), both poring over an old manuscript. But within minutes, other witches had been summoned and Lysandra had been whisked away for treatment.

Now, as Roshni tried to explain to the others exactly what had happened at the lake, Merry was waiting. Leaning against the wall, scratching bits of dried blood off her fingernails, straining her ears to hear what was being said about her in low voices.

Not that she needed to hear; the glances the other witches were giving her made everything clear enough.

The only good thing was that Denise wasn't there.

Mum and Gran arrived. Gran looked awful; grey and stooped. Mum got her settled in a chair near the empty fireplace and hurried across to Merry.

'Are you hurt? When Rosh called—'

'I'm fine, Mum.'

'But what were you doing, sneaking out of the house –'

The rest of Mum's lecture got lost as Roshni called everyone to order.

'As I've explained to most of you already, Merry attempted to use *be haele* to heal the fracture within the point of intersection.' As the noise level within the room increased, Roshni raised her voice. 'She did this with my permission. Unfortunately, although the spell was working, it appears that...' She hesitated, then drew herself up, squaring her shoulders. 'It appears Merry's magic has a side effect. Her spells are killing the land. They are turning living things into glass.'

There was a clamour of questions. But Roshni ignored them, holding up her hand for silence. 'So,' she continued, 'we seem to have two separate problems. First: the fracturing of the barrier at the point of intersection that I believe to have been caused by Ronan, at least initially. Dealing with this is our priority, especially since there was another abduction last night. The witness reported a sense of overwhelming terror.'

'Another elf?' somebody asked.

'Probably.' Roshni shuddered, as if she were remembering the elf she'd seen at the lake the other day. 'Unfortunately, the wards we have erected round the lake don't seem to be effective at keeping out creatures that don't exist in our world. We'll have to start patrolling the lake in shifts.'

There were murmurs of dismay from the other witches.

'Um… where was I?' Roshni frowned. 'Oh – the second problem. Merry is probably the only one of us with power to re-seal the gateway, but clearly, she shouldn't be using magic right now. We cannot risk more damage to the land.'

'She shouldn't be using magic in any case.' The comment came from Belinda, a witch Merry had always thought of as a motherly sort of woman. But now she had her arms crossed and was frowning at Gran. 'I know she's your granddaughter, Eleanor, but Merry lacks judgement. She's reckless; she doesn't listen; she doesn't follow rules…'

Every word was like a blow to Merry's stomach.

Mum gripped Merry's hand tightly. 'Belinda, that's not fair. Merry's still only seventeen.'

'She's a seventeen-year-old with too much power and not enough sense,' Belinda snapped back. 'Roshni, you're acting head of the coven. You have to do something.'

Merry couldn't stay silent any longer.

'What happened to Lysandra was an accident!'

Roshni had her eyes closed, her fingers pressed to her

temples. When she looked back at Merry, her face was grave. 'I know you didn't intend any harm, Merry. But I told you to stop. And you didn't. You have to stay away from magic, at least until this crisis is over and we have time to work out what exactly is going on with your witchcraft.'

Merry shoved her hands into the pockets of her jeans. 'Fine. I'll try not to use it.'

'That's not good enough,' Belinda replied. 'How do we know Merry isn't directly responsible for the damage to the point of intersection? That it isn't another side-effect of her spells? And she says she killed Ronan, but there's no proof. How do we know he isn't still alive, and sending these elves and what-not to attack us?'

Roshni glanced at Gran, but she was leaning her head in one hand and didn't look up. Eventually Roshni said: 'We don't know the answer to any of those questions for certain.'

There was muttering from some of the witches. A couple of them even edged further away from Merry, as if whatever was wrong with her magic might somehow be catching. Roshni had bowed her head, almost like she was praying. But then she seemed to come to a decision. She gazed at Merry, her face carefully neutral.

'Very well. Meredith Cooper, it is the decision of this coven –'

'Rosh,' Mum murmured, 'please don't do this…'

'– that you should be temporarily bound, to prevent you using any magic. If you refuse, your refusal will be reported to the Stewards.'

Merry didn't know what to say. All she could think was: how have I ended up here?

Roshni spoke some words of Latin and a glowing violet filament appeared, floating and twisting in the air above her head. It looked almost like a single strand of witch fire. 'If you agree to be bound, you must hold out your wrists.'

Mum was whispering in Merry's ear. 'Sweetheart, just do what they say. Then they'll be responsible for fixing everything, and you won't have to worry about this any more…'

That would be nice: not having to worry. Merry stared up at the strand of light, mesmerised, and began to stretch out her arms. The filament split into two parts that floated towards her.

Mum was still whispering to her. 'And the coven will be responsible for dealing with Ronan too, if he is still alive—'

'No!' Merry snatched her wrists away, hiding her hands behind her back.

'No?' There was a strange expression in Roshni's eyes.

'I'm the only one here who's faced Ronan. I'm the only one who knows what he's capable of. And I'm not giving up the ability to protect my family.'

'And you understand the consequences of your refusal?'

Merry paused, listening to her heart thudding in her chest.

'I understand.'

'Very well.' Roshni waved her hand and the strands of light disappeared again.

As the witches began discussing and arguing among themselves, Merry turned to her mother. 'I can't be here any more.' She ran out of the room as fast as she could.

Several hours later, Merry was knocking on Ruby's front door. She didn't know exactly how she'd got there. After leaving Mrs Knox's house she hadn't wanted to go home, so she'd walked into town. She'd wandered through the gardens round the castle. She'd drifted down the high street, watching normal people getting on with their lives: working, shopping, buying coffee, catching buses. She'd stood on the bridge and watched the Tillingbourne river meandering its way out to the farmland nearby. During the day she got hungrier and hungrier, but she didn't have her phone, or her purse. And at some point, she left the town centre, wandered back out into the suburbs…

She knocked on the door again.

Ruby's mum opened it.

'Merry.' Her eyebrows raised as she looked Merry up and down. 'Whatever's the matter?'

'Nothing. I mean, I'm fine, thank you, Mrs Summers. Um… is Ruby in?'

Merry slipped past as Mrs Summers opened the door wider. 'She's just back from school. I'm guessing you weren't there today?' Was Merry imagining it? Or was there something faintly accusing in the older woman's tone? 'Ruby told me you'd been ill, of course.'

'Yeah. I had glandular fever. But I'm much better now.'

Mrs Summers didn't look convinced. She was still studying Merry's face, her lips pursed.

'So, is Ruby upstairs?'

'Yes. You can go up.'

'Thanks.' Merry kicked off her shoes and ran up the stairs. She could tell Mrs Summers was still watching her. It was a relief to turn the corner on to the landing.

Ruby was, as predicted, lying on her bed with her headphones on. She jumped up when Merry came in.

'Bloody hell, Cooper! What have you done to yourself? You look even worse than yesterday.'

Merry surveyed her reflection in the full-length mirror on Ruby's wardrobe door. Her hair was unbrushed, her outfit gave the impression she'd got dressed in the dark (which she had) and there were blood stains on her hands and on one sleeve of her jacket. Her lips were cracked, and an angry red spot had erupted on her chin. No wonder Mrs Summers had been staring.

'Sorry. I've just had a really, really bad day.' Merry's stomach growled.

Ruby shook her head.

'Honestly, Merry. I don't even know why you're out of bed, given the state you're in.' She bit her lip. 'Go and clean up. I'll fetch some biscuits, and some juice. Then you can tell me what's happened, OK?'

Merry nodded. As Ruby thudded down the stairs, she went into the bathroom, found a flannel and began scrubbing at her face. There was a comb too, so she dragged that through her hair, wincing and swearing at all the tangles. It wasn't much of an improvement, but better than nothing.

Ruby was back in her room, sitting on the swivel chair in front of her desk. She chucked Merry an unopened packet of chocolate digestives. 'That's all I could find. So what's happened?'

Merry sat on the bed, gulped down the glass of apple juice Ruby had brought up and opened the biscuits, trying to figure out what to say. How could she possibly explain to Ruby what she'd been through that morning, when Ruby didn't know – didn't want to know – anything about the bits of Merry's life that involved witchcraft and curses and death?

'Merry?' Ruby prompted.

'There's stuff happening… I mean, I've got involved with things that are –' The lump in Merry's throat was too large for her to continue. She blinked away the tears prickling her eyes. 'I'm sorry.'

Ruby hurried across to the bed and threw her arms round Merry. 'Hey, it's going to be OK.'

'No, it's not.'

Merry heard her friend sigh.

'Is this…' Ruby began, 'is this to do with your gran? With the… the witches?'

Merry gasped and pulled away. 'You know? I wondered, but…'

'Yeah.' Ruby was looking down at the silver rings she wore on all her fingers, twisting them round and round. 'Well. I'd heard the rumours, ages ago. And I saw you, earlier in the summer.'

'Saw me doing what?'

'Magic. It was after school one Friday last term. I'd forgotten to print something out so I went back to the library. And there you were, and these books...' Ruby shook her head. 'They were floating. Back and forth, between the shelves.'

'Did it... Did I freak you out?'

'No. Because you looked happy. So I figured it was all right.'

'Oh, Rubes...' Merry hugged her best friend tightly. 'I was happy. But now, there's some really bad stuff happening, and my magic seems to be screwing everything up, and I'm scared – I'm so scared—'

'That's enough!' It was Ruby's mother, standing behind them in the doorway. 'Merry, you need to leave.'

'But, Mum,' Ruby said, 'you were the one who told me about the rumours, and about Merry's gran. You never seemed to care.'

'Because the coven hid their existence as much as possible. And they used to help people. But these last few months...'

Mrs Summers had a water bottle in her hand. She held it up in front of her like a talisman. 'They've brought evil to the town. There have been murders, attempted murders, people going missing – you can tell your grandma, Merry, that not all of us are blind. I know there's something bad happening. And I'm sorry for you, child. But you're to stay away from my daughter from now on.'

Merry stood up to leave – what else could she do? – but Ruby grabbed her arm.

'This is ridiculous, Mum. Merry's my best friend!'

'I know that. But I have to keep you safe.'

'By threatening her with holy water?' Ruby gestured to the bottle in her mother's hand. 'I know what you've got there. She's not a bloody vampire!'

Mrs Summers ignored Ruby's protest. 'Ruby, we're leaving for your grandparents' in Norfolk in half an hour. You'd better start packing. Merry, please leave. Now.'

'But, Mum—'

'Ruby, it's OK.' Merry gently prised Ruby's hand away from her wrist. 'It'll be better, if you're not here. At least I'll know that you're safe.'

'But, Merry,' Ruby's voice was wobbly, 'what's going to happen?'

'I don't know. I love you.'

'I love you too.'

Merry left the room before Mrs Summers decided to throw the holy water all over her. Her legs felt wobbly, and she clutched the banister tightly as she walked down the stairs, Ruby's mother at her heels. In the hallway, she paused.

'I would never hurt her. You know that, right?'

Mrs Summers nodded. 'I know. But someone else in your world might. And I can't take that risk. Do you understand?' Her dark eyes glittered in the dim space.

Merry was pretty sure she knew what her own mother would do, if the situation was reversed. 'Yeah. I understand.'

As soon as Merry was outside the house, Mrs Summers shut the front door. Merry could hear the bolts being driven home, the chain put on. She went and sat in the bus shelter opposite, and waited. A little over half an hour later, Ruby and her mum emerged from the house with two suitcases. A couple of minutes more, and they'd driven down the road in the direction of the motorway.

Ruby was gone.

I've lost her.

★ ★ ★

Leo was sitting at the far end of the garden, watching the house and the road beyond slip into twilight. The street lamps had flickered into life about ten minutes ago. A little longer, and he would be all but invisible to anyone watching, swallowed up by the shadows beneath the trees.

And that would be fine by him.

Ronan had watched him all the time, directly or magically. Now he was home, Mum was being almost as obsessive, checking where he was, asking all the time whether he wanted to talk about things. He understood why, but it was a relief to be entirely unobserved.

Besides, there was no way he wanted to be in the house right now. When Mum and Gran had come back from wherever they'd been this morning, Gran was exhausted and Mum had been strangely quiet. Then Roshni had turned up and Mum had got hysterical, blaming the other witch for something to do with Merry. Still, Roshni had taken all the abuse and stayed to look after Gran, while Leo had finally persuaded his mother to calm down. Mum had made various doom-laden, half-articulated comments about Merry being punished for something. But nobody would tell him exactly what was going on. Roshni had left a little while earlier, and Mum and Gran were both in their bedrooms. And as for Merry…

She hadn't come home, and no one knew where she was. He'd called her from the landline, but her mobile had sounded from her room; she'd left it on her bedside table. That had been about six hours ago now.

Leo's phone was next to him on the bench. He glanced at it, considering. After months with no social media – no electricity, no hot water, no glass in the windows, not much of anything, really – he was in no hurry to rush back into communication with the modern world. It felt... scary. Overwhelming. He'd started carrying his phone around again because that was what he used to do; it was what everybody did. But he hadn't actually used it.

Perhaps he should now, though. He switched it on, squinting against the sudden brightness. The Lombards (plus Cormac) were still in town staying at the hotel. It was hard to imagine Finn wanted to be anywhere near Tillingham right now – as far as Leo knew, Merry had ignored all his texts and calls – but Finn's dad was staying to help fix whatever was going on at the lake, so maybe Finn had been ordered to stick around too. Leo checked the number on the piece of paper in his hand and texted Cormac.

I've got some questions. You around tomorrow?

The response came quickly:

Sure. I was planning to come over in any case to check on you. See you after breakfast.

Leo switched his phone off again. The darkness surged back.

FOURTEEN

THERE WAS A crash: the alarm clock, hitting the wall. Its insistent beeping stopped.

'Oh, Jesus –' Leo grabbed the glass of water from the bedside table and chugged it, spilling half of it over himself. He leant back against the headboard, gasping. Ronan had haunted his dreams every night since he got home; being asleep was almost more tiring than just staying awake.

There was daylight filtering into the room. Kicking the tangled bedsheets away from his legs, he stumbled over to the window and drew back the curtains, blinking. Broad daylight, despite the cloud. The alarm clock was on the floor near his feet and was still working, though there was a crack right down the centre of the plastic casing.

There's probably some metaphor there, if I had the energy to think of it.

It was nearly eight. Leo put the clock on his desk, yawning widely. He hadn't turned his light off until he heard Merry get home, at about three in the morning. And the rest of the house was quiet. Everyone was probably exhausted after yesterday's drama. He looked down at his soft, comfortable bed…

… and dragged himself off to the bathroom.

Just as well. He'd been downstairs in the kitchen for about ten minutes when the doorbell rang. Cormac was standing on the doorstep, clutching his messenger bag.

'Come in.'

'Thanks.' The wizard stepped into the hallway, shaking the drizzle from his hair, drying the lenses of his glasses. 'I was really glad you texted last night. I thought, after what happened between Finn and Merry the other day…' He flushed. 'I thought you might not want to speak to either of us again, to be honest.'

'Yeah, well. I'm still not sure I want to talk to Finn. I'm kind of surprised he's talking to you.'

'He's mostly ignoring me.' Cormac shrugged. 'Can't say

I blame him. And at least he hasn't tried to turn me into a frog.'

Leo led the way through to the kitchen. 'Tea?'

'Please. Have you been taking the drops I gave you?'

'Yes. Milk?'

'No, thanks. And? Are they helping?'

'Um… yes, I think so. Yeah.' Leo turned away to rummage in a cupboard. 'D'you want a biscuit? I know Mum's stashed a new packet somewhere in here. Or there's probably some cake left…'

'Nothing, thanks.' Cormac came to stand next to him. 'Leo, can I take a look at the marks?'

'I s'pose. But they're honestly fine.' Leo sighed. 'Let's go upstairs. I don't feel like dealing with any of my family right now.'

Up in his room, Leo put down his tea. 'OK, let's get this over with.' He pulled his T-shirt over his head. 'See? Definitely better.'

Cormac was frowning. 'Leo, they're worse.' He shook his head. 'This shouldn't be happening. There's no reason for it.' He began rifling through his bag again, muttering to himself.

Leo squinted down at the marks on his chest. He'd tried to avoid looking at them before. Or thinking about them. But Cormac was right. The spots seemed to be linking up into the outline of something else.

The rune that Ronan had burnt into his skin, back at the lake?

'It's Ronan, isn't it? He's coming back.' Leo pulled his T-shirt on and sank down on to the bed, dropping his head into his hands. 'That's why I keep having nightmares about him. That's why that elf turned up at the lake. Ronan's not dead. He's coming back, and he's trying to take me over again, to make me into that thing…'

'There's no reason to assume that—' Cormac broke off, and Leo heard him swear under his breath. The wizard came and sat on the bed next to him. 'Dreams are just dreams, usually. And it's no wonder you're having nightmares after what you've been through. But the truth is, we don't really understand what's happening, with those spots on your chest, or at the lake. Finn and my uncle are going to consult with the coven again this morning. They're worried too.'

Leo thought about Mum and Gran yesterday. 'Everyone is.'

'I know. But, in the meantime, I want to try a cleansing spell. I don't have the right equipment with me, though, so I'll need to come back.'

Leo turned to look at the wizard. 'Is there any point? Everything seems to be going wrong.'

'Yes, there's a point. Even if it's only to show that we've not given up. You know what they say. While there's life, there's hope. What doesn't kill us makes us stronger. Tomorrow is another day.' Cormac smiled. 'I could go on, you know.'

Leo couldn't help smiling back.

'That's OK. I suppose you're right.'

'Good. So, what did you want to ask me? You said you had questions?'

'Oh, yeah. Well,' he reached for his mug of tea, 'it's about Finn, really. Merry's in a bad place. She got into trouble with the coven yesterday and took off. Didn't turn up again until the early hours of this morning. And I know she blames herself for what's happening at the lake. So, I just thought…' He paused, trying to work out if there was a less blunt way of phrasing his question, before deciding there wasn't. 'Look, if Finn really is the manipulative bastard that my sister thinks he is right now, then I don't want him within a hundred miles of her. But if he's not…' He shrugged. 'She could do with something to make her happy. She could do with someone else to trust.'

'Well…' Cormac waved his hand at a pencil balanced on the edge of the bedside table; it began looping through the air in lazy arcs. 'Since Merry dumped him on Saturday, I'd say Finn's mood has been a variation on the theme of obnoxious. He's either glowering at us – me in particular – or trying to kill us with sarcasm.'

'Because he's in trouble with his dad for not persuading Merry to marry him? I still can't believe your uncle thought that was a good plan, by the way.'

'It's a terrible plan, morally, practically…' Cormac snatched the pencil out of the air and replaced it gently on the table. 'It sucks on every level. But after Cillian was born a pleb, my uncle became obsessed by the idea that the Lombards were losing their magical ability. It happens to most Kin Houses, eventually; we've lasted longer than any other family. So he came up with this plan to inject fresh magical genes, I suppose, by having Finn marry a witch. But Finn was never seriously going to follow through with it. He agreed in the end because it gave him an excuse to follow Ronan to England. His real concern was always his brother: he was desperate to find a way to wake Cillian from the coma he'd fallen into.' Cormac pulled his glasses off and began polishing them again. 'Finn can be an arrogant pain in the bum sometimes, but he's a good guy deep down. He was destroyed by what happened to Cillian. And as for Merry… I honestly think he came to care about her. That he still cares about her.'

Leo picked absent-mindedly at a spot of Blu-Tak on the wall next to his bed. 'He helped Merry rescue me.'

'He did. And he would never have done anything like that to keep his dad happy. Not in a million years. It could only have been for Merry. And for you. And he ended up losing his magic because of it.' Cormac shuddered. 'He said it was like a limb had been amputated.'

The Blu-Tak came away in Leo's fingers, revealing the bare plaster underneath the grey paint. 'OK. I'll talk to Merry. Though I'm not promising anything.'

'I understand. And thank you. It's so hard for us to meet people, usually. Witches – generally speaking – don't like us. Fair enough, given the history, and the snobbery. As for dating ordinary people…'

'Is it forbidden?'

'No. But it doesn't need to be. It's too hard, being with someone that you can't be honest with. Knowing that if you do tell them the truth, they'll either think you're mad and dump you, or think you're scary and dump you, or become insanely jealous that they can't do the same things as you. And then dump you. So, we mostly end up dating and marrying within the Kin Houses. It's acceptable, but suffocating.'

Leo wondered if Cormac was speaking from experience. The wizard was chewing on his bottom lip, still polishing the lenses of his glasses over and over. And then the colour flamed into his face as he said without looking up:

'My last boyfriend was non-magical.'

Oh…

Leo felt himself blush: it was the last thing he'd expected Cormac to say. Panic tightened his chest as he tried to decide whether he should have known Cormac was gay, at the same time as figuring out how on earth to respond. *That's nice*, or *Hey I'm gay too, in case no one's mentioned it*, or *Does that mean you're single at the moment*, or…

But he had to say something quickly because he could see that Cormac was getting even redder, that the wizard was starting to feel like an idiot for having shared something so personal.

'Well,' Leo cleared his throat. 'It could be worse. My last boyfriend was a psychotic male witch who kidnapped me.'

Cormac looked up at him, both eyebrows raised. Then he laughed.

Leo laughed too, not because anything to do with Ronan was remotely funny, but because he could hear the mixture of relief and surprise and happiness in Cormac's voice.

'At least he didn't dump you because you were too boring,' Cormac added. 'That's what happened to me. Dumped by text. I think he's dating a dentist now.'

'A dentist? Seriously?'

Cormac nodded, that same mischievous expression in his eyes Leo had noticed the other day. 'Honest to God. Though I believe he does orthodontics as well…'

They both started laughing again. Leo realised it was the first time he'd laughed for months. And that just made him laugh even harder.

* * *

Laughter.

Someone in the house – unlikely as it seemed, given the circumstances – was laughing.

Merry glanced at her alarm clock. It was nearly eleven-thirty. She swung her legs out of bed, pulled an old hoodie on over the top of her pyjamas, and went to investigate.

The laughter was coming from Leo's room. She paused outside: Leo and another bloke, by the sound of it.

One of Leo's old friends? She leant closer to the door. It was Cormac.

Her own brother, laughing and joking with a Kin House wizard. With a Lombard. Her magic fizzed from her fingertips up through her wrists and forearms before dispersing, displaced by a dull heaviness that settled in her chest.

Downstairs, Mum and Gran were in the kitchen, but they weren't talking. Mum was leaning against the counter near the stove, texting someone, a stack of books on the worktop behind her. Gran was sitting bolt upright at the table, tapping away at her laptop, her lips clamped together in a narrow line. They both looked up as Merry entered.

'Morning.' Mum's eyes flicked across to the clock on the wall. 'Just about. I made fresh coffee, if you want some.'

'No, thanks.' Merry got some juice from the fridge, grabbed a croissant from the bread bin and sat down, wondering how long it would take Mum to ask the obvious question. She began counting in her head.

One thousand, two thousand, three thousand, four thousand, five—

'I was really worried yesterday, by the way.' Mum's tone was injured. 'You didn't tell us what you were doing, you didn't have your phone –'

'Bronwen, honestly…' Gran sighed.

'– so where did you go?'

'Just into town. Then Ruby's, later on. But she… she was busy, so I didn't stay long.' Merry couldn't bear to tell anyone how Ruby's mum had thrown her out. 'Then I went up to the North Downs. I needed to get some air.'

Mum raised an eyebrow. 'Did it help?'

'A bit. What are you doing, Gran?'

'Emailing other covens. Roshni and the others tried to repeat what you attempted yesterday morning with the healing spell. But just singing the spell as it's written didn't work. Whatever it is you did, they couldn't replicate it. They've started patrolling the lake instead, as Roshni suggested.' Gran took her glasses off and rubbed her eyes. 'More black holly trees have appeared overnight.'

Merry's gaze drifted to the garden, where the first hint of autumn was gilding the leaves of the beech hedge. There were a few berries already hanging from the hawthorn tree in the corner, and the autumn flowers were beginning to bloom: pink cyclamen, purple Michaelmas daisies, bright red begonias. The idea of a deadly black holly tree erupting in the middle of such a peaceful scene sent shivers down her spine.

'Still,' Gran continued, a note of forced optimism in

her voice, 'someone, somewhere, must know something useful: how to fix the point of intersection. Or how to enable you to use your magic without... damaging things.' She replaced her glasses and peered at the computer again. 'Most covens keep records. Something will turn up.'

Merry just nodded and started eating her breakfast. She understood: her grandmother couldn't do much magic right now, but she couldn't stand to be doing nothing. She wanted to keep fighting.

The kitchen was silent again apart from the click of the keyboard. Merry finished her juice, put her plate and glass in the dishwasher and turned to leave.

'Just a minute.' Her mother's voice called her back. 'I have to ask: you do understand why the coven want you not to use your magic right now, don't you? You were quite right to refuse to be bound, but—'

'I'm not an idiot, Mum. I was there when Lysandra got impaled by a glass branch. I saw what my magic was doing.'

Mum flushed. 'Of course. I'm sorry.'

'It's fine, Mum. It doesn't matter.'

Her mother looked surprised. Maybe she'd expected Merry to be angrier.

In the hallway, Leo was saying goodbye to Cormac. Merry waited, loitering by the coat stand, until Leo closed the front door. But instead of going back up to his room, her brother turned towards the kitchen.

'Oh. What are you doing there, Merry?'

'Hiding from Cormac, obviously. I don't want to see another Lombard as long as I live.' She walked away and began to climb the stairs, but Leo followed her.

'It's not his fault that his uncle's a jerk. Or that Finn was keeping secrets.'

'Isn't it?'

'You know it isn't. And he came over to help me, to see if the drops are working…'

Merry stopped. 'I'm glad Cormac's helping you. He seems like a decent guy.'

'He is, I think. And as for Finn, perhaps you should just talk to him, give him a chance to—'

Merry held up a hand, cutting her brother off. 'I don't want to hear about Finn. He's lied to me too many times now. How can I be with someone I can't trust?'

Leo didn't reply.

'That's what I thought.' She carried on walking towards her room. But just before she shut the door Leo called out:

'People make mistakes, Merry. Sometimes the only thing to do is forgive them. Just think about that, will you?'

'Why do you suddenly care about Finn so much?'

'I don't particularly care about Finn. But I do care about you.'

Leo turned into his own room before she could answer.

There was a text message from Finn on her phone. The fifteenth he'd sent since yesterday. She deleted it without reading it, just like she had all the others. Then she brought up his contact details, her finger hovering above 'Block this Caller'… and put the phone down without completing the action. Just like she had all the other times.

She was tired again. Too tired to want to think about any of this. Closing the curtains, she got back into bed and fell straight to sleep.

Merry was freezing when she woke, and no wonder: at some point during the night she'd kicked off the duvet, and her pyjamas were damp with sweat. She felt like she'd spent the last so many hours running, though she'd actually just been dreaming. A long, complex dream about the Black Lake, and Ronan, and her magic, all mixed up with fairy tales: a man, whose face she couldn't see, spinning flax into gold, and a spindle with a wicked-looking silver needle at one end…

Maybe she'd just been in her room too long: she'd slept

most of yesterday, and all night too. Jumping up, she threw the bedroom window open and stuck her head outside. The morning air was cool and damp. She breathed in the earthy smell of the garden, listened to the few cars passing on the road outside. But nothing dispersed the strange heaviness of her limbs. The drowsy unreality of her dreams still weighed her down.

The Black Lake still called to her.

She sighed, and gave in.

Merry thought about using the broomstick spell; it wasn't as if she'd agreed to be bound. But the image of Lysandra, impaled by a glass branch of Merry's making, was still too fresh in her mind. So, she walked instead. The woods were hushed; no birdsong, no humming of insects, not even a breath of wind to stir the air. It wasn't particularly warm, but by the time Merry got near the lake she was sticky with sweat. She found herself studying the undergrowth on either side of the path, watching for any hint of movement. There were no wolves in England: she knew that. But, at the same time, she half expected to see one from the corner of her eye.

What she did see were black holly trees. They seemed to be sprouting up everywhere, smaller than in the other world, but with the same black bark, dark-green leaves and cruel, silver-tipped spines. Even the ordinary holly trees in the wood seemed to be changing: black branches growing through the ordinary, slender green limbs. Black leaves crowding out green ones. It was like her normal world was being slowly suffocated, crushed out of existence.

Finally, the lake came into view. No one seemed to be around; perhaps whoever was on patrol right now was round at the far side. The lake itself was unchanged from when Merry had last seen it, two days ago. No better, but no worse. She walked closer, drawn by the pulsating images. It reminded her of something she'd seen on a school trip once: a montage made up of lots of small photographs, all allegedly of the same scene, but taken from slightly different angles and elevations, with different focal points, layered together to create a single picture, both unified and disjointed.

If she looked at it too long, it would probably make her head ache.

Merry was near enough now to feel the warding spells that had been placed round the lake. Non-magical people could have walked right through them without noticing anything. But to her eye there was a slight shimmer in the air, like the heat haze rising from a sun-baked street.

Her own power kindled in response, making her skin tingle. She could almost hear it whispering to her, begging to be used…

'Merry?'

'Leo! You made me jump.' She waited for her breath to settle. 'What are you doing here?'

'I got up and you weren't in your room. I thought you might need some help.'

'But how—'

'You've got your phone with you today. You're broadcasting your location to the world. Well,' he smiled a little, 'at least to me and Mum.'

'Oh. But are you OK, being here? I mean…' She gestured at the lake.

'It's making me feel a bit sick.' He turned his back on the lake. 'But otherwise… There are lots of memories here. Not all of them are terrible.'

'We always seem to end up back here, don't we?'

'Yeah.' Leo fell silent. Merry knew he was thinking about Ronan, just as she couldn't be in this place without thinking about Jack.

A breeze crept across the back of Merry's neck, raising goose pimples on her skin.

'You should go home. It's not safe for you to be this

close to the point of intersection any more. If something else from the other world comes through, you won't be able to defend yourself.'

'But I want to help you. And you still haven't told me what you're doing.'

'Well, nothing, really.' She shivered. 'I had this weird dream, and…'

But her brother wasn't listening. He was staring over her shoulder, his eyes wide.

'I think… I think something's coming.' He pointed.

Merry spun round. One patch of the strange composite lake was twisting and fragmenting even more than usual. She raised her hands. 'Stay back.'

They waited, Merry trying to calculate in her head how long it would take to use a broomstick spell on Leo – whether she'd have time to send him home safely and still fight whatever it was that was about to come through the gateway. Ahead, the wrenching of reality got so bad she had to shield her face, squinting through her fingers to see what was going on. But still, she couldn't tear her gaze away from the lake –

The awful writhing stopped, and the lake returned to normality – or as near to normal as seemed possible at the moment.

And there, collapsed on the grass by the edge of the lake, was… Jack.

Merry sprinted over to him, Leo at her heels.

'Jack, what's happened? What are you doing here?'

Jack's eyelids fluttered open. 'Ronan,' he wheezed. 'I was sent to warn you. Ronan is coming.'

FIFTEEN

MERRY SAT BACK on her heels.

Ronan's alive. After everything I did, he's still alive.

She was surprised by her own lack of surprise. As if, deep down, she'd always known that Ronan had survived. Leo was staring at Jack, his face ashen. 'Leo, can you help me get him up? We need to find out what's gone on.'

Leo gazed at her blankly. But then he nodded and slipped an arm round Jack's shoulders, propping the other boy up.

'Jack, talk to me. What's happened?'

Jack opened his eyes again. 'Meredith sent me.' He was speaking in modern English, just like her Jack had when he'd emerged from beneath the lake.

Merry studied his face. His hair was longer than when she'd last seen him. His face was thinner, and he looked exhausted. 'How long has it been for you? Since Leo and I came back home?'

'Three months, at least. For the first few weeks all was quiet. We thought it was over. But then... then he reappeared. He took Helmswick, killed the king, and Carys...'

Merry caught her breath. Carys was dead?

'Oh Jack, I'm so sorry.'

He was shaking his head. 'That is not the worst.' He struggled to sit upright. 'The black holly continues to spread like poison throughout our lands. Strange things are appearing, like the... the... What was it, by the cottage?'

'The lamp post?'

Jack nodded. 'And Nia is delirious most of the time—' He lurched forward suddenly, groaning. Beads of sweat were forming on his brow.

Merry touched his forehead. She glanced at her brother. 'He's burning up.'

Leo frowned, lifting Jack's wrist to take his pulse. 'Jack, what's happened to you? Are you sick?'

'I – I just need rest.' Jack's eyes fluttered open. 'The journey through the gateway has weakened me a little, that is all.'

'How long has it been since you ate anything? And how long since you last slept?'

'It doesn't matter. There's not much time.'

Merry put one hand on his shoulder. 'Jack?'

Jack sighed. 'A week, perhaps more. Rations are scarce, and we have little time to rest.'

Merry's insides twisted with guilt. She'd failed to kill Ronan, she'd damaged the gateway, and then she'd just left the people in the other world to get on with it...

She rubbed one hand over her face, trying to concentrate. 'Leo, we need to get him back to our house. But I'm not supposed to use any magic...'

'I'm on it,' said Leo, standing up, pulling his phone from out of his jacket pocket. 'Cormac will come and get us.'

Between them, Merry and Leo got Jack to the nearest car park. Soon after a car pulled up and Cormac got out.

Followed by Finn.

Merry hissed at Leo. 'What's he doing here?'

Her brother shrugged.

Finn's hair was rumpled, and there were dark shadows beneath his eyes. He smiled at her, tentatively. Merry looked away. Aside from shock that he'd actually dared to turn up, she didn't know what she was feeling.

Cormac crouched down beside Jack.

'Hello, Jack. I'm Cormac. I'm sort of a doctor; a leech, I guess you'd call it. D'you mind if I take a quick look at you?'

Jack seemed too tired to protest and sat quietly while Cormac examined him. Cormac closed his eyes briefly, placing both hands on Jack's chest.

'Right. You have a mild ailment – what we'd call a virus. Just a moment.' Cormac took a wooden bowl, a bottle of water and Tupperware box out of his bag. Filling the bowl with water, he tipped some green powder from the box into the water, which immediately started to fizz. Merry inhaled deeply; the mixture smelt like spring, or like the air after it has been washed clean by rain. Helped by Cormac, Jack drained the bowl quickly; a little colour came back into his cheeks, and the wizard began repacking his bag. 'Right. There's another potion I'll prepare when we get back to the house, but it's mostly rest and food that you need. Are you feeling well enough to travel?'

Jack smiled weakly. 'Yes. Thank you.'

Cormac clapped him gently on the shoulder. 'No need to thank me, Jack. Any friend of Leo – and Merry's, of course – is a friend of mine. Finn, can you give me a hand?' Together, the two wizards hoisted Jack from the ground.

Merry breathed a sigh of relief. For a Lombard, Cormac was OK.

It was Jack's first time in a car. He sat in the back seat next to Merry, and grabbed her arm when Cormac turned on the ignition and pulled away. Despite his exhaustion, he sat wide-eyed and awake the entire way back, watching Cormac or staring out of the window.

On Merry's other side, was Finn. He didn't look at her; just kept his gaze directed firmly out of the other back window. He didn't say anything, either. Merry decided that was fine with her. She didn't want to talk, anyway. She couldn't get her head round the idea that Carys was dead. Carys, whom she'd only seen a few days ago, who had been so stubborn, so determined not to give in to Ronan… Merry squeezed her eyes shut. No way was she going to cry in front of Finn.

Thankfully, they were soon back at the house. Leo had

phoned Mum in the car: she was waiting on the porch when they arrived. She smiled at Finn and Cormac, but her face couldn't seem to settle on an expression when it came to Jack. Merry guessed her mother was feeling overwhelmed, and she didn't blame her. The cursed teenage prince whom Merry had killed only a few months ago had now shown up at her house. It was a lot for Mum to take in.

Inside, Mum disappeared into the kitchen, muttering something about chicken soup. Cormac and Finn went with her, so Leo and Merry helped Jack into the sitting room. Gran was waiting for them, sitting bolt upright in one of the armchairs. Her face was gaunt, and she was gripping the arms of the chair so tightly that her knuckles showed white.

'Jack,' Merry began, 'this is my grandmother. She's the head of our coven. Gran, this is—'

'I know,' Gran interrupted. 'Are you well enough to talk to me, Jack?'

Jack nodded.

'Good. So tell me: are you certain Ronan is alive?'

'Yes. I've seen him.'

Gran's shoulders drooped, as if she'd been hoping that there had been a mistake.

'And,' Jack continued, 'I know what he wants. We captured one of his creatures, and Meredith forced it to talk to us.' He glanced across at Merry and Leo. 'He is coming for you. For both of you. He wants revenge. Perhaps he has other wishes too, but if so, the creature didn't know of them.'

No one spoke. Merry tried to force some words out, to say something brave, defiant. But the memory of Ronan at the lake, laughing at her as he held a sword to her brother's throat, overwhelmed every attempt at rational thought. Fear flooded her body, suffocating her; she got up and opened a window.

'But I don't understand,' Gran said. 'Ordinary people cannot use the points of intersection to travel between worlds. How did you get here, Jack?'

'The gateway has been damaged, and Ronan has been working to make the damage worse. The barrier between our worlds is now so weak that Meredith was able to send me through. Ronan will soon be able to bend the gateway completely to his will, to control it. You will not be able to keep him out.'

Leo had dropped his head into his hands. Merry put her arms round him, comforting him, trying to convey reassurance she didn't feel herself.

'What are we going to do?' It was Mum, standing in the doorway with a tray of food. Finn was hovering behind her. 'How can we stop him?'

Gran straightened up, as if knowing that the worst was now about to happen gave her strength. 'What we're not going to do is panic. Bronwen, give the food to Jack and then call Roshni and tell her to summon the others. Finn, please contact your father and ask him to meet us at Sophia Knox's house.'

'Of course. My family has already suffered at Ronan's hands. We'll do whatever we can to defeat him. Whatever it takes.' He paused, looking wistfully at Merry. 'You don't have to face this alone.'

Merry felt her heart swell painfully. She stared into Finn's eyes, trying to find the truth in them. She wanted so badly to trust him.

The doorbell rang. Mum gasped, almost as if she thought Ronan was standing on the front doorstep. 'Whoever could that be?' She hurried into the hallway. A few moments later she reappeared, with another woman behind her. Merry recognised the newcomer: she was a witch named Helen. And she was a friend of Denise's.

'Helen is insisting on talking to you.' Mum's voice was brittle. 'I've told her this is not a good time but—'

Helen pushed past. 'Eleanor, please.' The woman was twisting her hands together; she shot a look of mingled fear and distaste towards Merry. 'I need to speak to you about Denise. I'm really worried about her.'

Merry stood up. 'I'm sorry, Gran, but I don't think I can be here right now.' She left the room without another glance at the newcomer.

Mum caught up with Merry as she was halfway up the stairs. She'd shut the sitting-room door behind her. 'Merry, where are you going? What about the coven meeting?'

'I'm not exactly part of the coven any more, am I, Mum? I'm not allowed to use any magic. And you heard what Jack said: Ronan's after me and Leo. There's bound to be somebody at the meeting who suggests just handing the two of us over.'

Mum's eyes blazed. 'If anyone dares suggest such a thing I'll curse them, I swear.'

'No – I don't want you to get into trouble. But you see why I don't want to go. And I just couldn't sit there and listen to that woman badgering Gran about Denise…' Merry took a deep breath. All her emotions seemed too close to the surface right now, as if whatever she was feeling might seep through her pores at any second. 'I'll fight Ronan, if he turns up. I don't have the energy to fight the coven as well.'

Mum looked doubtful, but she nodded eventually. 'OK. What are you going to do?'

'I'll go to the gym, I think. I need some exercise. And some normality.' Merry turned to go, but Mum clutched at her hand.

'Don't disappear again.'

'I won't. I'll see you later.'

When Merry got home, Leo was sitting at the kitchen table, drinking a can of Coke and reading something on his laptop. He shut the screen down as Merry walked in.

'How was the gym?'

'It was OK. I did some boxing. Pretended the punch bag was various people I don't like.' It had been quite therapeutic, while she'd been actually using her fists. But nothing had been solved, of course; her problems were waiting for her as soon as she'd walked back into the changing room. 'What have you been up to?'

'Nothing much. Preparing for the end of the world. Contemplating death. Wondering whether now is a good time to start smoking again.' He smiled bleakly. 'Normal stuff for a wet Saturday afternoon. Everyone else went off to the coven meeting, even Finn and Cormac, so there wasn't much else for me to do. You hungry?'

'Not especially.'

'I think you should eat something anyway. Something full of sugary goodness to keep your energy levels up.'

'OK.'

Leo took a tub of ice cream out of the freezer and passed it to Merry, together with a spoon.

'Thanks,' said Merry. The ice cream was her favourite – chocolate fudge. She started half-heartedly hacking away at the frozen top layer.

'So,' said Leo, 'how about Finn? You decided to forgive him yet?'

'I don't think so.' She stabbed the ice cream a bit more. 'Nothing's really changed since the last time I saw him.'

Her brother shrugged. 'Maybe not, but I can't stand to see the poor bloke wandering around like a lost puppy. He's clearly pining for you.'

'So?'

'So maybe you should throw him a bone?'

Merry pulled a face. 'Since when did you become Team Finn? Especially after he—' She clamped her mouth shut. There was no reason she shouldn't tell Leo that Finn had stopped her killing Ronan in the first place. No reason at all. But still… 'He lied to me, Leo. He was planning to trick me into falling for him, to *use* me –'

'I'm not Team Finn. I'm on your side, Merry; I always have been, and I always will be. Nothing is ever going to change that. But, Finn's dad's plan was just that: his dad's. Cormac says Finn was never intending to go through with it, and I believe him. He also says Finn cares about you. And I believe that too.' Leo sipped his Coke. 'More importantly, I think you care about Finn. If I'm wrong, tell the guy to get lost. Or I'll tell him to get lost for you. But if I'm right…' He reached across the table and squeezed her arm briefly. 'Maybe you should talk to him. I just want you to be happy, Merry. And I think he makes you happy.'

Merry sighed and took another spoonful of ice cream. She was hungrier than she'd realised. Another thought occurred to her. 'You're not just saying this because you fancy his cousin, are you?'

Leo choked on his drink. 'What? What makes you think I fancy Cormac? Just because we're both gay doesn't mean that we're automatically going to fall for each other!' His voice dropped. 'Besides, the last thing I'm looking for right now, after what happened with Ronan, is another relationship.' He shook his head in bewilderment. 'Geez. If you can call what Ronan did to me a relationship.'

'I'm sorry.' Merry pushed the tub of ice cream across the table to him as a peace offering, cursing herself silently for being so tactless. 'Don't be cross. But he obviously likes you. He seems a really nice bloke, too, even though he is a Lombard. And you of all people deserve a really nice bloke.' Leo was still scowling, though he had taken a spoonful of ice cream. 'Oh, c'mon, Leo. Don't tell me you don't fancy him just a little bit?'

There was the sound of the front door opening, voices in the hallway. Leo rolled his eyes at her and hurried out of the kitchen.

Merry pulled the ice cream back across the table and carried on eating.

'Merry?' It was Roshni, standing in the doorway. 'May I join you?'

'I s'pose.'

Roshni hesitated briefly, then sat down in the chair Leo had just vacated. 'Your grandmother's tired after the meeting; Bronwen and Leo have taken her upstairs.'

'OK. Is Jack here?'

'He is staying with Sophia, for now. We've persuaded him to rest for a little before he attempts to return through the point of intersection.' She shifted uncomfortably on the chair. 'Do you mind if I make everyone some tea?'

'Go ahead. Not for me, though.'

Roshni waved her hand to turn the kettle on, just as she had the last time they'd sat at this table together. 'Would you like to know what happened at the coven meeting?'

Merry shrugged.

'Well,' Roshni continued, 'the first thing you should know is that Denise has been reported to the Stewards.'

'What?'

'Helen turned her in.' There was a certain satisfaction in Roshni's voice. 'Denise has been acquiring books of prohibited magic from somewhere, and Helen claims she saw her practising a spell on somebody from the town. Helen has asked to rejoin the coven.'

'She still doesn't like me,' Merry said, remembering how Helen had looked at her earlier.

'She doesn't have to like you. What's important is that the Stewards will take into account Denise's behaviour when considering her complaint against you.' Roshni sighed. 'I feel for Denise. To have to bury one's own child… It's unthinkable. And clearly, it has affected her deeply. But she's beyond our help now.'

'What about Ronan? Is the coven going to do anything?' The doorbell rang, but Merry ignored it.

'There's not much we can do, other than wait.' Roshni rubbed her eyes, stifling a yawn. Obviously Merry wasn't the only one who was having trouble sleeping. 'We have to stay focused on what we can achieve – preventing mass panic in the town as more people realise that at least some of the fairy stories they grew up with are real, and getting rid of the black holly before it can hurt anyone. Stopping further attacks by creatures from the other world, if we're able.' She stood and got some mugs out of a cupboard. 'We hold the line, and we prepare our defences. And when Ronan arrives, we'll be ready. And we'll face him together, Merry: no one suggested handing you and Leo over to Ronan. No one.'

Merry realised she'd been clutching the edges of her chair so hard that her hands hurt. She relaxed as relief washed over her.

'Thanks, Roshni.' The doorbell rang again. Merry put the lid on the ice cream and shoved it back into the freezer. 'I'd better get that.' She hurried through to the hallway and opened the door.

It was Finn.

'Can I come in?'

'Um...'

'Please? I won't take up much of your time, I promise.

I just want to talk to you, that's all. After everything we've been through, I can't bear to leave things like this. Just five minutes. Please.'

Merry remembered what Leo had said earlier and wondered whether her brother had deliberately ignored the doorbell. 'OK. But Roshni's here. Let's go into the garden.' Grabbing her jacket from the stand by the door, she led him round to the back of the house. The rain had given way to sunshine, and there were long shadows stretching across the lawn, but there was a chill in the air too; a reminder that the days were getting shorter.

She turned to face him. 'Well?'

'I want you to forgive me. To really forgive me. For lying to you when I first came to Tillingham. I don't want you to forget about it, or pretend it never happened. I want you to forgive me, and then I want us to move on.'

Merry stared up at him. 'So, this is all about what *you* want?'

'No!' She could hear the exhaustion and frustration in his voice. He stopped, and took a deep breath. 'I screwed up, Merry. In a big way. I know I did. But all I've done since then is try to put things right. Try to be there for you. And now you're shutting me out because of something I was never going to do anyway…'

'Really? You were never going to do what your dad wanted? Because you put on quite a good show when you arrived here.'

'That was different! I was trying to get to Ronan. And I'm not proud of how I behaved, or what I did, but at least I was doing it to save my brother. I never had any plans to get it on with some girl I'd never met before, despite what my father wanted.' He faltered for a moment, his fists gathered into tight balls. 'But then I actually started to care for you. For real.' He ran both hands through his hair. 'Screw it, Merry: I'm in love with you. What more do I have to do to prove it?'

The bottom of Merry's stomach seemed to drop away. Her voice, when she found it, seemed to come from somewhere off in the distance. 'You're in love with me?'

'Of course I'm in bloody love with you. Why else do you think I went back with you to try to save Leo?'

'To make up for what you'd done. To prove to Leo that you weren't a complete waste of space. That was what you said.'

'And all of that was true. But mostly, I did it for you.'

Merry looked away, trying to think through what Finn was saying. She heard him sigh.

'Merry, if you don't like me any more – if you don't

love me – then tell me so. Say the words. And I'll go, right now. No more arguments.'

Did she love him? The sun was setting, splashing glowing golds and pinks across the western sky: there wasn't much time left. Merry tried to imagine how she would feel if she sent Finn away. If she never saw him, never spoke to him again.

And it hurt. It hurt like someone trying to cut out her heart.

She looked back at him. 'When I heard you with Cormac, he was talking about marriage, and babies…'

'You're seventeen, and I'm nineteen. I know as well as you do that we're not ready for that kind of stuff. I'm not asking for a declaration of life-long commitment and I'm not asking you to promise anything. All I want is to be with you. To make you happy. I swear. And it's killing me that you won't allow me to do that.'

'But – but how do I know you're telling the truth? That you're not saying all this because your dad wants you to?' Merry couldn't help it: a tear escaped the corner of her eye and slid down her cheek. All the emotion she'd tried to hold in check over the past few days was bubbling up inside her, threatening to brim over like a river in flood, to wash her away, to drown her. 'I just don't think

I could bear any more shocks or disappointments, Finn. I really don't.'

Finn took her face gently between his hands, so she was staring up into his blue-grey eyes. 'I love you, Merry.'

The question was unspoken, but it was there.

'I love you too.'

Finn closed his eyes and bent his head, resting his forehead against hers.

'I don't know if either of us will survive what's coming next. But I won't leave you. Not for a minute. And that's how you'll know I'm telling the truth.'

He kissed her. And she kissed him right back.

SIXTEEN

'**Y**OU LOOK TERRIBLE.'

Merry opened one eye. Leo was bending over her. And she… she was lying awkwardly on the old sofa in the kitchen. She pushed herself up, yawning and rubbing her eyes and wiping the slobber off her cheek. 'Time?'

'Quarter to nine.'

No surprise, then, if she did look terrible. For the last five nights, she and Finn had been out for hours at a time, patrolling by the lake, so that the rest of the witches could work in the town. It turned out Ruby wasn't the only ordinary person who could sense the destabilising presence of the other world and its creatures; lots of people could. It was making them upset and angry, even the ones who hadn't seen any black holly or who claimed not to believe any of the strange rumours swirling around Tillingham. Trying to avoid complete panic, by keeping the whole population of the town (and its surrounding villages) in a state of blissful ignorance, was almost a full-time job. Merry still wasn't supposed to do any magic, but the coven had given her an exemption if she and Finn encountered any unicorns, elves, or any other magical creatures trying to come through the gateway. She was pleased to be allowed to participate in keeping the town safe, but the night shifts were exhausting. Her head was full of cobwebs.

'Shall I make some coffee?' Leo asked.

Merry yawned again. 'Please.' Standing up, wincing at the stiffness in her legs, she located Finn. He was asleep with his head on the kitchen table. She limped over to him and shook his shoulder.

'Hey.'

Finn groaned, but didn't move.

'D'you want some coffee?'

He raised his head, blinking drowsily. 'Huh?'

Leo put a mug of coffee down in front of him.

Finn inhaled deeply. 'Coffee.'

'Yep.' Merry sat down next to him as Leo passed another mug of coffee to her.

Finn sat up properly, sniffing the air again. 'Bacon?'

'Uh-huh,' Leo called from where he was standing by the stove. 'Bacon sarnies. You want?'

'So badly.' Finn took a sip of coffee. 'Bloody hell, that's good. I could actually kiss you right now.'

Leo chuckled. 'Yeah. I'll pass. Though I appreciate the sentiment.' The sound of sizzling fat grew louder. 'How was it last night?'

'Cold. Boring.' Merry could have added 'disturbing'. The pull of the other world had increased; all the witches had noticed it. So had Finn and Cormac. But no one else seemed to feel it as intensely as Merry did. Being at the lake, simultaneously revolted by the visual representation of the broken gateway, and beguiled by the magic of the other world – it was weird. 'Mind you, I guess boring is a good thing, in the circumstances. Have you seen Mum this morning?'

'Briefly. She and Jack went out about half an hour ago. There's more black holly in the park by the river.' Mum had learnt the *mortiferis* spell, so now she and Jack, armed with an incredibly rare obsidian axe from the Lombard family vaults – much bigger than the axe Merry had been able to produce from Gran's knife – were responsible for clearing the black holly trees that were springing up afresh every night. At least a dozen ordinary people had been injured by the holly already, sent into that unbreakable unconsciousness that would hold them alive in its grasp even as their bodies slowly withered and decayed. And there was nothing anyone could do to help them.

Leo put a bacon sandwich down in front of her. Merry pushed it away.

'I'm not hungry.'

Her brother pushed it back towards her. 'Eat it. You can't function on nothing but coffee and adrenaline. Not for any length of time.'

'He's right,' Finn mumbled, his own mouth already full of breakfast. 'And this is really—' The end of his sentence was lost in gasping and coughing as Cormac materialised in the corner of the room. 'What the hell, Cormac?' Merry slapped Finn on the back until he'd recovered. 'What's wrong with the front door?'

Cormac winked. 'Jealous, cousin? If you'd just take the trouble to learn the spell…' He walked across to Leo, still standing at the stove. 'How are you this morning? Did the cleansing spell help?'

Merry noticed that her brother's hand went automatically to his chest. And the frown lines across his forehead seemed to have become permanent. He may not have been out casting spells all night, but she wondered how much sleep he'd had.

'Um…'

'Honestly?' Cormac persisted.

Leo shrugged. 'It's not any better. But it's definitely not any worse. I've been checking carefully.' Cormac sighed and pinched the bridge of his nose. 'Hey, it's fine. Not worse is good. And you've got plenty of other stuff to worry about right now.' Cormac was working on an antidote to the black holly poison, as well as trying to construct amulets that would protect people from the auras projected by elves. But his concern for Leo, as far as Merry was aware, hadn't wavered. She liked him for it.

'Well, I'll have a think, see if I can come up with anything more effective.'

'D'you want some breakfast?'

'I've eaten, thanks. I'm off to the big house; some people were injured in a brawl last night, so I've to help your grandmother make up some more healing salve.'

Cormac meant Mrs Knox's house. Gran was staying

there at the moment; she still couldn't cast many spells, but she had enough magic to prepare the healing salves and potions that she was so good at.

Merry took another sip of coffee, enjoying the warmth seeping into her tired limbs, took a bite of her bacon sandwich and stood up. 'OK. I need to check in with Roshni and the others too. Finn? Leo?'

Her brother shook his head. 'I'm going to wait here for Mum and Jack. They should be back soon.'

Finn stood up, draining his coffee mug. 'I'll come. Shall we tag along with Cormac or would you like me to drive you?' He stood behind Merry and slipped his arms round her waist, leaning down to murmur in her ear. 'We could go down to the coast afterwards. Have a romantic walk along the beach.' He kissed the side of her neck lightly, making her shiver.

Cormac made a retching noise. 'It is way too early in the day to be watching whatever this is. I'll see you at the house. Leo,' he winked, 'I'll call you later.' Merry saw his lips move in the opening of *Intervolitare*, the wizards' version of the broomstick spell. And then he was gone, a breeze rippling through the kitchen as the air rushed in to fill the space where Cormac had been standing.

'I guess we're driving.' Merry turned her head to kiss Finn's cheek. 'But no beach trips today; there's far too much to do.'

Finn groaned. 'Fine. I'll get my keys...'

At Mrs Knox's house, the work was being done from the old ballroom as usual. There was a large map floating on the end wall, centred on the lake and showing Tillingham and the surrounding region. The area round the lake directly affected by the other world had been highlighted in red. But a much larger area was also marked out: the space where the destabilising influence of the other world was being felt by ordinary people, where black holly was spreading and random attacks by elves had been reported. This area seemed to be growing every day. Round the sides of the room were trestle tables where spells and potions were being worked on. At one table Gran was sitting, giving instructions to Cormac. On another table was a long branch of black holly, being carefully examined by two witches and a wizard who looked up and waved at Finn.

'Oh, Zach's here – that's great. Who knew Ronan would be the source of so much inter-magical cooperation?' Finn commented. 'I'll just go and say hello.' As he strolled towards the table with the black holly, Merry went to see her grandmother.

'How are you feeling, Gran?'

'Hello, sweetheart. Surprisingly well, thank you.' She smiled at Cormac. 'This young man is a treasure. So gifted when it comes to healing potions.' Merry remembered her own attempts at healing spells and salves earlier in the summer, and couldn't entirely suppress a twinge of jealousy. Until Gran added, 'For a wizard.'

Cormac blushed and grimaced, as if he couldn't quite work out whether he was supposed to feel flattered or insulted.

'Well, I'll go and fetch the, um…' He pointed at a piece of paper in this hand, a list of some sort. Pushing his glasses back up on to the bridge of his nose, he hurried out of the French windows that led to the garden.

'He's nervous of you, Gran. What else have you been saying to him?'

'Nothing at all. I simply explained—'

Gran broke off as a commotion arose at the other end of the hall. Roshni and Mrs Galantini walked through the door. In between them, draped in silvery strands of light extending from the witches' hands, was a man. The trio moved slowly into the centre of the room and the witches let go of the strands, the loose ends forming a loop so the man was surrounded by a glowing silver chain, unable to move. Everyone else gathered round.

'Who is this? Gran asked.

The man was dressed in dark trousers and the remnants of a dark blue top. There was a long, yellow bruise down one side of his face, partially concealed by several days' worth of stubble. He had other injuries too. Merry squinted; there was something about the man that seemed familiar...

'It's that policeman. The one at the lake, who was taken by the elf.' She pointed at his top. 'See, they've ripped the sleeves off, where it said "police".'

Lysandra pushed through the ring of witches and peered at the man's face. 'Merry's right.'

'Well, we found him outside.' Roshni was kneading one shoulder, wincing. 'He was trying to get past the wards. He threw a hammer at me.'

That seemed odd: the man wasn't angry. He wasn't anything: his face was entirely emotionless. Almost entirely... Merry edged closer to the glowing strands. There was a hint of horror buried deep at the back of the man's otherwise vacant eyes. She'd seen that look before.

'There's something controlling him.'

'Are you sure?'

'Pretty sure. Has he said anything?'

'Not so far.'

There was something clutched tightly in the man's hand. Something metallic. Merry reached through the glowing filaments and tugged it gently out of the man's palm. It was a bracelet. The twisted silver bracelet that Ronan had given to Leo shortly before he snatched him away.

'Merry?' Roshni was peering at the bracelet as it lay in Merry's open hand. She went to pick it up—

'It is not for you.' The man's voice was oddly toneless. But he was watching them now, his eyes flicking from one to another. 'It is for him. It is a token.'

'For Leo, you mean?' Merry asked. 'Did Ronan send you?'

'I am Ronan.' There were exclamations from the witches, and many of them brought their hands up, ready to cast a spell. 'I am on my way. I have aligned the worlds, and I will be here very soon. Before the sun sets today. And when I arrive, you will have to choose.'

'Choose what?'

'Choose obedience. Or choose death.'

The man pulled his lips back, a parody of a grin. 'By

the way, Merry, have you guessed my name yet?' His face went slack for a moment. Then, eyes wide, he began to scream, over and over and over.

Roshni flung her hand up, murmuring a sleeping spell. The man slumped, unconscious, still held upright by the loops of silver fire about his body. She lowered him carefully to the floor – the magic chains vanished – and glanced up at Merry, questioning.

'That was what Ronan said to me, the night he took Leo.' Merry gripped the bracelet hard. 'Guess my name, and I'll let him go. Just like the fairy tale.'

'Obviously.' Roshni pressed her hands to her cheeks, staring down at the sleeping man. Merry nudged her.

'I suppose you'll want Gran and Cormac to stay here, see if they can find a way to fix whatever Ronan's done to him. And the rest of us, as many as we can gather, we should probably go to the lake. I guess that's where Ronan is going to show up.'

'Er… yes. Yes, the lake.' Roshni shook herself. 'OK. Sophia, will you send out a message?' Mrs Knox nodded. 'And Finn…'

Finn appeared beside Merry, taking her hand in his. 'I'll call my dad.'

★

It took longer than Merry expected to get everyone organised. Some had to be left behind to protect the town and the villages nearby, and to keep ordinary people away from the lake. The wizards, and witches from other covens, who had promised support, had to be given time to arrive in Tillingham. But finally, two hours or so after the possessed policeman had spoken to her, they were standing near the Black Lake.

Not that it was really recognisable as a lake any more. There was just a swirling maelstrom, flashing with colour. It seemed to have depth. Merry felt its attraction deep in her gut. Around her, other witches and wizards were staring at the space where the lake had been, leaning forward, hands up as if to touch the scene in front of them.

'Lucky you guys put those ward things up, huh? Leo's voice was light, but he couldn't hide the tension in it. Merry had wanted him to stay at home, but he had insisted on joining them; he said it was scarier to wait around to see if she would come back or if Ronan was going to turn up instead. So, her brother was here, and her mum and Jack and Finn.

Lots of people to go for, if Ronan really wants to hurt me…

Roshni and some of the others were testing the wards,

adding strengthening spells here and there. But apart from that, there was nothing to do but wait.

The time dragged on. Initially tense, prepared for immediate attack, people began to flag. Some sat down. Some brought out bottles of water and cereal bars. Others approached Roshni, clearly wondering whether there had been a mistake. But she and Finn and Jack were all still standing, ready.

The difference, she realised, was that they had seen Ronan. They knew what he would do, given the opportunity. To everybody else, he was still… abstract.

It was almost a relief when a gap opened in the turmoil of the lake, and figures began to emerge. Humans, mostly, many with that same blank expression the policeman had worn earlier. But also a handful of elves; there were involuntary murmurs of horror from some of the waiting witches and wizards, despite the protective amulets that had been hastily constructed. Finally, Ronan himself, flanked by two others. One, a blank-faced woman, carrying a white flag. The other, Gwydion. Merry felt her mouth twist in disgust. The wizard looked more than half dead: eyes sunken in his head, clumps of hair missing, open sores on his face and the backs of his hands. She couldn't understand how he was still walking.

Ronan and the woman with the flag approached the edge of the wards. All the witches and wizards were now back on their feet, hands raised, some already holding globes of witch fire ready to be used as a weapon. Ronan raised his fingers and brushed them across the shimmering, barely-there surface of the nearest ward, snatching them back and laughing as the magic crackled against his skin.

'Why are you here, Ronan?' The question was from Roshni.

Ronan gestured at the white flag. 'I'm here for a chat, obviously.' He smiled, looking around at the countryside beyond the lake, taking a deep breath in and out. 'It's so good to be back in Tillingham. The weeks I spent here, I think I was actually happy...' The smile faded when he spotted Merry. 'But happiness never lasts, does it?' He shrugged. 'Power is so much easier to hold on to. And I do wonder, now I think about it, whether power isn't better than happiness. What d'you think, Merry?'

'I think you're wrong.'

'Course you do.' He began pacing up and down behind the wards. 'You don't care about power at all. You won't mind if people try to take it away from you. And even if your coven leader orders your wrists to be magically bound, so that you can't do any spells, I'm sure you wouldn't object.' He gave her a sideways glance, and Merry felt the blood flaming into her face and neck.

But that was at a coven meeting. How could he possibly know?

'Admit it, Merry: you're just as much a power-hungry freak as I am.' Some of the other witches were now staring at her, brows furrowed with doubt.

'Leave her alone!' Finn stepped in front of her, his hands raised. 'She's nothing like you.'

'Finn! Grand to see you again. How's your brother?' Before Finn could do anything other than gasp, Ronan switched his attention back to Merry. 'What did you have to promise him in return for his help? Your firstborn child?' He laughed. 'But has he spun enough glittering lies to get you into bed yet?'

'Shut up, you bastard!' Finn's voice was thick with hatred.

'Drop the act, Finn. You know as well as I do the sacrifices your father has demanded: Cillian told me everything. Anything to keep the Lombards going, eh? Anyway, down to business, I suppose. I'm touched, though. I hadn't expected to see so many of you here to negotiate the terms of the surrender.'

'There will be no surrender.' Roshni raised her hands and the wards flared with colour. 'You cannot stay here,

Ronan. Not as you are. The other world doesn't belong here. The instability will destroy everything in the end. You know I'm right.'

'I know that life is short and uncertain, even for people like us. My reality is here,' he waved a hand to indicate the broken gateway between the worlds, 'and now. I'm not going to worry about the future.' He tilted his head, eyebrows raised.

'But, we can help you.' Merry could hear the tension in Roshni's voice. 'We can find a way for you to get more power without stealing it from others, without—'

'Helping me now, is it?' Ronan sneered. 'Like my mother's coven wanted to help her by locking me up and throwing away the key? And would you expect me to be grateful for the scraps of magic you're charitable enough to give me? No, thank you. I don't need your help any more. I've more power than I know what to do with. More power than you've ever seen.'

Roshni straightened up. 'Then you are determined to fight us?'

'I'd much rather not, to be honest. I think we should at least try to strike a bargain first.'

'There's nothing to negotiate. Either you leave voluntarily, or we will drive you out.'

Ronan laughed. Beside her, Merry felt Leo shiver, and she took his hand.

'Have you forgotten that I control the point of intersection now? Besides I've not come empty-handed. Here are two of my bargaining chips.' Ronan clicked his fingers. Two elves came forward, both dragging a prisoner. Meredith and Nia.

Nia seemed not to know or care where she was. She was singing and talking to herself, swaying on the spot and rocking what looked like a large doll back and forth in her arms. But Meredith…

She was obviously too weak to stand: the elf was almost holding her up. One arm was in a rough sling, and there was a blood-stained bandage wrapped round her head. Beneath the dirt, her skin was waxy.

Jack gave a strangled cry and began running towards Ronan, drawing his sword. But Roshni raised her hand, murmuring the beginning of a spell, and he fell backwards as if he'd run into something. 'Wait, Jack!'

'Listen to the witch, Aetheling. Although, I suppose you're no longer an Aetheling, not since I killed your father. You're a king now, not a prince. Still,' Ronan wagged his finger at Jack, 'you haven't heard what I want yet.'

'Well?' Roshni crossed her arms. 'They are but two, Ronan. The lives of many are at stake.'

'True. I hope you remember that.' Ronan cleared his throat. 'These are my terms. I will withdraw from this place, and I will place a temporary barrier in between our worlds. No more elves. No more hard-to-explain disappearances, or murders. No more magical influence from the other world worming its way into people's heads. The plebs you care so much about won't remember that I was ever here. And I really don't want much in return.'

'We're not giving you anything,' Roshni snapped back.

'You will, unless you want me to allow the elves free access to this world. You know and I know that you can't keep them out.' He paused, but Roshni didn't speak. 'So, my first demand: you're to turn over Merry – an easy choice, I would think, given all this is basically her fault. And secondly, I want Leo. He belongs to me, and he is to take his place at my side, as he promised.'

'No.' Merry's voice came out weak and scratchy, but she could tell from the twitching of his face that Ronan had heard her. 'I don't care what happens to me, but I'm never going to let you anywhere near my brother.'

'Why don't you let him decide that?' Ronan turned to

Leo. 'Please? One way or another, this is going to happen.'

Leo loosened Merry's grip on his arm.

'Leo, don't…'

Without replying, moving stiffly, her brother walked a few paces closer to Ronan. 'Why? You don't really love me. You can't.'

'But I do. You're mine.' Ronan sounded like a child disputing ownership of a toy.

'People don't belong to other people. That's not love: it's slavery.' Leo took one more step forward. 'Please, if you ever cared for me, leave us alone. Find someone who wants to be with you.'

Anger blazed in Ronan's eyes, disappearing just as quickly. 'You're the only one I've ever cared for, Leo. I won't give you up. I can't. But,' he stretched out his hand, 'if you come with me now, I'll be merciful. I swear I won't hurt your family.'

'Leo, don't believe him—' Merry didn't get to finish her sentence: Cormac was pushing his way to the front of the crowd.

'He's not going anywhere with you,' the wizard shouted. 'You convinced my cousin, Cillian, that you were his friend, and he believed you. Even when you were feeding him poison and pretending it was medicine, I expect. I'm not about to let you hurt Leo in the same way.' Cormac grabbed Leo's hand and yanked him backwards.

Merry could see Ronan's gaze darting back and forth between Leo and Cormac. 'No.' His face twisted with rage, and he snarled. 'No!' Pulling the knife from his belt he flung his arm out sideways, plunging the blade into the chest of the person nearest him.

Nia.

SEVENTEEN

SILENCE. THE DOLL Nia was holding slipped from her fingers. She raised her hands to touch the hilt of the knife protruding from her chest and laughed: one high, clear peal of laughter that rang through the still afternoon air. And then she collapsed.

'Nia!' Meredith cried out, struggling to free herself from the grasp of the elf restraining her. 'Nia!' But her sister did not answer.

Leo gazed at Cormac, frozen beside him, staring through the slight shimmer of the ward at the body of the dead witch, only a few metres away. Cormac's chest was rising and falling rapidly, his grip on Leo's arm almost painfully tight. Meredith began sobbing quietly, and Cormac flinched. A quick glance behind confirmed that most of the other witches and wizards had also been shocked into inaction, caught between fear and revulsion.

And yet, Leo reflected, it was a quick death. Merciful, almost, compared to others Ronan had forced him to witness.

Only Merry was different. His sister's eyes glistened with tears, but she was also gritting her teeth and clenching and unclenching her fingers, and Leo could see the ends of her nails glowing.

Ronan himself was breathing heavily, eyes closed, his face dark and blotchy. But as Leo watched he seemed to regain control. The colour faded from his face. He opened his eyes and shot a look of unalloyed ill will at Cormac.

Dread slithered down Leo's spine, and he wished Cormac had stayed with Gran, where he would have been safe.

Ronan leant down to examine Nia's body. He wrenched the knife out of her chest, provoking anguished screams from Meredith, and picked up the doll she had been cradling. 'I would have given you everything, Leo. My wishes would have become yours, and you would have been happy. Instead, the witch is dead because of your… stubbornness. I hope you're satisfied. Because you will still be mine, in the end.'

His voice could have frozen rivers. Leo shivered and remembered the warmth of the hours he'd spent here with Ronan before. Had every word been a lie? Every action, a deceit? Or had there been some ember of truth, the remains of a soul still clinging on inside?

Not that it mattered now. If there had been anything, it was surely gone, burnt away to cinders.

Ronan had turned away from him.

'Very well. Leo refuses to sacrifice himself for the good of others. I hope you've all noticed that. Luckily, I'm flexible. I'll take an annual tribute instead: one witch and one wizard, both under thirty, to be sent through the barrier every autumn equinox. Until such time as Leo comes to his senses.'

'You're insane.' Roshni strode to the edge of the ward. 'There will be no tribute and no bargain. We will—'

Ronan, eyebrows raised, put his knife to Meredith's throat. Roshni held up her hands, backing away slightly.

'The second part of my demand is non-negotiable. I can't resist Merry's power any longer. It sings to me. I can feel it vibrating across my skin. I can see it glowing in the darkness behind my eyelids. Her power is no good to you here.' He shrugged. 'And she took Leo from me, so obviously, I have to take my revenge. Turn her over to me, and I will reseal the gateway as I promised. If not…'

Merry crossed her arms and lifted her chin. 'Really? And what if I refuse? My brother is safe from you.'

'Well,' Ronan pulled a face, 'he is, and he isn't.' Leo's entire body tensed. 'Did you really think I wouldn't have an insurance policy?' Lifting the doll, he positioned the point of his knife against it. 'Old magic, this. And costly. But still so effective.'

Leo, watching his sister's face, saw confusion give way to fear. She swung towards him. 'No, Leo—'

Ronan slashed the knife across the doll.

Leo grabbed at his left shoulder, gasping at the pain that had exploded across his skin. 'What the…'

Blood, warm and red, was flowing between his fingers and down the back of his hand.

★　★　★

Her brother staggered, held out his hand and stared at it. The blood was spreading across his T-shirt like ink on a paper towel. He looked up at her.

'Merry?'

And then Mum was there, throwing her arms round Leo, begging him to lie down. Cormac was trying to examine the wound. The other witches and wizards were shouting and some of them were already aiming spells at Ronan, but the wards were in the way and the magic was just sizzling uselessly across the surface. Even the elves, who could pass through the wards, stayed well back, out of the reach of the hexes and curses. Jack was slashing at the invisible barrier with his sword until most of the blade shattered and broke. Finn was yelling, urging the others to get the wards down, to attack, but Merry knew it would take too long because Ronan was lifting the knife again –

'Don't worry, Merry. They're just surface wounds. For now.' He slashed down and Leo collapsed, groaning and clutching his shin, blood soaking through his jeans.

'Stop it! Stop hurting him!' Merry raised her hands and sent silver filaments streaming from her fingertips, forming a cage round Leo and Cormac.

Ronan laughed. 'That won't help you this time.' He struck again and Leo moaned as a long gash ripped down the length of his forearm.

Merry screamed as her body trembled and pain shot up her arms. She hurled the magic towards the ward in front of Ronan, ignoring the cracking and burning of the grass round her feet, ignoring the yells of the others. The only thing that mattered was to get to Ronan – to stop him, to hurt him back. And her enemy started to retreat. Bright fissures began to spread across the surface of the nearest ward, a branching tracery filled with liquid light, hanging in mid-air. Ronan, no longer laughing, raised the knife again. At the same time the elves holding Meredith forced her to her knees and held a sword above her neck.

'Stop, Merry, right now!' Ronan called. 'Lower your hands. Or I'll end this.'

Someone was in front of her, grasping her wrists. 'Merry, you must stop. Please.'

She looked up into his eyes. Brown, with little flecks of gold.

'Jack?'

'Yes. Lower your arms, please.' His voice was low and gentle.

'But…'

'We will fight him. And we will destroy him. But not today.'

Merry looked past Jack to where Ronan was standing, the point of his knife aimed very clearly at the doll's heart.

Behind her, Leo was crying, and Cormac and Mum were both talking to him, telling him he was going to be OK. She sobbed and ground her teeth. But she let Jack push her arms down to her sides.

Ronan walked up to the damaged ward.

'Such power.' Pressing his hand, fingers spread, against one of the glowing fractures, he breathed in deeply. 'I can't wait to take it from you.' He held up the doll. 'You have two nights, Merry, because I'm generous. Two nights to make your goodbyes. By sunrise the day after tomorrow I want you back here to surrender to me. If not, I'll kill your brother. Bit by bit. And then I'll set the elves free to plunder this world as they like, and I'll make sure they kill everyone else you care about. You'll be left with nothing. But it's your choice.'

A gap opened in the pulsing, nightmare landscape of the lake. Slowly, Ronan's followers began to file back through it, disappearing into the darkness beyond. On their side of the ward, Merry and the coven and the others watched, silent.

Not completely silent. Nearby, someone was laughing.

Her heart thumping in her chest, Merry turned round.

Denise was pointing at Leo, and grinning. 'Now you know how it feels!'

'Shut up, Denise!' Roshni stalked over, her hands raised. 'Unless you'd like to tell me how Ronan knew about what happened at our coven meeting the other day?'

Merry closed her eyes as the two witches argued. Her legs, her arms – every bit of her – was trembling, weak. But not too weak to deal with this.

Denise had retreated before Roshni's anger. She was standing right in front of the damaged section of the ward now. And the gap into the other world was still open.

Quietly, Merry began to sing a shifting spell. Denise stopped shouting, and her eyes bulged. She stumbled backwards until she was pressed against the fractured ward. Merry raised her voice and Denise began to squirm and cry as the cracks in the ward spread and joined and grew –

The ward shattered and vanished, and Denise flew backwards into the dark space on the other side of the lake. The gap snapped shut, swallowing her scream.

Nia's crumpled body lay alone by the edge of the lake.

'There you are.' Mum, clutching a mug of tea, sat down next to Merry. They were back at Mrs Knox's, and Merry had been sitting for the last hour on a garden bench, as far as possible from the house and from everyone else.

'How's Leo?'

'Fine, physically at least. For now.' Mum sniffed. 'Your grandmother and Cormac between them have done a good job of healing him; you'd barely know he'd been injured.' She wrapped her hands more tightly round the mug. 'But, he's so scared, Merry. He…' Her voice wobbled. 'He says it would be better for you to kill him, to stop Ronan using him. He says if *you* killed him, instead of Ronan, he knows he wouldn't suffer—' She was crying too much to say any more.

Merry took the mug out of her mother's hands and put her arms round her. 'I'm not going to let Ronan hurt him, Mum, I promise. I'm going to figure something out.'

Mum dabbed at her eyes with a tissue. 'The others are trying to find a way to shield him. But this kind of old magic…' She trailed off, half-shrugging and opening her hands.

Old magic. That was how Ronan had described it. And Gran. Poppet magic (spells involving the use of dolls or puppets) had been on the prohibited list for over five hundred years. It relied on possession of some part of a person's body – nail clippings, or a lock of hair, for example – things that Ronan had had ample time to collect.

'I still don't understand why the net I put round Leo

didn't help. It worked before. OK, so he's linked to that horrible doll thing now, instead of to another person, but still…'

That's the trouble with banning things and covering up the bad stuff that used to be done. People forget. And then if it happens again, no one knows what to do.

Mum was staring down at her hands, twisting the ring she wore round and round. The skin on her finger was inflamed.

'Come on, Mum.' Merry stood and tugged her mother upright. They walked slowly through the garden back to the house, neither speaking. Mum was still fiddling with the ring, Merry was thinking about poppet magic and blood magic and wondering what other types of magic were prohibited (or frowned upon). What other half-forgotten knowledge was around that might help her, if only she had access to it?

Gran was resting in the sitting room. After settling Mum in there with her, Merry went in search of Jack.

She found him in the dining room. Nia's body was lying on the long mahogany table, surrounded by lit candles. The witches had washed her and combed her hair and had charmed away the rents and stains on her clothes. They'd placed a pillow under her head and covered her in a sheet, drawn up to her neck. Her long tresses looked very dark against the bloodless pallor of her skin. Jack was sitting in a chair at the foot of the table, eyes closed, his broken sword across his knees, and Merry wondered if he was praying. He looked up as she approached.

'She knew she was to die. She told me so, before I came to this place.' His voice was rough. 'I told Meredith I would protect her. That I would protect them all...' A muscle in the side of his face began twitching as he tightened his palm round the jagged remnant of his blade.

'I'll free Meredith if I can. I promise. But I need to ask you something.'

Jack nodded.

'When your mother was killed, Ronan cut her heart out. Did that happen to anyone else, as far as you know?'

He shook his head. 'Our scouts found many bodies. But none with that particular injury.' His gaze returned to Nia. 'I will watch over her tonight. And at dawn, I will place her on a pyre. Will you be here?'

'If I can.'

Jack bowed his head again. Merry stood watching him for a moment. She was reminded so strongly of the first night she'd met him by the Black Lake. His clothes were different, but the anguish in his face...

And the broken blade. Just like he used to carry. And Nia and Carys both dead, but Meredith still alive…

Was her world fighting back? Trying to reassert itself against the other world and its alternative version of the past?

But if that's so, Gwydion should be free.

Merry hurried out of the room back into the garden, carefully avoiding the ballroom where the others were still working. Why had Ronan brought Gwydion to the lake? She began pacing up and down. Gwydion had been tied to that grotesquely carved chair, just like Jack had been. But it seemed he wasn't being sent to cut out people's hearts. What exactly was Ronan doing with him?

More blood magic, perhaps, but how can I—

'Merry?' It was Finn. 'Sorry. I didn't mean to startle you.'

'That's OK. I was just,' she massaged her temples, 'just trying to think through some stuff. Where've you been?'

'Making plans with Dad. He's going to go and visit some other wizards, see if any of them have any useful information on the type of magic Ronan's using. I thought I might go and check out the books at home.' He plucked a leaf from the tree next to them and twirled it in his fingers. 'I can bring them straight back here. Or you could come with me, if you like.'

'Um… Do wizards have prohibited magic?'

330

'Huh?'

'I mean, is there, like, a list of spells you're not allowed to do?'

'Er…' Finn scratched his head. 'Well, the Kin Houses have agreed that some spells ought not to be used, but…' He pulled a face. 'It's more of a suggestion.'

'So you have books on blood magic at your house?'

'Yeah. Quite a few, I think. I've never read them.'

Merry started pacing again, Finn watching her, his eyebrows raised. She didn't want to leave Leo. But there wasn't anything useful she could do here, not right now.

'Will your mum mind? If I come with you?'

'She's gone to France. She has no magic, so Dad thought it would be safer.'

'Oh.' For a moment, Merry had forgotten that the women of the Kin Houses weren't magical. 'Let's go to yours, then. But you'll have to take us there. I'll tell Mum and Gran what I'm doing. Meet you back here?'

Finn nodded and ran towards the house.

Mum wasn't best pleased at the idea of Merry disappearing off. She didn't say it, but Merry knew what she was thinking: that she might lose her daughter forever in less than forty-eight hours. But Gran… Gran was strong, and supportive, just like she always was.

'You have to let her go, Bronwen. It's a good idea. We could apply to the Archivists for permission to study the prohibited texts, but we don't have time. Go.' She squeezed Merry's hands. 'We'll look after Leo, and keep working on a shielding spell, and on some way to stop Ronan's elves getting through the wards.'

'Thanks, Gran. Where's Leo?'

'Asleep. Cormac has given him something to help him rest.'

'OK. Well, when he wakes up...'

Gran nodded. 'Take your time. Be thorough. And trust your instincts.'

Merry hurried to her room to throw a few things into a bag, then raced back into the garden. It didn't feel like she had much time left at all. Finn was waiting there, a piece of paper in his hand.

'Cormac wrote the *Intervolitare* spell out for me.' He blushed faintly. 'I'll learn it properly, if we manage to survive this.' He held out his hand. Merry took it and closed her eyes as he chanted the first line of the spell. The sudden spaciousness washed over her, sending her insides tumbling...

Solid ground beneath her feet again, and Finn's hand still tight in hers. She opened her eyes and blinked.

When Finn told her his family had some books, she'd been expecting a few shelves in a regular room. But this was an actual library, straight out of a TV period drama. Three of the four walls were lined with tall, white-painted, gothic-style bookcases, topped with pointed arches and little spires, while the fourth wall was pierced with seven wide, arched windows. In front of each window was a table and chair. There were sofas and armchairs and little side tables clustered in groups, and a large circular table in the centre of the room. A Wedgwood blue carpet matched the colour of the walls above the shelves. The books themselves all seemed to be bound in dark leather. Merry glanced up, and was unsurprised to discover the ceiling was fan-vaulted, the ribs picked out with silver leaf that glimmered in the evening sunshine.

Finn was looking smug, and Merry realised her mouth was hanging open. She shut it quickly and shrugged. 'Nice library. So where are the books on blood magic?'

'This way.' He led her to a section of shelves in one corner of the room. Merry put up her hand to take one of the books but Finn grabbed her wrist. 'Wait – the shelves are protected. Only accessible by family members over sixteen.' He held his hand just in front of the bookcase, fingers spread wide, and murmured a couple of words in a language Merry didn't know. The air rippled. 'OK. Now everything in this case is accessible. I'll open the others as we need them.'

'What would have happened if I'd touched them?'

'An alarm goes off. And you get hit by a particularly vicious stinging hex. Brings you up in hives.' Finn rubbed his arm and winced. 'It's not much fun.'

'Um, OK.' She ran her fingers along the spines of the books, but there were no titles she recognised. 'Any suggestions?'

He pursed his lips. 'Start at the top and work down? And just remind me what we're looking for?'

'Anything that describes how and why blood magic is used to control people, I guess. Gwydion isn't being used in the same way Jack was, so I want to find out exactly what his role is in all this.'

Finn nodded and pulled two books down from the top shelf. He handed one to Merry. 'Here you go. I'm going to ask Mrs Norris about dinner.'

'Mrs Norris?'

'Our housekeeper.' Merry obviously didn't conceal her surprise very well, because Finn flushed. 'What? It's a big house.'

'I didn't say anything.' She tapped the book. 'I'll get

started.' As Finn left the room she opened the book and scanned the title page: *The Haematochairon*. The pages were blotched with age and looked hand-printed. Sighing, she settled herself on one of the sofas. This was probably going to take a while.

Five hours later, Merry was ready to hurl the leather-bound books through the nearest window. They'd taken a break when dinner was brought in (by actual *uniformed servants*, just like they were suddenly on the set of a *Downton Abbey* episode), but other than that she and Finn had been silently working their way through the bookshelves. And so far, neither of them had turned up anything that sounded useful. There had been lots of stomach-churning descriptions of blood-magic rituals, lots of (often unbelievable) claims about what a skilled practitioner of blood magic might accomplish, but nothing that shed any light on what Ronan might be doing with Gwydion. Adding the volume she'd just finished to the pile next to the sofa, she groaned, running both hands through her hair.

'I'm so tired. And angry. But mostly tired. And we're running out of time.' She swung her feet off the sofa and slumped forward, hands on knees, rubbing her sore eyes. 'I really thought we'd find something useful.'

Finn was next to her, his arm round her shoulders. 'Don't give up. Maybe the next few books will have something relevant. Or maybe the others will find a way of shielding Leo.'

'I really doubt it. You heard what Gran said about the kind of magic Ronan's using.' She dug her fingernails hard into the skin of her forehead, wanting it to hurt. 'Somewhere along the line I've missed something. I just don't know how I'm going to fix this.'

'Look at me.'

Slowly, Merry shifted round so she was sitting facing Finn, with one leg tucked up under her, her gaze still lowered.

Finn lifted her chin and took her hands in his. 'You are not the only person responsible for this. Gwydion was the one who brought the evil from the shadow realm in the first place. Meredith was the one who bound you to a future you never asked for. Ronan was the one who freed the King of Hearts from beneath the lake. And I...' He swallowed and dragged his lower lip through his teeth, 'I was the one who stopped you killing Ronan when you had the chance.'

'But I was the one who went back for Leo. I broke the gateway.'

'You don't know that. It might have been broken by Ronan. If you'd never gone back for Leo this probably would have happened anyway. Ronan would have found a way back, eventually. But my point is, you don't have to do this alone.' He leant forward and kissed her softly, making Merry's heart flutter and sending waves of heat through her core.

Her stomach rumbled.

Finn pulled back fractionally, so their faces were still almost touching.

'Let's go,' he brushed his lips across her neck, making her draw in her breath quickly, 'and explore the kitchen.' The next moment he was on his feet, pulling her up off the sofa.

The kitchen turned out to be a good five-minute walk from the library. They'd gone down one very grand staircase, along several corridors and then down another staircase (less grand). Nobody was around; when Merry mentioned this to Finn he explained that the staff all went home by eight at the latest unless they'd specifically been asked to stay. Merry shivered and drew closer to him.

'So you mean we're completely alone in this huge house?'

'Completely.' He winked and she laughed, despite Ronan and Gwydion and the other world. 'Here we are.'

Finn flicked the light switch. They were in a large, modern kitchen full of high-tech appliances. Finn went to check out the contents of the fridge; he waved his hand and various jars and tubs floated over to the kitchen table.

'Have a seat.' He summoned a bread knife from the other side of the kitchen. 'I'm going to make you my famous chicken-with-everything sandwich.'

'Famous?'

The smile faded from Finn's face and he glanced down at the scar on the inside of his wrist. 'Cillian used to enjoy it.'

Merry's chest tightened and she squeezed Finn's free hand. 'Then I'm sure I'll love it.'

As Finn worked, Merry found a sheet of scrap paper and tried to summarise all her experiences of blood magic, everything about Gwydion and Ronan that she was certain of.

Gwydion was forced to eat Edith's heart, but he's been in chains each time we've seen him. So he's not controlled by the King of Hearts in the same way Jack was.

Other people are being controlled, but Jack said no one is cutting out hearts like he had to.

Something is happening to Gwydion that is gradually destroying him, draining him of life…

She paused, biting the end of the pencil.

Something draining him, like he was a battery.

But Gwydion was just a man, even though he was also a wizard. He couldn't *generate* the sort of power that Ronan was wielding. So where was it coming from?

Finn put two sandwiches and two glasses of water on the table and sat down next to her.

'Thanks.' She took a bite: it *was* good. Chicken, and spring onion, and Swiss cheese, and – 'What's in the sauce?'

'Mayonnaise base with a few spices and other things thrown in.' Finn grinned. 'My own invention. I could reveal it to you, but then I'd have to kill you.' He started telling her about how he'd got into cooking, describing various disasters – exploding things (chocolate ganache, and profiteroles, for example) seemed to feature heavily – and Merry asked him more about Cillian and what they used to do together.

It was surreal. Sitting here, discussing food and childhood with Finn as if everything was normal.

She kept chewing and swallowing automatically, but the flavour of the food had disappeared, and her stomach felt like it was closing up…

Picking up the glass of water, she drained it quickly.

'Are you OK?' Finn asked.

Merry shrugged, and he sighed and reached across to smooth her hair back off her face. Staring into his grey eyes, she remembered the other times they'd faced each other like this. The first time she'd met him, when he'd broken into Gran's house. The first time they'd kissed, sitting in the car he'd fixed for her. The first time he'd told her he loved her. Finn had made her life so much more complicated. And he'd hurt her. But he'd also saved her.

She glanced down at the list she'd been making earlier, and scrunched it into a ball. Then she took Finn's hands and stood, drawing him up with her.

'Where are we going?'

Reaching up on tiptoe, she wrapped her arms round his neck and whispered into his ear.

'I don't want to go back home tonight. I want to stay here. With you.'

She felt a tremor go through Finn's body, and he pulled her close, burying his face in her shoulder. After a moment, he murmured:

'Are you absolutely sure?'

'Yes.'

'And if you change your mind, at any point, you'll…'

'Yes. I'll tell you.'

Taking her hand, Finn led her out of the kitchen and back along corridors and up staircases until they reached his bedroom. He let her in and shut the door behind them. Merry glanced around, briefly taking in the high ceiling and the space and the general air of disorder, and went to sit on the end of the bed. Finn sat next to her, tapping one hand on his knee, breathing quickly.

'So… what now?'

Merry almost laughed. Compared to everything else happening in her life, this seemed so… uncomplicated. 'I want you to kiss me. And then… We'll just see what happens.'

Finn turned and took her in his arms again. He kissed her: her mouth, her jawline, her neck, her collarbone. And together, they slipped backwards on to the bed.

Light, shining through her closed eyelids. Finn next to her, curled round her, his chest rising and falling against her back, one arm draped round her waist. She was warm and weightless and her skin tingled all over. She didn't want to wake up, to come out of this cocoon of contentment and safety. She didn't want this to be the only night that she and Finn spent together.

But the light was too strong for moonlight. She forced her eyes open. The pale grey of early morning had crept beneath the curtains and was throwing shadows on to the walls and ceiling. Mostly, the room looked like any other teenager's room. Shelves, a wardrobe, a desk with a laptop on it. Posters on the wall. But there were stranger touches too: various odd-looking instruments that might have been scientific. A pair of scales. Some sort of crystal ball that was splitting the light into a spectrum of colours, fanning them out across one corner of the room.

Merry watched it for a bit, thinking about prisms, about how light flowed through the crystal to make a rainbow, how electricity flowed through a bulb to make light. Conduits, turning one thing into another. A kind of alchemy, though that had never been real magic…

'Why are you frowning?' Finn was awake, propped up on one elbow, looking down at her. 'You're not upset, are you?'

'No.' She smiled. 'It was amazing. All of it.'

'You were amazing.' He began kissing her again and she pushed him away gently.

'I'm just trying to figure something out about Gwydion, that's all.'

'Oh. Do you want to hit the books again? Shall I make you some breakfast?'

'A coffee would be good. But then we should go home. I need thinking time instead of books right now. I think.'

'Whatever you say.' Finn dropped a kiss on her forehead and slid out of the bed. 'There's a bathroom through there.' He pointed to a door on the other side of the room. 'I'll give you some space.' He padded out of the room.

Merry stretched, holding on to the warmth of the bed for another minute, and went back to contemplating the rainbow on the ceiling. The different-coloured shards of light were pretty. But they were quite dim. Nowhere near as strong as the sunlight...

What if Gwydion wasn't like a battery? What if he was more like a prism? Was that the right comparison? One King of Hearts, harnessing the power of the shadow realm. But that power then being split between Ronan and his servants, like light split by a prism. Power that made Ronan indestructible – how else could he have survived the black holly in the tower? – and also allowed him to control the people he captured... She frowned, her heart racing, trying to untangle the tendrils of thought waving around in her mind, worried that if she thought too hard the idea would just evaporate like rain on a hot day.

Even if she was right, how did it help her?

Scrambling out of bed, Merry hurried to the shower. She wasn't sure of the answer to that last question, not yet. But at least she had somewhere to start.

EIGHTEEN

IT WAS QUIET back at Mrs Knox's house. Mum let them in and led them through to the sitting room. Gran and Cormac were there: a huge pile of books lay open on the coffee table in front of them, together with several discarded mugs of coffee and a plate of sandwiches.

'Where is everyone, Mum?' Her mother looked tired. So did Gran. Merry wondered if they'd been working all night.

'Oh, everyone's busy. Some of the coven are in town, keeping people calm, some are working on the wards. And Leo went with Jack, a couple of hours ago now. He wanted to build a pyre for that poor girl...' Mum's eyes filled with tears, and Merry gave her a hug.

'Where's my dad, Cormac?' Finn asked.

Cormac glanced up from the book he was reading. 'Back at the hotel.'

'He's holding a meeting with the Kin Houses,' Mum added, her face brightening slightly. 'Quite a few have shown up to help, as well as members of the other covens. It will even out the numbers a bit, tomorrow.' She took a sip from her coffee mug, hugging it to her chest. 'How did the two of you get on?'

'We didn't find anything in the library.' Merry yawned. 'But I did have some thoughts this morning. What about Leo? Did you discover anything to protect him from that horrible doll Ronan's made?'

'Not as such,' Gran said, the worry lines prominent on her forehead. 'That type of magic hasn't been openly practised in this country for hundreds of years, though Ronan obviously stole the knowledge from somewhere. Although we know the theory of poppet magic, none of us know the exact spell that Ronan used. And without that, we can't override the magic remotely. Nor can we just destroy the doll – not without risking killing Leo. The only solution is to get our hands on it: to get it away from

Ronan, then figure out how to destroy it later. At least Ronan won't be able to make another doll, now he doesn't have access to Leo.' Gran sighed. 'According to the theory.'

'So that's it?' Finn asked, his voice incredulous. 'And how are we supposed to get the doll from Ronan? Ask him politely? Or are you suggesting that we just hand Merry over, like he wants?'

'Of course not, Finn,' Cormac cut in. 'Ronan can't be trusted: you and I both know that. He probably won't give up the doll anyway. But we do need to get hold of it, one way or another. I can heal any superficial wounds Ronan inflicts upon Leo, but I can't bring him back from the dead.'

Finn started arguing again with his cousin. Merry wandered over to the china cabinet behind the nearest sofa. She could just about make out her reflection in the glass in one of the doors. She didn't look much different from the person she'd been a few months ago – the person she'd been when she'd discovered the trinket box in the attic, just before she found out about Jack, and the family curse. But she was different inside. More powerful. Perhaps a little wiser. But older too. Tired.

Finn and Cormac were still arguing, and it sounded like Mum had joined in.

She had to get the doll from Ronan.

She had to stop Gwydion being used as a prism, if that was what he was, to channel the King of Hearts and the power of the shadow realm.

She had to destroy the King of Hearts, or trap it somewhere so inaccessible that this time no one would ever be able to reach it or harness its power again.

And if she did all that, she might, finally, be able to kill Ronan. And surely, if Ronan was dead, the gateway would repair itself? *When a witch or wizard dies, their enchantments are usually dissolved…* That was one of the first lessons in her wisdom books. Usually, not definitely. But still.

'I'm going.'

The arguing stopped.

'What? Where?' Mum asked, not understanding.

'I'm going to hand myself over. To do what Ronan says.'

'What? No!'

'Are you out of your mind?'

Both Mum and Finn were shouting at her. But it didn't matter. Merry knew what she had to do.

'I need to get close to Ronan. It's the only way I can get my hands on the doll *and* deal with Gwydion, so it's the only way I can kill him. If I die in the process, I die.

But one way or another this has to end.' She turned to Gran, hands spread out. 'You know I'm right. Ronan has control of the point of intersection. If I can kill him, then the barrier between the worlds can be rebuilt. This is the only way to protect our world. It's the only way to save Leo, and Meredith, and everyone else.'

'No way, Merry. You're not sacrificing yourself to save me. I'd rather die first.'

Merry swung round. Leo and Jack were standing in the doorway behind her. Jack was supporting her brother a little. Leo was very pale, dark smudges under his eyes.

'And exactly how are you going to stop me, big brother?' Merry tried to smile at him as she raised her hands and murmured a few words of a protection spell.

'What are you doing?'

'Casting a spell to stop you harming yourself.' Merry raised an eyebrow at him. 'Just in case you were getting any ideas.'

Leo looked appalled. He opened his mouth to say something, but Merry cut him off.

'I can't afford to spend time worrying that you're going to do something stupid. I'll take care of Ronan. You've got to trust me.'

'But, Merry—'

'Please, Leo! There's more at stake than just you and me right now.'

'But we need a proper plan,' Mum cried. 'The Kin Houses, other covens – they may be able to think of something to defeat Ronan. Something that we've missed…'

'Your mum's right. There's got to be another way.' Finn started forward, panic in his eyes. 'Merry, you can't do this!'

'Yes, I can, Finn. And what's more, I have to.' She appealed to Gran again. 'What was that you said to me, Gran, when you first told me and Leo about the curse? That day in your kitchen, remember?' Her grandmother nodded, her gaze steady. 'You said the burden of defeating Gwydion and ending the curse had been passed to me, and to me alone.'

Gran smiled faintly. 'I remember.'

'Well, then. Nothing's changed. I killed Gwydion in this world, but that didn't properly end the curse. I left the King of Hearts under the lake where Ronan could summon it. And when we were in the other world and Gwydion *begged* me to kill him, I wouldn't, because I couldn't forgive him. I wanted him to suffer. And because Gwydion was still alive, Ronan didn't die, despite me filling his entire hall with black holly.' She shrugged. 'I've made mistakes, and now I'm paying the price, and that seems… fair. Tomorrow, I'll go to the lake and set things right. If I can.'

Everyone was staring at her. Everyone looked horrified. Apart from Jack. He was solemn, but there was something in his eyes: confidence? As she gazed at him he dipped his head, bowing slightly. It was a small gesture, but Merry knew what it meant. Of all the people in the room, Jack truly understood the meaning of duty, of sacrifice. And it would make it a little easier tomorrow, if she knew he at least was on her side.

Merry looked round the room. 'What about everyone else? I really need you guys to trust me.'

'I trust you, darling.' Gran's voice shook a little, but she kept her head held high. 'And I'm very proud of you.'

Merry swallowed hard.

'I'm proud of you too,' Mum huffed. 'But I still think we're rushing into this. It's not even as if we have a plan…'

'Mum. I have a plan.'

'What?'

Merry sighed. 'I. Have. A. Plan.'

'You do?'

Merry forced a smiled. 'Of course I bloody do. I wasn't going to just wing it, you know.'

'Oh.' Mum looked flummoxed. So did Finn, and pretty

much everyone else. 'Well. I suppose that's a little bit different.' Mum reached for her coffee again, and Merry could see that her mother's hands were shaking ever so slightly. 'But would you mind sharing it with the rest of us?'

'Sure,' said Merry, taking a deep breath. 'Why not?'

Not long after, Roshni and the rest of the coven arrived at the house, together with Finn's dad and some other Kin House members. Merry reluctantly ending up sharing her plan with them all, standing in the front as they crowded into the ballroom. Her face was hot, and she couldn't quite figure out what to do with her hands; public speaking wasn't really her thing. Also, the plan wasn't exactly fool-proof. There were definitely some holes in it.

'So,' said Roshni when Merry had finished, looking at her appraisingly. 'You're basically going to pretend to go along with what Ronan wants, so you can get close enough to Gwydion to stab him with a knife coated in black holly juice. And you think that once Gwydion is out of the way, so to speak, it will be possible to kill Ronan.' She rubbed her fingers along her jaw. 'There are a lot of variables. It's a gamble. But it could work.'

'It will work,' Jack announced decisively from the back of the crowd. 'It has to.'

'I don't like it.' Finn shook his head in response. 'It's really risky. You have to do too much on your own, and it relies heavily on Ronan not realising what you're up to. He's not an idiot.'

'I know that, but he is arrogant.'

'But you have no clear idea what he's going to make you do tomorrow. He might not even let you get close to Gwydion. And you'll be out there on your own…'

Merry had a suspicion about what Ronan was going to try to make her do. But she couldn't face talking about it in front of all these people.

'I won't be on my own. I'll have you guys behind me. Literally. If the plan doesn't work, then you'll just have to hit Ronan and his army with everything you've got. You all knew it might come to that.'

'Of course, none of us objects to doing our part, young lady,' Finn's dad interjected. Merry would have been cross if she hadn't been distracted by Finn rolling his eyes at him. 'However,' Mr Lombard continued, 'what happens if Ronan manages to drain you of your power? He would present a significantly greater challenge in those circumstances.'

Merry bit her lip. She'd spent a lot of time thinking about this, always coming up with the same unpalatable solution. 'Well, you'll have to find a way of… neutralising me, before Ronan can do that. Some kind of spell that would get through any barriers he might try to put up. Something he wouldn't be expecting. Maybe something we could enact in advance?' She almost laughed at herself. She couldn't believe she'd used the word 'neutralise': it sounded like something out of one of her favourite sci-fi films. But somehow, she couldn't quite bring herself to suggest out loud that her allies should kill her. She shivered a little. At least Leo wasn't there. He hadn't said a single word to her since she'd hit him with the protection spell, and now he'd taken himself off somewhere with Cormac…

'To neutralise you? Merry, do you even know what you're saying?' Mum was wringing her hands, almost crying. Finn attempted to pat her on the back, rather awkwardly, but Merry loved him for trying.

'Mum, of course I do. But you saw what state Gwydion is in. Better to die than be used as some kind of magical battery by Ronan. Better to die than be enslaved by him. Besides, it won't happen. You have to trust me.'

'Trust you? Merry, you're my child. As powerful as you are, you're not indestructible. And you're only seventeen. I can't lose you.'

'I know, Mum, but we need to be practical. We need a contingency plan.'

Mum shook her head. 'I'm sorry, Merry.' Her voice broke. 'I can't sit here and listen to this.' She stood up and hurried into the house.

With a nod from Gran, Lysandra ran after her.

Merry's chest ached with sadness. She glanced over at Finn, hoping for some comfort, but he looked just as distressed as her mother had done.

Thankfully, someone else stood up and started speaking. It was Mrs Knox. 'I have a suggestion. If I may.'

'Of course, Sophia,' said Gran, sighing. 'Go ahead.'

'I think we should create a doll. Another doll, I mean. One for Merry.'

'What? You can't be serious…' Finn interrupted, earning himself stony looks from Roshni and his dad.

'Go on, Sophia?' Gran leant forward.

'It would allow us to control the situation. If it looked like Merry was losing to Ronan, we could…' Mrs Knox hesitated, looking nervously from Merry to Gran. 'We could end it. Destroy the doll.'

Gran's face was bland, although Merry could see her hands gripping the arms of her chair. 'That would certainly work. But none of us knows exactly how to make such a doll. That knowledge has been forgotten, or hidden away over the centuries…'

'Not sure you're quite right about that.' Mrs Knox's face turned a deep shade of pink. 'I may know someone who can help. Possibly. And she can be here in an hour.'

'Right,' said Gran thoughtfully. 'In that case, you'd better invite this person over.'

Merry had hoped that she'd get a break while they were waiting on the mystery person – that maybe she and Finn could go for a coffee somewhere. But Gran had other plans. She'd asked the coven to put some additional protective spells on Merry, just in case. Merry wasn't sure they'd achieve much, but she understood Gran's motivation: the coven members wanted to help, to feel that they were doing something other than waiting for Merry to save them. Or not. So, Merry stood and let them sing over her, and mark her with runes, just like they'd done before she went to face Gwydion. At the end of it, as most of the coven dispersed, many of them hugged her. And even Helen wished her luck.

Mr Lombard had gone back to his hotel, taking Finn and Cormac with him (at least temporarily – they'd both asked already if they could stay at Merry's house that night), and he gave Mum a lift home too. Jack took off, promising her he'd see her at the lake; he wanted to scatter

Nia's ashes on the North Downs. Only Merry, Gran, Roshni and Mrs Knox were left. Just as well, since they were the only ones the mystery visitor would speak to.

The mystery person turned out to be Mrs Knox's niece, Tabitha, who worked as an assistant in the Archives: the place where all dark magic books were supposed to be stored. As soon as she arrived, she insisted on all the witches present swearing an unbreakable magical oath of secrecy.

'I'm sorry, but I simply can't afford for this to get back to the Archivists,' Tabitha said, for about the tenth time. 'I'm supposed to log any books that get found and put them into storage. I'm not supposed to take them home. And I'm definitely not supposed to learn how to do any of the magic in them.' Tabitha bit her bottom lip nervously. 'It's become a sort of hobby, really. But if anyone found out about what I've been doing…'

'But no one will, not now that we've each of us taken an oath,' Gran said. 'So there really isn't any need to worry, is there?'

Tabitha looked unconvinced. 'I do want to help, Mrs Foley. Aunt Sophia's told me about Ronan and what he's doing. But I love my job and I can't risk being reported to the Stewards.'

'Honestly, Tabitha,' said Mrs Knox, trying, but failing,

to keep the irritation out of her voice. 'No one here is going to report you. And if Ronan keeps the point of intersection open, there probably won't be any Archives for you to work at. So tell us what you know. Unless you want me to talk to your mother about your "hobby"?'

Tabitha blanched. 'No, no, I'll tell you.' She turned to Merry. 'It's not as complicated as you might think, actually, making a doll like the one Ronan has made for your brother. The incantation that I know of is a bit of a faff: it's in Gaelic, and it has lots of verses. And there are some fiddly bits in terms of the supplies, so to speak, the sequencing of events, and so forth.'

'What supplies do you need?'

'Something you really love. It can be an object you've owned for a long time, or even a photo of a person you love, though I think the person has to be dead, otherwise their energy messes the spell up. And then something with your DNA in it. A fingernail. Lock of hair. That sort of thing. Oh, and a doll to put it all into. The larger the better, if the spell-caster wants to be able to hurt specific parts of a person's body...'

Two hours later and a 'Merry' poppet doll had been created. Tabitha had supervised while Roshni, Mrs Knox and Gran performed the spell. The doll that they'd used was a hideous Victorian-style one that Merry's father had given to her years ago; she'd shoved it in the back of a cupboard and never played with it. Just looking at it made her shiver. Knowing that it had now been imbibed with a 'part of her spirit', as Tabitha put it, made it even creepier. Mrs Knox had 'volunteered' (at Gran's insistence) to look after the doll, and to take it into battle with Ronan tomorrow. They'd known each other for over fifty years; Gran knew she could trust Mrs Knox only to use the doll as a last possible resort, if Merry's plan failed.

'Not that you will fail, darling. I'm sure of that.'

'Thanks, Gran. I wish I felt as confident as you.'

'You don't need to be, Merry. I am confident enough for both of us.' Gran had hugged her tightly.

Now, Merry was sitting by herself in the garden back home. She and Mum, and Leo and Gran, had all left Mrs Knox's house after the doll was complete. It was quiet after the bustle of the morning. Restful.

Finn appeared, a glass of lemonade in his hand.

'You're back, then?' Merry asked.

'Yep. And Cormac. Dad got tired of us practising spells on each other. How are you doing?' He dropped a kiss on to the top of her head before sitting down in the garden chair opposite.

'OK. Knackered. Kind of wishing tomorrow would never come. But also wishing it was here already. I just want to get it over with.'

'I know what you mean.' Finn propped his chin in his hand, watching her. 'And once it is all over, I'd like to take you out to dinner. We've never had a proper date. I'm going to have to fix that.'

'What, take me somewhere flashy in that oh-so-subtle sports car of yours?'

'Absolutely,' Finn replied, grinning.

Merry grinned back at him, remembering the first time Finn had given her a lift in his shiny red two-seater. Leo, proud owner of an ancient black Peugeot, had not been impressed. Her smile faltered. 'A date would be good. Assuming I survive.'

Finn reached across and took Merry's hand. 'Don't say that. OK? Of course you're going to survive. I'm going to be with you, every step of the way. And so are your family and several covens of witches, by the looks of it. Not to mention most of my family and friends. You're not going to be on your own. You know that, right?'

'Yes. I know.' She squeezed his hand back.

Suddenly Finn was down on his knees in front of her, kissing her madly, hugging her so tightly that she almost couldn't breathe. Finally, they broke apart.

'Do me a favour, will you?'

Finn nodded, looking into her eyes. 'Anything.'

'Sleep in my room with me tonight. I don't want to be alone.'

Finn reached up and smoothed a strand of hair back behind her ear. 'Of course.' He kissed her again. 'I'm meant to be on one of the sofas in the living room with Cormac tonight, but it's not much of a sacrifice. He snores.'

Merry laughed and slapped him on the arm. 'Well, you'll have to be back down there before Mum gets up. Poor Cormac. I like him. Where is he?'

'Following Leo round like a mooncalf, as usual.' Finn sat on the bench next to her, slipping his arm round her waist. 'Cormac's crushing on your brother pretty hard.'

'Leo likes him too, I think. But this whole thing with Ronan...'

'I know. But Cormac's happy to play a long game. He's a really good guy.'

Merry lifted her face for one more kiss. 'I have to go and do stuff.'

'Secret plan stuff?'

'Partly. Also, Mum and me and Leo are going to pick up a takeaway from our favourite Chinese restaurant in Guildford. It's an hour round trip, but the food is so good…'

'I could have cooked something.'

'That's OK. I'm kind of looking forward to the drive, actually. You know. Quality time.'

He squeezed her arm. 'I understand. What about your gran? Can we do anything for her?'

'Leave her in peace to finish her book – I think those were her words. She's probably having a nap, to be honest, but you'd better not tell her I told you.'

'Fair enough. Off you go, then. Cormac and I will cope.'

'I'm sure you will.'

Mum and Leo were waiting for Merry in the kitchen. Merry hadn't spoken to her brother since she'd put the spell on him to stop him harming himself. She nudged him with her elbow.

'Hey. Are we OK?'

Leo shook his head. 'No. I'm still furious and I refuse to forgive you.' He smiled. 'I'm kidding. I *am* still furious. But of course, I forgive you.' He punched her softly on the shoulder.

'I'm glad. And don't worry about tomorrow. I'm going to finish Ronan off properly this time. He won't hurt either of us again. You'll see.' She smiled at him as brightly as she could, hoping she sounded more convinced than she felt. 'Have a little faith in me, OK?'

'I do have faith in you, Merry. You'll kick Ronan's backside. I know you will.' He turned to their mother. 'By the way, Mum: no kidnapping us and driving us to Northumberland this time. OK?'

Mum blushed. She didn't really like to be reminded of how she'd dragged them up to Northumberland in an attempt to keep Merry safe from Gwydion; it hadn't exactly gone to plan. 'OK. No kidnapping. Much as I'd love to.' She shook her car keys. 'Come on, then. I'd like to eat dinner at some point this evening.'

The drive to pick up the food was surprisingly relaxed. The three of them decided to pretend that tomorrow was already over, and talk about the future. Merry said she was going to go back to school, hang out with Ruby again and try being a normal teenager. Leo was considering taking up his place to study medicine in London, after a few more weeks' recovery time. Mum was planning a family holiday, somewhere hot. It was almost like old times, except that Merry could hardly remember the last time they'd all sat together and chatted like this. Pretending that everything was normal, at least for sixty minutes, was nice.

When they were nearly back home, Merry asked her mother to stop the car. She walked a little way into the woods, found a black holly tree – it wasn't difficult – and cut off the thickest branch she could find with Gran's obsidian knife.

They watched *Wonder Woman* while they ate dinner; it was Merry's choice.

Finally, it was time for bed. Merry waited until Mum, Gran and Leo had all gone up. Then she said goodnight to Cormac and went up to the bathroom, taking her time to shower and brush her hair. When she got into her room Finn was in her bed, waiting for her.

She didn't say anything when she saw him there, looking up at her. She simply crossed the room, got under the duvet and turned the light off. And then he held her, tightly wrapped in his arms, for the rest of the night.

NINETEEN

WHEN MERRY WOKE up, Finn had gone. She stretched out in her bed and glanced at the clock. Not long now before she had to get up. They had to be at the lake soon enough.

She slipped out of bed, wrapping the duvet round her shoulders. One other thing had occurred to her during the night. Going to her wardrobe, she pulled the trinket box out from the bottom shelf. The braid was on top; she tied that round her wrist. It had protected Merry from Gwydion before because it had been made from Queen Edith's hair and he'd sworn that he would never harm Edith — that was before she had refused to marry him, obviously. Merry had no real expectation that the braid would provide any protection from Ronan, but the feeling of it against her skin comforted her. Next, she took out the manuscript and spread it open on the floor. The directions it had given them in the other world, the route to Meredith's cottage, were still visible.

I guess this particular quest isn't over yet.

Merry cleared her throat.

'*Eala*, manuscript.'

The same word she'd spoken appeared on the page, in the same spidery handwriting.

'How can I stop Ronan?'

No response.

'How can I stop Gwydion?'

Still no response. Perhaps the manuscript had already told her everything it knew about that wizard. There was one more question she wanted to try.

'How can I mend the point of intersection?'

The writing began to spill across the paper again.

Give back to the land what you have taken from the land.

'But I haven't taken anything.' She racked her memory, but the only thing she could think of was her seashell collection, and that was long gone. 'Give back what?'

But the manuscript remained stubbornly blank. She

sighed and shoved it back into the trinket box. It was time to get dressed.

They arrived at the lake, singly and in groups, and ranged themselves along the remaining wards. Gran had decided they shouldn't repair the ward that Merry had destroyed; she reasoned that they needed to be able to fire some spells at Ronan to provide cover for Merry. As Merry walked forward to take her place, Gran caught hold of her hand.

'I won't be at the front, Merry. I haven't enough magic and I'm not strong enough. Cormac and I will stay back here again, to help with any injuries.'

Merry nodded. 'That's a good idea, Gran.' She kissed her on the cheek. 'I'll see you later.'

'OK, darling.'

Merry turned away and walked to where Mum, Leo and the others were waiting for her, wondering how long she would have to stand there until Ronan turned up.

But her enemy was punctual. Ronan had changed back into modern clothes: jeans and a T-shirt. He grinned at her, his eyes twinkling, looking so much like the guy who'd helped Leo into the house two months ago that Merry's stomach churned with the horror of it all.

Beside her and around her she heard murmurs of dismay. Ronan was surrounded by his bodyguards, or court, or whatever he called them. Elves and blank-eyed humans, captured by Ronan in the other world and possessed by the King of Hearts. Witches and wizards from the other world who supported Ronan, all of them branded with his sign, the same rune he'd burnt into Leo's chest. Merry gasped as she recognised Denise among them, the mark defacing her skin still a livid red. So many more than had been at the lake before. He had brought an army with him.

'Merry,' Ronan stepped forward. 'I'm glad you've seen sense.' He clicked his fingers and the ranks of his followers parted. Men came forward, carrying what looked like a long tree trunk. Merry could see it had been carved all over, just like the chair Gwydion had kept in the room beneath the tower. Ronan waved his hand, sketching a rune in the air, pale and barely visible against the lightening sky. The ground shook as the wooden column buried itself up to its middle in the earth. The crowd parted again and elves appeared, dragging Gwydion between them, just as they had dragged Meredith. As they began chaining the wizard to the column, Ronan held his hand out to Merry.

'Shall we get this over with?'

'Not yet.' She scanned the crowd of people in front of her: Meredith was there, held fast between two elves but still alive. Still standing. 'There is one condition.'

Ronan raised an eyebrow. 'You're in no position to be making demands.' He waved a hand towards one of his dead-eyed servants, who had the Leo-doll in one hand, and a long needle in the other. 'If any of you moves without my say-so, poor Leo dies.'

'There is one condition,' Merry repeated.

Ronan forced a laugh. 'Fine. What do you want?'

'In return for my cooperation, you have to give up Meredith.'

'And why would I do that?'

Swallowing hard, Merry pressed on. 'Because if you refuse, I'll kill Leo myself. And then I'll come after you.'

The smile faded from Ronan's face. His gaze switched to Leo, who was standing, pale but calm, between Roshni and Mum, and then slid across to the doll. 'You'd never do it,' he sneered. 'Kill your own brother?'

Merry pressed on, ignoring the question. 'Give up Meredith, and I'll surrender my power to you. Willingly. And I know how much you want it…' She tried to relax, to allow the power trapped underneath her skin to expand outwards, hoping that Ronan would be able to sense it more clearly. It seemed to work: he quivered, eyes half closed, running his tongue quickly over his lips.

'Very well. You can have the witch.' Ronan glanced at Jack. 'I took most of her power. And she's injured, and almost certainly beyond a cure. I suppose His Majesty there may as well get to hold her as she dies.'

Jack made a guttural sound in the back of his throat, and Merry could see the tendons of his hand sticking out as he gripped his sword hilt. But he didn't break the line.

Ronan gestured to the guards holding Meredith, and they hustled her towards the broken-down section of the ward. His lips moved as he murmured an incantation, and the iron manacles round her wrists fell away. 'Meredith, you're free to go.'

Her eyes found Jack, and she took a halting step towards him. Then another, and another, until she was staggering as fast as she could through the gap. Jack held on until she was clear of the wards, then ran towards her, scooped her up in his arms and hurried to where Gran and Cormac were waiting. Merry watched, until she saw him lower Meredith on to the ground, with Cormac kneeling next to her, then turned back to face Ronan. Cold sweat was running down her back. She concentrated on the weight of the knife, hidden with an invisibility spell and concealed in her pocket, crushing her fingers into her fists so that no one would see them trembling.

'Now, Merry.' Ronan was grinning again. 'Time for your side of the bargain. I hope you've said your goodbyes?'

She nodded. Behind her, Mum murmured her name, half sobbing. Merry closed her eyes briefly, clamping her lips shut. But she didn't dare look back.

Forward. I've got to go forward.

She began walking, very aware of the muscles in her legs flexing, of the blood pounding through her veins.

I can do this. I can.

Ronan's grin grew wider. 'That's it. Quickly now.'

Merry sped up. Another few seconds and she was past the ward and Ronan was only a metre away. She stopped.

'Good.' He closed the gap between them. 'Now, kneel.'

'No, I—'

Ronan glanced at the servant holding the doll, nodding slightly, and behind her Merry heard her brother cry out in pain. She dropped to her knees, wincing as she landed awkwardly on the uneven turf. Ronan held his hand in front of her face. There was a large gold and sapphire ring on his middle finger. She kissed it.

'Ah, obedience is a wonderful thing.' He grabbed her upper arm, hauled her upright again and dragged her to where Gwydion was chained to the wooden column. Up close, the wizard looked even worse. There were weeping fissures running across his skin, his eyelashes and eyebrows had fallen out, and he stank: like meat gone bad. As Merry grimaced and turned her face away, Ronan just laughed and pushed her closer. 'Now, you two have met before, so we can skip the introductions. Merry, have you guessed yet what I want you to do?'

Merry shook her head, trying not to breathe through her nose.

'I want you to kill him. I want you to take this knife,' Ronan pulled a dark metal knife out of his belt, 'and I want you to cut out his heart.'

Gwydion began to shout inarticulately, stifled by the gag in his mouth. Merry stared at him, mesmerised by the horror in his eyes. Everything about him made her skin crawl, but she couldn't look away.

Ronan was watching her. 'Not feeling sorry for him, surely?'

'No. I killed the version of him that lived in this world.' Her mouth was dry; she ran her tongue across her lips. 'This Gwydion is from the other world, but I want to kill him too. He is at the root of everything. He is to blame for all of this. For the destruction of everything I love. I want…' She gritted her teeth. 'I want to rip out his heart. I want to watch his blood flow across my hands.'

'Yes…' Ronan's eyes were bright. 'I knew you were like me, deep down. There's a shadow that lies across your soul.' She could hear his breathing: fast, and uneven. 'This will be better. Much better.' Pressing the knife into her right hand, wrapping her fingers round the hilt and holding them there, he leant closer, whispering. 'Don't resist the darkness, Merry. Embrace it. Surrender willingly. Kill him, and eat his heart and give yourself to the King of Hearts, to the shadow realm. Perhaps it will not destroy you, as it has Gwydion. You can rule with me, instead. All the power, all the freedom you want. And you won't even have to prick your finger on a spinning wheel…'

Merry stiffened. 'That was you that I dreamt about? You put those thoughts in my head?'

'You flatter me. The inclination, the desire − that was already there. I just spun it into a dream.'

Merry felt her face burning, felt the eyes of everyone behind her boring into her back.

Just breathe. He can put stuff into my mind. Doesn't mean he can take stuff out. Otherwise he'd have stopped me by now.

Unless he's playing me.

Another heartbeat passed.

Could he be playing me?

Ronan stepped back again, and there was no time left to worry. 'Now, Merry. No more delaying.' He nodded at the man with the doll, and again Leo moaned in anguish. Merry jerked forward as if she'd been stung, bringing the knife up in front of her. Gwydion was struggling, trying to twist away from the approaching blade. But the iron chains held him fast. She edged closer until she was pressing the point of the blade against Gwydion's clothing. Gripping the worn fabric in her left hand she half cut, half tore away a long strip of material, laying his skin bare.

'That's right,' Ronan hissed. 'Now slice through his flesh.'

Gwydion groaned, half fainting, his eyes rolling back in his head. Merry adjusted her grip on the hilt. Bringing her left hand down to her side, she dropped the piece of cloth and slid Gran's obsidian knife out of her pocket at the same time as raising her right hand, as if to strike down with the blade. She ran over the first few words of a summoning charm in her head.

Out of the corner of her right eye she could see Ronan, his eyes wide, glittering. And the servant holding the doll was just a little further off.

This was it.

Her power was thrumming, vibrating deep in the centre

of her core, driving out fear and uncertainty, drowning every sensation apart from the ache in her fingertips. The magic wanted to be used, to be set free.

She couldn't draw back now. Not even if she'd wanted to.

With one movement, Merry slashed Gwydion across the chest with the poisoned obsidian blade and twisted, bringing the knife in her right hand round, slamming it into Ronan's thigh and leaving it there. While he shrieked and staggered, Merry sang the first line of the summoning spell: the doll hurtled through the air into her open palm.

Ronan had fallen to one knee and was trying to yank the knife out of his leg, screaming at his servants to attack.

But it was too late. Merry had dropped the obsidian knife and now she was singing a shielding spell, the same type she'd used at the lake before when she'd protected Leo from Ronan. The silver filaments poured from her fingertips, encircling her and Gwydion. Ronan got back on his feet and began sending spell after spell searing through the air between them – fire runes and hexes and curses Merry had never seen before – striking the shimmering net over and over.

Between the net she'd cast and the spells Ronan was using, Merry couldn't see much beyond the point where

Ronan was standing. But she heard a shout go up from the coven and the others on their side – Finn and Jack yelling, urging those nearby to attack – a roar of defiance from Ronan's elves, and the witches and wizards who followed him. And all the time Ronan kept up his assault, trying to find a way round her defences. But the barrier held.

Finally, as the shouting and fighting and the clash of spells behind him intensified, Ronan let his hands fall. He was breathing hard, and Merry could see blood soaking through his jeans.

'You won't win, Merry. You still stabbed him. He'll be dead soon, and the thing inside him is loyal to me. *I* released it from under the lake. *I* gave it form again.' His gaze drifted down to Merry's feet. 'And you won't be able to stay behind that shield forever, freak.'

Merry glanced down. Within the circle of the net the grass was intact. But, where the silver threads met the earth, it had changed: turned to the same tiny, crystalline shards she'd seen before. In places even these were disappearing, melting into molten glass that was running in rivulets across the scorched ground beneath.

'You're right. But I don't need forever. He's not going to die.'

Ronan gave a shout of disbelief. 'You stuck the knife in him. I saw you.'

'I scratched him. The blade was coated in poison from black holly. All I needed to do was get it into his system.' She glanced at Gwydion. His head was hanging forward, and she could see his eyelids fluttering. 'He'll be asleep soon. The sleep that no one ever wakes from. Sleeping and sleeping and slowly, gradually, withering. Eventually he'll die. But by then, the thing inside him will have withered and died too. It's trapped, Ronan. And this time it's going to stay trapped until it has faded into nothingness.'

'No…' Ronan stared down at his hands. The man standing nearby, the one who had been holding the doll, fell to his knees and slowly toppled sideways. 'No!'

All around, the other enslaved humans collapsed like trees felled at the roots.

Merry's heart raced. She was right: Gwydion was a – a *conduit*, a gateway between the shadow realm and the human world, and without him, without the King of Hearts, Ronan's access to the power of the shadow realm was cut off. He was vulnerable. He could be killed.

'It's finished, Ronan. You won't be able to hurt my brother any more—'

She could have bitten off her tongue. Ronan blinked,

as if he'd forgotten about Leo's existence. He stared at the doll, still lying at her feet, and then looked away towards the gap in the wards.

'You might be right.' He grinned at her. 'But then again…' Backing away, he began writing fire runes in the air. A sheet of flame erupted from the ground in front of him. Even behind the silver net Merry could feel the heat; she threw her hands up, shielding her face, squinting at the place where Ronan was standing.

Had been standing. He'd vanished.

TWENTY

RONAN HAD GONE, and he obviously still had enough residual power to keep casting spells. To hurt Leo.

Damn it –

There was an elf nearby, watching her with its head tilted to one side, a spear raised in one hand, seemingly untroubled by the fire Ronan had conjured or by the ring of scorched earth gradually creeping outwards from the silver net. Merry picked up Gran's knife – carefully – and stashed it back in her pocket. The doll... There was no way she could safely dismantle the spell. She frowned and bit her lip. It would probably be safer to leave it here, behind the net. No one else would be able to get to it, unless she was killed.

Guess I'd better not get killed.

The elf was still watching her. And Ronan's fire was still burning…

Merry remembered the lake, and the springs that had surrounded this place before the lake. There was water somewhere, down beneath her feet. And she knew how to use water.

She began singing a summoning spell. Her eyes were fixed on the elf, keeping its attention. But in her head, she was thinking about water pressure, and bottomless wells.

There was a rumbling sound from below ground. The elf frowned and slowly knelt, pressing one hand against the grass. When it looked up at Merry again its eyes and mouth were wide, and it jumped up to run—

But it was too late. Water spurted high in the air as the earth cracked open. The elf stumbled and fell into the rapidly widening chasm, and the ground where Ronan's fire was burning collapsed into the void after it. There was a hiss and a dense white fog drifted upwards, hanging in the air for a moment before melting away on the breeze.

Merry waved her hand and a gap opened in the silver

net. Backing up as far as she could, she sprinted towards the newly formed chasm and jumped across it, rolling as she hit the ground and scrambling upright. The net had closed instantly: Gwydion, and the Leo-doll, were both protected within it. But from here she could see the damage to the grass – the still unexplained crystallisation. Her spell to get rid of the elf and the fire had made it much worse. The breach in the point of intersection was worse too: the other world was clearly visible now, even closer than before. She sighed; Gwydion's loss of consciousness hadn't solved either of those problems. But maybe killing Ronan would.

The fighting was concentrated around the gap in the wards, but she couldn't see Ronan from here. She started to run.

There was Jack, blade flashing in the dawn light, fighting two elves. There were Finn and his dad, hurling spells against two robed wizards from the other world. As Merry watched, Edward Lombard cried out, his skin erupting in bloody hives, but Roshni came out of nowhere and hit one of the wizards with a ball of witch fire. There was Mrs Galantini, and Lysandra, but there was no sign of Mum or Leo. And where was Mrs Knox?

Merry spotted her: white-faced, her hands raised and

lips moving silently in what Merry guessed was a shielding spell. Behind Mrs Knox, gripping his sword in both hands, was Leo. And in front of her, writing a fresh fire rune in the air, stood Ronan.

'Get away from my brother!'

Ronan swung round and flung the fire rune in her direction. Swiftly Merry murmured a counter spell, but Ronan was close to her and the fire rune was strong; the force as the two spells collided knocked her backwards even as the fire rune itself crackled away into the air.

She pushed herself on to her hands and knees, shaking her head, trying to clear it. Ronan was still sprawled on his back.

'Merry!' It was Gran, panic in her voice. Merry looked up. Denise was there, a black mist spilling out from her fingers, swirling and coiling in on itself. Merry raised her hands and sent a binding charm at the other witch, followed immediately by a stinging hex. Denise blocked the first spell but the second hit her square on and she fell backwards, squirming and moaning. Merry grinned and stood up, turning to tell Gran that it was OK, that she didn't need to worry—

Too late, she saw Ronan, back on his feet.

She saw the fire rune, less than a metre away from her.

And Gran, throwing herself in the path of the spell…

The fire rune hit, knocking Gran backwards into Merry's arms.

'Gran!' Merry gabbled out a shielding spell and looked down at her hand: it was covered in blood. There was blood all over Gran's blouse, blood mixed with a thick black liquid.

'Gran – Gran,' Merry shook her grandmother by the shoulder, pressing her other hand against the bleeding wound in her chest, trying to remember or construct some spell to reverse what had happened. But the blood kept flowing, welling up between her fingers, staining her nails red. 'Somebody, help me! Where's Cormac? Gran, please…'

Gran lifted one hand to grasp Merry's wrist. 'It's OK, baby angel.' She sounded like a faint echo of herself; Merry leant closer. 'It's OK, Merry. No one gets to live forever, not even me.' Her eyelids fluttered. 'But I've realised. You have to heal…' Her voice faded.

'Gran, I don't understand!' Roshni was on her knees next to her, pushing her out of the way, spitting out spells as fast as she could. Where was Cormac?

Gran's grip on Merry's wrist tightened. 'Heal the land, my darling. You have to…' She gasped and winced, '…you have to give back, give back to the land…' Her arm fell to her side.

'Don't die, Gran, you can't die. Please. Please.' Tears blurred Merry's vision. 'Please.'

Gran smiled faintly 'Be strong, Merry. Be—' Her whole body stiffened. Roshni began hurling spells at her, screaming them out –

The rigidity passed, and Gran's head fell back.

'Gran?'

No response, no pulse. She was dead.

Roshni slumped forward, silent, resting her head against Gran's chest. Nearby, a woman's voice – Mrs Knox? – began chanting something in Latin. A spell, or a prayer – Merry didn't know, or care. She had to find Mum, and Leo. She had to tell them…

Someone was laughing. A horrible, grating, hysterical cackle.

Ronan.

Merry got to her feet. Witch fire ignited in both her palms, the globes surrounding her hands, amethyst tendrils running all the way up her arms. Gritting her teeth, she began to run at Ronan.

His laughter faded and stopped. He began to back away, casting fire runes at her – hexes – curses – blocking spells.

But Merry threw the witch fire at everything in front of her, incinerating his incantations faster than he could cast them, burning them up in sheets of violet flame as if they were nothing more than wisps of paper caught in a bonfire. From the corner of her eye she could see Finn and his dad and other witches and wizards still casting spells at those of Ronan's supporters who hadn't yet retreated towards the other world. She spotted Jack, swinging his sword round in a wide arc and slicing the head of an elf away from its body. Then Roshni was next to her, and Mrs Knox, and other coven members, hitting Ronan with spell after spell, forcing him to exhaust his power.

Ronan's spells were getting weaker as the magic that the King of Hearts had given him started to run out. He was sweating and gasping, his arms were covered in gashes, and there was a burn down one side of his face, puckering the skin.

'Go on, then,' he screamed at her. 'Take your revenge, if you can. It won't bring her back.' He half smirked, half grimaced in pain. 'It won't bring any of them back.'

He was right, of course. What he and Gwydion had done, between them... Even when the other world disappeared, and the point of intersection was repaired, the people who had died wouldn't return. Nothing would be the same. The same as it had been, or the same as it might have been. Ronan cast another spell at her, and again she batted it away.

'It's over, Ronan. The power you took from the shadow realm won't last much longer. Give up.'

'Give up? You want me to make it easy for you?' He spat at her. 'You're going to have to kill me.' A witch, one of Ronan's supporters, was lying injured on the ground nearby. He gripped her head, digging his fingernails into her face, and she started writhing and screaming and Merry realised he was stealing the woman's magic, just like he'd taken Gran's magic, and Flo's…

No. This has to end.

She began running towards him again, summoning her own power, bringing it to the surface. Her nails throbbed and the skin on her arms stung so much that tears came to her eyes. She blinked them away in time to see Ronan drop the woman's body. He ignited witch fire in his hands, raised his arms and began singing an amplifying spell –

Merry launched her magic towards him in a stream of white sparks, letting it engulf him, letting it do whatever it wanted. The magic surrounded Ronan, extinguishing his witch fire and overwhelming him, hiding him from view. Beneath Merry's feet the ground was glowing and cracking, and Ronan was screaming in agony, shrieking like an animal caught in a trap… but Merry didn't care. She concentrated on the power flowing through her hands, embracing the pain in her nails because the more it hurt, the more damage she was doing to Ronan.

The screaming stopped. And Merry realised it had stopped because Ronan was nearly dead. She could feel his magic fading – vanishing – and she let her hands fall to her side. The air began to clear, and she could see that where Ronan had been, there was now a statue.

She'd turned him into glass.

The statue still looked like a man: a man kneeling on the ground, his hands up over his head, his face contorted in pain. It was like something in an art gallery. Horrifying, yet beautiful at the same time; translucent, bathed in the early-morning light. Merry turned her head away. She couldn't bear to look at it, to look at him, for one more second. Raising her arms again, Merry cast a shielding spell round the statue. Ronan had hurt enough people while he lived; she wasn't about to let him hurt anyone now he was dead. Then she conjured a final ball of witch fire, and hurled it at the statue.

The fire hit.

The statue glowed purple-white, and exploded.

Nothing was left of Ronan, apart from a fine crystalline powder, glistening, drifting downwards on to the scorched earth.

He was gone. It was over.

Merry took a deep breath, trying to control the trembling in her limbs.

It is over, isn't it?

She turned in a circle, peering at the land around her. Ronan was dead. Everything should start to turn back to normal, back to the way it had been.

But the other world was still there. Still. Merry could see it, could see the jagged edges of the broken gateway.

Why hadn't it gone away?

Jack was nearby, sword still drawn, the body of a dead elf at his feet. He limped over to Merry.

'You're injured,' Merry said.

'It's a scratch, nothing more.' He stared at the lake. 'Why is it still here? Why are *we* still here?' He gestured to the elves and the witches and wizards marked with Ronan's sign. Some were still fighting, but more were fleeing towards the breach.

'I don't know. Gran said I had to heal the land, to give something back. And the manuscript said the same thing, but I don't know what that even means...' Merry directed

388

a binding charm towards a witch from the other world who was still fighting one of the Kin House wizards, sending her sprawling. 'Gwydion's asleep, so there's no more access to the shadow realm. And Ronan is definitely dead. I have all this power, but I don't know what else I'm supposed to do.'

'I do.' It was Meredith. She was still pale, and there was a fresh bandage round her head, but her colour was better. In response to Merry's raised eyebrows she smiled slightly. 'The young wizard, Cormac, is a fine healer. He may be a great one, in time.' Her smile faded. 'But the sickness that lies upon the land is beyond his reach. And it is my fault.'

Jack brushed Meredith's hair away from her face. 'It's not your fault. It was Ronan who broke the gateway, who planned to make this… bridge, between the worlds.'

'True.' Meredith shrugged slightly. 'But I am the reason the land cannot heal itself now that Ronan is destroyed. In this world, I made the oath to destroy Gwydion. I tied my bloodline, and all of my descendants, to the land.' Her gaze flicked back to Merry. 'I am the one to blame.'

'What?' Merry dragged the back of one hand across her eyes. She was too tired for people to be talking in riddles. 'What exactly are you saying?'

Meredith's voice was full of sorrow. 'I swore the oath

on this land.' She pointed at the ground. 'I swore on the bones and the soul of it. I bound the oath to the land, and I bound you to the oath, and that is where your power comes from.' She sighed. 'You draw it directly from the land, and you have taken too much.'

Merry stared at the earth beneath her feet. She'd felt the power of the land when she'd first used the point of intersection to follow Ronan and Leo. She'd felt it, she'd harnessed it, and she'd assumed that everyone was able to do the same...

Roshni had told her she was killing the land. And Ronan kept telling her that he and she were alike.

Is that why things have been turning to glass: because I've been sucking the land dry? Stealing magic from it, just as Ronan stole from other witches?

'You have to put it back, Merry.' Meredith touched Merry's cheek gently. 'Or at least try...'

Merry nodded.

I think I know what to do. Please, let it work.

She turned. 'Roshni?' The other witch was there instantly. 'I'm going to try something else to heal the point of intersection. I don't know what's going to happen, so you and the others have to protect Gwydion, keep him here.' She pointed towards the net she'd spun, still sparkling in the sunlight. 'And the doll – the thing Ronan was using – that's there too –'

'I understand.' Roshni took Merry's hands in hers, gasping as Merry's magic flowed across her skin. 'Do what you need to, and we will take care of everything else.' Roshni stepped away and began organising the other witches and wizards.

Merry turned to Jack and Meredith. 'If this works... I guess you won't be here any more.'

'We will return through the gateway to our own land, before you make your attempt,' said Meredith, looking worriedly at the lake. 'It will be safer.'

'Will you be able to fix what Ronan did there?'

'In time, I hope.' Meredith smiled at Jack. 'A good king can work wonders, or so I've heard.'

Jack flushed a little. 'I hope to earn that title, one day.' He dropped his free hand on to Merry's shoulder. 'Thank you again, Merry. You've rid us of Ronan and Gwydion, and we will not forget you. I will not forget you.'

Merry's breath caught in her throat. She leant forward and kissed Jack's cheek, and then Meredith's. 'Stay safe, both of you. I'll miss you.' There was nothing else to say. As Jack lifted Meredith into his arms, Merry began to run back towards the lake.

She reached the water and then jogged for a little along the edge of the lake; whether to find an easily accessible spot, or to put off what she had to do, she wasn't sure. When she came to a flat space where the land jutted into the lake, she stopped and looked back. There was no sign of Jack and Meredith. They'd gone, returned to the other world.

There was no reason to delay any longer.

Merry lay on the ground at the edge of the lake and thrust her arms into the water as far as she could reach. The coolness felt good: it soothed her sore skin and aching nails. Through the murk, she could see her hands glowing faintly. The aura of magic gilded her skin a glimmering gold-green.

But there was no time left to wonder at the beauty of what she was about to give up. Closing her eyes, she let go. She imagined her power flowing out of her pores, flowing into the water like blood. And there, in response, was a gentle, drawing pressure, like something sucking softly at her fingertips. The hum of the magic began to subside. It faded from beneath her skin, contracting into her body. It vanished from her veins, so she could no longer sense it pulsing through her limbs and organs. It slid away from her bones. And all the time she could feel the pull of the lake against her hands.

Twisting her head, she peeked out from beneath her lashes. It was working: she could see the hole between the worlds closing, collapsing in on itself. The people and creatures from the other world who were still left here were being dragged into the fissure like they'd been picked up by a hurricane.

Her magic was almost gone now. All that was left was a small, bright ball of power, pulsating in the centre of her chest – the magic that was hers alone, unconnected with Meredith's oath, or the generations of witches who had worked to make Merry into a weapon that could finally defeat Gwydion. But the gap in the gateway hadn't yet closed completely. And the lake was still tugging at her fingers.

Did she have to give up everything? Could she not keep just a fraction of magic for herself?

Can I not be a witch any more?

Gran's voice echoed in her head, something she'd said to her earlier in the year: *Did you think the craft was just something to be used, Granddaughter? That it was an easy way of getting what you wanted? That there would never be a price to pay?*

Merry swallowed. Perhaps this was how it had to be. Perhaps this was the only way to get to the point where everybody lived happily ever after.

She took a deep breath, screwed her eyes shut, and pushed.

There was a loud rushing sound. Merry looked up in time to see the breach between the worlds shrink down and shrink down until it was a tiny black dot…

And then it was gone. There was grass beneath her – proper, green grass, none of it crystallised or burnt away – and the lake glittered in the early-morning sun.

It was – truly, finally – over.

Merry shuffled back from the edge of the water. Her body was shaking, like she'd just run a marathon; actually getting up and walking was out of the question. Instead, she lay on her front, head resting on one arm. There was nothing more for her to do. Nothing more she could do. It hurt to think about that right now so she concentrated on the prickle of the grass beneath her skin, on the earthy scent of the ground, on the nearby voices growing in volume as the coven and everyone else began to realise…

It's over, it's over.

Someone was calling her name, and there were footsteps getting closer.

Merry rolled on to her back.

Denise stood over her. Still here, still alive, and holding

a sprig of black holly above Merry's head. She raised her arm, her lips pulled back into a grimace—

A sword blade erupted through the witch's stomach. The grimace faded, her face slackened. And the holly slipped from Denise's grasp.

'Merry, shielding spell!' It was Leo, shouting at her.

He doesn't know…

Merry put her hand up automatically, batting the holly away from her face. But one of the long, silver spines sliced open the tip of her finger.

'Merry, no…' Leo was kneeling next to her. He scooped her up into his arms, yelling for help, and grabbed her injured hand. 'Hold on, I'll suck the poison out—'

'No.' Merry pulled her hand away. Her eyelids were heavy; the venom was quick. Like general anaesthetic… There was water on her face: Leo, crying. 'Don't.' Her voice sounded far away in her own ears, and she wondered if her brother could hear her. 'Don't cry.' The light was fading, and Leo seemed far off, as if she was being sucked away from him down a dark tunnel. He was shouting at her, something about fight, or fighting… She tried to move her hand up to his face, to make her mouth work, to tell him that she loved him, to tell him goodbye…

But the paralysis was complete, and the darkness was

rushing up to swallow her, flowing into her eyes, her ears, her nose, her mouth, until the air had gone and she was drowning in night.

Drowning,

drowning,

drowning…

TWENTY-ONE

'**M**UM?' **LEO SHOOK** his mother's shoulder gently. 'Mum, you should go to bed.' It was early in the morning, but Mum had sat up all night in the chair next to Merry's bed. She must have fallen asleep at some point, but her hand was still draped across Merry's arm. 'Mum?'

His mother yawned and rubbed her eyes. 'What's the time?'

'About seven.'

'Only seven?' Her voice was flat and thin, and kind of raspy. All the crying; Leo had heard her, in the middle of the night. The blanket had slipped off her knees; she pulled it back up again, grasping Merry's wrist tightly, her hand covering the braid of hair that was still tied there.

He swallowed the lump in his own throat. 'Seriously, Mum, you need to get some proper rest. Let me take over now.' Mum still hesitated, chewing on her bottom lip. 'If you don't get some sleep then you won't be any good when she does wake up, when there's actually something to do.'

His mother nodded slowly. 'I suppose you're right.' She stood, clutching the blanket in her hands, avoiding Leo's gaze. 'And you'll stay here with her?'

'Of course.'

'OK. I'll, um…' She sighed and gestured at the door. 'Wake me, if anything changes.' She left, still not looking at him. No surprise there: Mum wanted to cling on to hope. Leo doubted there was any hope left in his eyes.

He settled himself in the chair and stared at his sister. She was asleep, supposedly. But surely sleep shouldn't look so like death? Her chest was rising and falling, but the gaps between one out-breath and the next in-breath were so long that Leo questioned every time whether the last breath was in fact *the last*. Her skin was bone white, apart from two spots of colour on her cheekbones, as if she were running a fever despite the chill that lay across her limbs. The cut on her finger from the holly thorn had been cleaned and dressed with healing salves again and again. But it was still open. Still bleeding.

'Why, Merry?' Why hadn't she shielded herself from the black holly? Why hadn't she magicked it away before it could touch her? He'd lost count of the number of times he'd asked that question over the last two weeks, but there had never been an answer. The tray with bandages, antiseptic wipes and salve was on the desk; Leo fetched it and began changing the dressing on Merry's finger. 'We held Gran's funeral a few days ago.'

Gran's funeral had been the third one that week. Lots of people had been there: all of the surviving coven members, witches from other covens, Kin House wizards. One of the Stewards had turned up to tell Roshni – better late than never – that no action would be taken against Merry. As though it would have made any difference now. The bodies of the people from the other world – except for Gwydion – had disappeared when Merry had sealed the breach. Presumably they'd been returned to the other world. The dead from the Kin Houses and from other covens had been taken back to their homes. Too much death, and too many funerals, over the last few months; enough for a lifetime.

But perhaps, there still needed to be one death more. Leo moved the tray and straightened the covers that lay over Merry's body, studying her face closely, as he had done for hours and hours of every day since they'd brought her back to the house. No sign there of consciousness, of any emotion. But how could he be sure? It was eternal sleep – that was what Roshni had told him; though that was an exaggeration. The natural processes were almost entirely suspended so that death took decades, or more than decades, to come. It was an immeasurably slow disintegration. He couldn't watch that happen to his sister.

And not even Roshni knew what was going on inside Merry's head. Was Merry dreaming? Black holly was a thing of the shadow realm, so Leo could more easily imagine horrific nightmares than pleasant fantasies. Or was she still awake, somewhere deep inside? Paralysed, but aware? Leo swallowed hard.

There was a knock on the door.

'Come in.'

Finn slouched into the room, his hands jammed in the pockets of his jeans. Finn's dad had gone home after Gran's funeral, but Finn and Cormac had both decided to stay on in Tillingham for the time being. They were spending the best part of each day at the house and going back to the hotel to sleep, though judging by the way Finn looked, he wasn't really sleeping.

'Any change?' Finn asked.

Leo shook his head. 'Cormac said he was trying out something new, yesterday…'

'It didn't work.'

Leo's stomach cramped as the last sliver of hope – the hope he'd been pretending not to have, for fear of the pain of losing it – shrivelled up and died.

The wizard slumped on a beanbag in the corner, staring at Merry, and Leo wondered if he was thinking about his brother.

'Finn, can I ask you something?'

'Sure.'

'When Cillian died…' Leo broke off, unsure how to phrase the question. It had only happened a few weeks ago, after all.

Finn dropped his head into his hands briefly. When he looked up, his eyes were glazed with tears. 'You want to know how I felt?'

Leo nodded.

Finn's gaze switched back to Merry. 'Lots of things. I felt like part of me had died. Like I'd failed him. Like my old life had ended, and that I was leaving my brother behind... It sounds ridiculous, but I had this very clear image: me in a boat, being carried away on the current of a river, and him standing on the riverbank, getting smaller and smaller until he disappeared from view.' He sniffed. 'And I felt guilty. Because I was relieved.' Finn's cheeks flushed. 'I was relieved that I wouldn't have to worry about him any more, or search for a cure, or go through the endless cycle of hope and disappointment.' He shook his head, half laughing. 'Hope springs eternal, and you can't bloody stop it.'

Leo nodded again, hoping to show Finn that he understood, that he sympathised. 'So...' He paused.

'Go on,' Finn prompted.

'So, if you had the ability to bring him back to life, but he would still be in the coma – you'd do that?'

Finn sighed and gripped his left wrist tightly. 'No. I'd give every atom of magic in my body to see my brother again, even for a moment. But despite being a selfish jerk, I don't think it would be fair. Lying there like he was...' He shook his head. 'Cillian wasn't living. He was just existing. He was trapped. And I wouldn't want to drag him back to that. He might be somewhere better now. I hope he is.'

'And hope springs eternal?'

'Yeah.' The wizard rubbed his face again. 'Why did you want to know?'

Leo shrugged. 'Just trying to think stuff through.' He stood up and stretched. 'I'm going to make some tea. You OK to stay here with Merry for a bit? Do you want something to drink?'

'Of course. And a coffee, please.'

Leo headed downstairs, kneading the muscles in the back of his neck. The kitchen was empty; Mum must have taken his advice and gone to bed. He filled the kettle up and switched it on, went to the cupboard to get out a couple of mugs—

'Hey, Leo.'

'Jesus, Cormac!' Leo knelt to pick up the broken pieces of pottery – the wizard had materialised in the corner of the kitchen. 'Seriously, can you just ring the doorbell next time?'

'Sorry, sorry. Here, let me get that…' Cormac murmured a spell and the scattered ceramic fragments swirled up off the floor into a tightly packed sphere. Leo took the lid off the kitchen bin and Cormac dumped the sphere into it with a flick of his hand. 'Sorry.'

'It's OK.' Leo's heart rate subsided. 'Um, Finn's upstairs.

I was just going to make us some drinks. You want something?'

'Tea, please.' Cormac reached out and touched Leo's shoulder lightly. 'How are you?'

Leo shrugged as he turned away to get some more cups out. 'You know. The marks on my chest have faded completely now, so that's good.'

'Yeah.' Cormac cleared his throat. 'Did Finn tell you? The antidote for black holly poison that I was working on last night—'

'He told me it wasn't working.' Leo leant on the counter and looked at the wizard. Cormac was biting the skin at the base of his thumbnail, his hair sticking up at odd angles like he'd run his hands through it far too many times. 'It's not your fault. I know you've been doing everything you can.' It was the truth: Cormac had been amazing over the last few days. He'd made healing potions for the injured, sleeping potions for those who couldn't sleep, and he'd spent every spare moment trying to find a way to wake Merry up. And he'd looked after Leo and Finn when they were too overwhelmed by grief to look after themselves. Leo held his hand out, and Cormac took two strides forward to grasp it tightly. 'Honestly, Cormac, if anyone's at fault, it's me.'

'That's not true.'

'It is. I saw Denise going after Merry. I should have got Finn or Roshni or somebody to chuck a spell at her. I shouldn't have tried to play the hero.'

'You acted on instinct.' Cormac let go of Leo's hand to grip his shoulders. 'Don't blame yourself.' He opened his mouth like he was going to say something else, before turning away to get out the tea bags. 'So, tea for me and you, and coffee for Finn, I'm guessing?'

'Yeah.' Leo watched as Cormac boiled the water and made the drinks. The ritual was vaguely soothing, until he caught sight of a box of Merry's favourite mint tea, unopened in the top of the cupboard. 'Do you think she's suffering? Like, having nightmares, or something?'

'No. I think she's unaware. Unconscious.'

'But are you sure?' Cormac didn't answer. 'Cormac? Can you promise me that she's not suffering?'

Cormac took his glasses off and began to wipe them on the corner of his shirt. Leo recognised the gesture now: it meant the wizard needed time to think. 'I can't promise, Leo. Nobody alive now has seen the long-term effect of black holly poison. And nobody who's been poisoned has ever survived to describe what it was like, at least as far as we know.' He took Leo's hand again. 'I think your sister is probably not suffering. But I can't say for certain.'

'And do you think anyone will ever find a way of waking her up? Before it's too late? Before her body is too…' Leo stopped and took a deep breath. He couldn't bring himself to say the word *decayed*. He didn't even want to think it.

'I don't know. Maybe. But…'

'But you can't promise that either.'

Cormac just shook his head.

'OK.' Leo exhaled slowly, riding out the rush of panic building in his chest. He sipped some of the hot tea; it scalded his mouth, but the pain actually helped him to focus, to reach a decision. 'OK.' He nodded and headed out of the kitchen.

'Leo?' Cormac followed him: up the stairs and back to Merry's bedroom. While Cormac hovered in the doorway, Leo walked up to the bed and leant close to his sister.

'Merry, please – wake up?' He shook her shoulder. 'Merry?'

Nothing changed. Squeezing one of her hands in his, he pressed his lips to her forehead.

'Leo?' Finn touched his arm. 'What are you doing?'

'Promise me you'll stay in here? That you'll stay with her?'

Suspicion and fear were growing in Finn's eyes, but he nodded.

'Cormac…' Leo led the other wizard along the landing to the door of the spare room. This was where Mum had insisted they store things after the battle with Ronan: the Leo-doll Ronan had created, the Merry-doll Gran had made, Gran's obsidian knife, and his sword, the one he'd used to kill Denise. The door had been magically sealed, warded, until the coven had time to deal with the two dolls.

'Can you get in here?' he murmured. 'Can you break down the wards?'

Cormac frowned. 'I can try, but why do you need—'

'Please, Cormac? I just—' Leo clutched the doorframe as a wave of nausea swept through him. 'I won't leave her like this. And I need you to help me.'

Cormac clamped his lips together, frowning at Leo. But then he nodded and raised his hands to the door, his eyes moving as if he were reading some invisible script written there. 'It looks like there's an alarm of some sort built into the wards. I'm not sure how much time you'll have.'

Leo nodded, but Cormac had already closed his eyes,

his lips moving silently through the words of a charm. Light rippled almost imperceptibly across the door. Cormac stepped back, breathing hard. 'Go.'

Inside the room someone had laid the dolls, the knife and the sword on a table. Both blades had been cleaned. Leo picked up the sword, the weight of the hilt familiar in his hand. He couldn't read the Old English inscription on the blade any more, but he knew what it said: true love.

And I'm doing this because I love her.

He positioned the point of the blade above the Merry-doll, roughly where he thought the heart would be.

'Leo,' Cormac laid his hand on Leo's arm, 'are you absolutely sure about this?'

Was he? Not really. He wanted his grandmother. He wanted Gran to tell him what to do. To tell him it was going to be OK. But she wasn't there. He'd never know if this was the right choice or not. But he could live with that. He couldn't live with the risk that he was leaving his sister to suffer.

'I'm sure enough. Please, go and be with her. And with Finn.' As Cormac left, Leo raised the blade. There were voices outside, in the driveway – Roshni, probably, coming to see who had broken the wards.

'Goodbye, Merry. Please, forgive me.' There was no time for anything else. Leo plunged the blade down as hard as he could: it pierced the doll and the table beneath.

There was a shriek of pain from Merry's room. His sister was screaming.

TWENTY-TWO

SHE COULD BREATHE again.

She dragged in huge lungfuls of air, gulping it down, but she needed more, because the agony in her wrist was growing and she needed to scream. She had to scream for someone to help her –

'Merry!' There was a voice in the darkness. 'What's wrong, what's happening?'

'Hurts…'

More air, while the voice kept questioning her, asking what was wrong, what hurt.

'Burns…'

She concentrated all her willpower on raising her left

arm, gritting her teeth against the intense pain, gasping out the words. 'It's... burning –'

'Oh, my God, the braid... Cut it off! Quickly...'

More than one voice now, and hands, touching her arm gently, spreading something cool over her skin. The pain began to fade, and the darkness withdrew.

Someone was nudging her, touching her wrist and her neck, her forehead. But it didn't matter. She could breathe again.

She could sleep.

Daylight, on the other side of her eyelids. Daylight, and she was lying on her side in her bed; she could feel the duvet tucked up round her neck. Arms, legs, fingers, toes – everything seemed to be intact. Though her left wrist felt stiff and sore. She moved her other hand across and felt a bandage wrapped tightly round it.

'Merry?'

She opened her eyes, blinking: Leo, in a chair next to the bed. 'Hey. What time is it?'

He began sobbing.

Merry pushed herself up in the bed, putting her arms round her brother as far as she was able. 'What's the matter, what's happened?'

'I thought – I thought I'd killed you. I stabbed the doll thing, and you woke up, and…'

Merry sank back against the pillows. 'You tried to kill me?'

Leo nodded, not looking at her.

'Because I'd been poisoned by the black holly?'

'Yes. Nobody knew what was going on in your head, and I was so scared that you were suffering – I couldn't leave you like that, I couldn't take the risk that you were in pain.'

'You were right. You were right, Leo. You did the right thing.'

He looked up at her, his eyes wide and glistening. 'I did?'

She nodded. 'It was horrible.' That didn't even begin to cover it. 'It was like… being in hell. I couldn't breathe, and—' She stopped, touching her throat. The nightmarish images had faded while she slept – properly slept – and she didn't want to recall them. 'There was no rest. Just pain, and horror, and it never stopped.' Leo clutched at her hand, crying again. 'You did the right thing, Leo, even if I hadn't survived.' Her stomach rumbled, and she wondered when she'd last eaten. 'Um, how did I survive? Did the doll we made not work?'

Leo grabbed a handful of tissues and began to dry his face off. 'No one's a hundred per cent sure, but Roshni thinks it's because I stabbed the doll with the sword. The hilt at least was originally made by Gwydion, and since he's not technically dead the enchantment that was already on the braid kicked in, protecting you from the effects of me... stabbing you.' He pulled an apologetic face. 'The full effects, at least. Cormac thinks you must have died briefly, which is why the enchantment from the black holly was lifted. The braid incinerated. It burnt you pretty badly. And you've been asleep for three days.' Merry looked down at her wrist. She'd miss her braid; it had connected her with Meredith, and with Jack.

'Hey, don't be sad.' Leo patted her hand. 'The braid protected you. It did what it was supposed to do.'

'I know.'

'And Cormac and Roshni think that we might be able to help the others who got scratched by black holly in the same way, by stopping their hearts and then reviving them. Not Gwydion, though, obviously. Not given that thing that's inside him still.'

'What's happened to his body?'

'It's been magically sealed up inside Mrs Knox's family vault with every type of protection the coven and the

Lombards can think of. No one's going to be summoning the King of Hearts again.'

Leo sounded like he really felt part of the magical world now. Hopefully it meant things were going well between him and Cormac. But it reminded Merry of what she'd lost. Mentally she prodded the space inside her chest, the last place she'd felt her magic. But there was nothing there, no spark. Just a void. She remembered how Finn had described it: as if something had been amputated. It felt to her more like some part of her had died – had just withered away. It didn't hurt at the moment; there'd been too much other pain and grief. But she suspected it would, eventually.

'Merry?' Leo squeezed her hand.

'My magic's gone.' For some reason Merry felt embarrassed admitting it; like there was something wrong with her now. Her face had grown hot. 'The lake took it, to heal the land and the point of intersection. All of it.'

Her brother's eyebrows had shot up. 'But... It'll come back, right? I mean, Gran's power had started to return.'

Gran... She knew her grandmother had gone; she remembered her dying clearly enough. But her absence didn't seem real, somehow.

More numbness. More pain saved up for later.

But then she heard Gran's voice in her head, almost as clearly as if she'd been in the room: 'A good witch doesn't try to cast fifteen different spells at once. Give yourself time, and remember that most things can wait until tomorrow.'

OK, Gran. Even though I'm not a witch any more, I'll try to remember.

'I don't think it will come back, Leo. This feels very… permanent.'

Her brother was staring at her, a stricken look in his eyes. 'Merry… I'm so sorry.'

She smiled at him.

'Hey, I'm alive at least. That's the important thing.' Sitting up again, she had to steady herself against a rush of light-headedness. 'That, and getting some breakfast.' She twisted round to look at the clock. 'Brunch, I guess. And where's Mum?'

'Oh –' Leo jumped up, knocking over the chair he'd been sitting on. 'I've got to call her; she went to Roshni's first thing this morning.' He ran to the bedroom door and ran back again. 'And Finn and Cormac – shall I call them too? They've been here every day, taking turns…'

'Finn's still here?'

'Yeah, of course.' He tilted his head. 'I mean, you guys are together, aren't you?'

Merry hesitated. They had been together, but now that she was just a pleb… She sighed.

One thing at a time, like Gran said.

'Sure. Let them both know. And the coven. And Ruby. But before everyone turns up and wants to make sure I'm not a zombie, I'm going to have a shower…'

Getting washed and dressed was exhausting. Merry had to keep sitting down to rest. Mum arrived during one of these rest periods – Roshni had brought her home with the broomstick spell – and for at least five minutes they clung together, crying. Tears of sorrow, tears of joy; too mixed up for Merry to tell which emotion was dominant. Then Mum sniffed and wiped her eyes and began drying and combing Merry's hair, helping her into the clothes she'd picked out, talking to her the whole time about how kind everyone had been, the other covens, and the Kin Houses who had turned up to support the Lombards; about how Roshni had bewitched the admissions people at Leo's university into believing he was off with the flu, since he'd missed the first week of term; about Gran's funeral. And when Merry started crying again, weeping about Gran and about the loss of her magic, Mum talked to her about all the other non-magical things that she could still do, all the talents she had, all the opportunities that would open up for her now she didn't have to be part of the coven. It didn't do away with the aching sense of loss, but it did help. Eventually, Merry was ready to go downstairs.

Mum took her by the shoulders. 'You and Leo have almost been the death of me over the last few months. I know I can't keep you wrapped up in cotton wool, but please…' Tears filled her eyes as her voice broke. 'Please, try not to get yourself killed any more. Or cursed. Or kidnapped. OK?'

Merry hugged her mother tightly. 'OK, Mum. I promise I'll try. It will definitely be easier, now I'm not—' She paused, waiting for the lump in her throat to go. 'Now I'm not a witch.'

Mum nodded and dashed the tears away from her eyes. 'There's my brave girl. Now, I've got a lot to do before this evening.'

'Why?'

'Roshni wants to organise a party.'

'A party? Is this really a good time? I honestly don't feel like it…'

'You don't have to stay for long if you don't want to.

But the coven has been through a lot of trauma recently. It will do everyone good to be able to celebrate together. And they specifically want to celebrate you. I think, just this once, you should let them have their way.'

Exactly the kind of thing Gran would say.

'And,' Mum continued, 'I'm going to get all your favourite food.'

'OK. I give in. Roshni can throw a party. But only if there's chocolate cake. And lasagne. Lasagne with lots of cheese on the top.' Merry's stomach rumbled again.

'You can write me a list.' Mum steered her out of the bedroom. 'But right now, you need to eat. Finn's been cooking.'

Merry drew back a little. She wasn't sure she was ready to talk to Finn. But the aromas wafting up from the kitchen did smell so good: bacon, and pancakes, and mint tea. Muffins too, if she wasn't mistaken. Her mouth watered.

One thing at a time, then. I'm going to eat some of Finn's delicious food, then I'll see how I feel.

She hurried downstairs.

'Go on, just have one more muffin.' Finn nudged the plate of muffins in Merry's direction. 'I made them specially.'

'And they're delicious. But I'm stuffed.' She smiled at

him. 'Leo should eat some more, though. He still needs building up.'

'Don't mind if I do.' Leo grabbed the whole plate and bit into another muffin, offering one to Cormac at the same time.

Finn rolled his eyes. 'Fine. Guess I'll start cleaning up, then.'

'No, Leo and I will take care of that.' Cormac waved a hand in the direction of the garden. 'Why don't you take Merry outside for some fresh air? It's a lovely afternoon.'

Finn flushed and shot his cousin a look, and Merry wondered if he was trying to avoid being alone with her. But then he held his hand out. 'Come on. You could probably do with some vitamin D.'

She slipped her hand into his and let him pull her up out of the chair.

Cormac was right: it was a lovely afternoon. Warm for the time of year, the thickly clustered red berries of the rowan tree dazzling against the blue of the sky. Insects were buzzing busily around clumps of Michaelmas daisies and tall red dahlias. Merry took a deep breath, inhaling the sun-warmed, scented air.

They sat down on the garden bench.

'Do you remember the first time we were out here together?' Finn asked.

'Yeah.' Merry smiled. 'I found you sunbathing without your top on. And then you wouldn't take the hint and leave me alone.'

'I remember. You sat there with your sunglasses on, ignoring me as hard as you could. But I wore you down in the end.'

They both fell silent.

'I want to make sure—'

'I wanted to say—'

Both stopped again.

'After you,' Finn prompted.

'Fine.' Merry looked down at the bandage round her wrist, tugging at a loose thread. 'I wanted to say, it's OK – if me losing my powers means that our relationship is over.'

'You'd be OK with that?' Finn's voice was flat.

The sound of an ice-cream van jingle floated across from a nearby road. Life in Tillingham getting back to normal.

'Actually, no – I wouldn't be OK with it. It would be a completely rubbish reason to break up with me. But, we've only known each other a few months. And I can't help any more with the whole making-magical-babies thing. Even if that was something we both decided we wanted to do, a long way down the line. So, if it's a choice between me and your family...' She shrugged. 'I'll live. And I'll try to understand.' She turned to look at him; he was sitting with his head bowed, staring at his feet. 'Well? Isn't that what you wanted to say?'

Finn shook his head. 'No, actually. What I wanted to say was, that I understand if you've changed your mind.'

Merry frowned. 'What?'

'What I mean is... That night at my house, it was amazing.' Finn's neck and face flushed red. 'But you thought you were probably going to die. And now you're not. I mean, you're not dead. So, if you've changed your mind about us...' He took her hand, still not looking at her. 'I wouldn't be OK with it. But I'll try to understand.'

Merry stared at him, before bursting into a fit of laughter.

'What? What's funny?'

'We are.' She tried to stop herself. 'We're both trying to be so pathetically self-sacrificing, I can't even...' The laughter took over again, but now Finn was laughing too.

'I'm sorry.' Merry dabbed her eyes with the bandage. 'But it was too funny.' She twisted round to face Finn. 'I told you I was in love with you before. And that hasn't changed, even though so much else has.'

'And I love you too.' He ran the tip of his finger down her cheek. 'With or without your magic.'

'What about your family?'

Finn squinted up into the sky. 'We might all be hit by an asteroid tomorrow. Or maybe Cormac will figure out how to produce a serum for enhanced magical ability in an easy-to-swallow capsule. Anything's possible. So I'm not going to worry about the future any more. I think we should enjoy the present instead.'

That made sense. The present was really all that anyone had.

Finn stood up.

'Where are we going?'

'Nowhere.' He took Merry's hands and drew her upright. 'But I want to kiss you, and I can't get close enough sitting down there.'

'Seems reasonable.' Merry slid her arms round Finn's neck as he pulled her tight against him, the familiar tingle of excitement and desire coursing through her veins as their lips met. They kissed hard and long, until Finn pulled away and buried his head against her neck. He was trembling, and Merry could feel his tears against her skin.

'I'm glad you're not dead, Merry Cooper,' he whispered.

'Me too, Finn Lombard. Me too.'

People began turning up not long after that, even though the party didn't officially start until much later. There were coven members, Finn's dad (Merry wondered if Finn had given him a lecture, because he seemed to be making an effort to talk to Leo), and Cormac's parents, among others. It was a bit exhausting: everyone wanted to talk to Merry, or to touch her, as if she was a sort of good luck talisman (or perhaps they really did want to check she wasn't a zombie). By late afternoon Merry needed to get away. She found Leo and Cormac up in Leo's room, immersed in an online role-playing game. She watched them for a couple of minutes; it was good to see Leo getting back to some of the things he'd enjoyed before Ronan.

'Leo?'

He jumped up straight away. 'What's the matter? Are you feeling all right?'

'I'm fine. But I'd like to get out of the house for a bit. Do you mind taking me for a drive?'

'No problem. Cormac…'

'You go. I should spend some time with my parents, in any case.' They kissed lightly on the lips. 'See you later.'

Cormac went downstairs and Merry turned to Leo. 'Much better boyfriend choice. Way better.'

Her brother grinned.

'Glad you approve. Where d'you fancy going?'

'This might sound weird, but…' she twirled a lock of hair through her fingers, 'I'd like to go to the lake.' Everything had started at the Black Lake. There seemed to be a certain harmony in returning there today, when her quest was truly finished. Closure, maybe.

Leo nodded. 'OK. I'll get my keys.'

Half an hour later, they were there.

Leo parked in the same car park they'd used earlier in the year, when they'd come to stop Jack going into Tillingham to attack people. Together they walked through the trees, the long shadows already shading into twilight beneath the dense canopy.

And there was the lake.

The breeze was chopping the surface of the water into glinting fragments. Without speaking, Merry took Leo's hand and led him up the slope to the top of the small cliff.

'I can't believe it was only six months ago that everything kicked off.' She shook her head. 'It doesn't seem real, all the stuff that's happened.'

'I know what you mean. Every so often, I think there's been a mistake – that I'll wake up and Gran will still be alive. And Flo… And Dan.'

Merry leant her head against her brother's shoulder, as he remembered his first love.

'Do you think it's really finished, this time?'

'Yeah. I think so. You beat the bad guys, Merry.'

'*We* beat them. Together.' She bent to pick up a stone and threw it as far out across the lake as she could, watching the arc of its flight and the splash as it sank beneath the water. 'Do you think Meredith and Jack got home OK?'

'I hope so.'

There was no way they'd ever know, for sure. But hope was something. Merry decided that she would hope for a happy ending for Jack. And she would hope for a happy ending for herself, and Leo, and everybody they loved.

And maybe – hopefully – that would be enough.

'Come on.' She put her arm round Leo's waist. 'Let's go home.'

ACKNOWLEDGEMENTS

WE BEGAN WRITING what turned into *The Witch's Kiss* in June 2014. Now, three books and countless drafts, revisions and middle-of-the-night editing sessions later, it's hard to believe that we've reached the end of Merry and Leo's journey. Their story has developed in ways we never imagined when we first started writing it, and we're so excited to finally see *The Witch's Blood* in print. But this book wouldn't exist without the encouragement and help given to us along the way by the fabulous people mentioned below.

Claire Wilson at Rogers, Coleridge & White, the best agent ever and our nominee for galactic overlord: she's always available (even when she's supposed to be on maternity leave!) and always super supportive. Our thanks also to Rosie Price who provided perspective, hand-holding and soothing vibes for a lot of the last year.

Michelle Misra, our editor at HarperCollins, for providing an absolutely seamless editorial experience, and for helping us give Merry and Leo the finale they deserve. We'd also like to thank Jess Dean, our publicist, Samantha Stewart and everyone else in the children's department at HC.

Lisa Brewster at Blacksheep Design for yet another stunning cover. We are in awe.

Our fellow RCW authors and members of 'Claire's Coven', especially Lexi Casale for all her support (and delicious cooking!).

Our other bookish friends (bloggers, writers and readers) who have been so lovely over the last couple of years. We'd particularly like to thank Zöe Collins, Perdita Cargill, Maja Diana, Rhian Ivory, Gary Collins, Peter Davey, Susan Mann, Chantelle at *Oh, the stories*, Rachel B, Suze and Anniek at *With Love For Books*, Kirsty Stanley, Hayley Fraser, Jemma Hadley, Odette Knappers, Giulietta Gigiliotti, Ciara O'Rourke, Amy Jade, Andrew Hall, Michelle Toy, and Maddie and Bee Halladay. We hope we haven't forgotten anyone!

A special shout out from Katharine to everyone in the Feminism 2.0 group – you know who you are! Thank you so much guys for listening and being there for me. It means a lot.

A wave to Janet McCarthy: thanks for giving Lysandra Blackheart her name!

Last (but not least), we'd like to thank our family for their boundless patience, reassurance and love. We couldn't do it without them.

Have you read the spellbinding first book in the series?

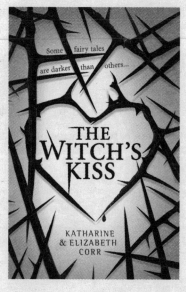

Merry used to dabble in witchcraft – and her gran runs the local coven – but, apart from that, she and her brother, Leo, are normal teenagers. So when Jack, a cursed prince, wakes beneath a nearby lake after fifteen hundred years Merry is shocked to learn that she's inherited the job of dealing with him. Aided by Leo, Merry tries to manage her power and figure out a way of breaking the curse. But as she gets to know Jack she realises she wants to save him – not destroy him. Will Merry lose her life as well as her heart? Or can true love's kiss really save the day?

The darkly magical sequel to
The Witch's Kiss **burns wickedly bright...**

It's not easy being a teenage witch. Just ask Merry. She's
drowning in textbooks and rules set by the coven,
drowning in heartbreak after the loss of Jack. But
Merry is not the only one whose fairy tale is over.

Big brother, Leo, is falling apart and everything Merry
does seems to push him further to the brink. And
everything that happens to Leo makes her ache for
revenge. So when strangers offering friendship show
them a different path they'd be mad not to take it...

Some rules were made to be broken, right?